Goodbye, Belvidere

His Eye Is on the Sparrow

Joyce Wheeler

Dear Readers,

In the first book of the Goodbye, Belvidere series, *A Hundred and Sixty Acres*, CJ Crezner was a young minister on a cattle drive in 1898. He found the virgin prairies of western South Dakota and the people who settled there fascinating, and to his family and his own surprise, he decided to stay—not as a minister but as a homesteader.

Love comes to CJ in two forms. Beautiful blonde Deborah Lynn Smith is a minister's daughter, who feels CJ should return to his family in Missouri. Dark-haired and feisty Joanna Swanson accuses him of running away and seems to care less what he does. Life gets complicated for CJ as he tries to sort out his problems. Fortunately, he has several mentors; and his outspoken landlady, Mrs. Ordin, sets him straight on many occasions.

He, of course, marries Joanna, and their life on the homestead with the ups and downs of weather, crops, cattle, and children weave a story of both fact and fiction.

The Crezners, Smiths, Swansons, Parker Vinue, and Tinners are all imaginary people. However, throughout both *A Hundred and Sixty Acres* and *His Eye Is on the Sparrow*, real pioneers are woven in as themselves and their line of work.

The first book ended with Joanna and her brother Simon leaving Belvidere on one of the first passenger trains. They are headed to Minnesota to visit their ailing mother, and it's a journey Joanna dreads. She and her mother have never had a good relationship.

His Eye Is on the Sparrow continues the story with a time lapse of several weeks. It begins, as did the first book, with CJ writing to his parents.

Historical fiction is a challenge. This might be a case where ignorance is bliss because had I known the hours of research needed, I might have had second thoughts of tackling the project. However, I've learned a great deal of history and have enjoyed fascinating conversations with folks whose parents and grandparents settled here during this time frame. I appreciate all the information they have given. Many, many thanks!

Sincerely,

Joyce Wheeler

www.prairieflowerbooks.com

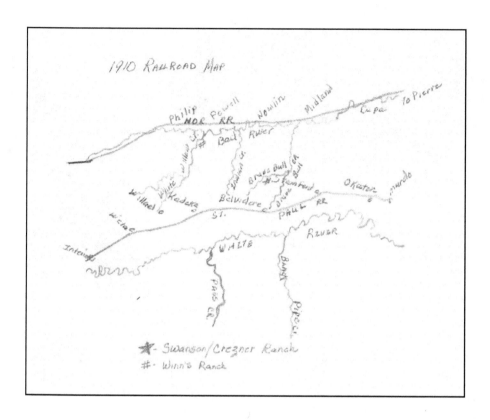

1910 RAILROAD MAP

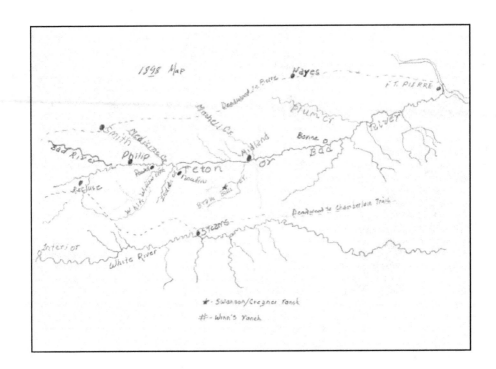

* - Swanson/Cregner Ranch
# - Winn's Ranch

1

May 1, 1907

Belvidere, South Dakota

Dear Mom and Dad,

Joanna has returned home. My wife continually surprises me. On a cold, damp April morning, two weeks after she and Simon left for Minnesota, a horse with its rider trotted into the yard. There was bedlam for several minutes when we realized the person under the hood of the yellow slicker was wife, mother, and aunt!

We were so elated to see her that we forgot to be ashamed of dirty dishes in the sink, unmade beds, piles of laundry everywhere, and clutter throughout her house. However, within a short time of her arrival, we were all working diligently to correct those oversights.

The best news is that Joanna's mother is feeling much better. I will let her tell you the details. As you know, Joanna and her brother Simon traveled on one of the first passenger trains to leave Belvidere. It was nice for them to have the luxury of train travel from here to Minnesota. Simon wanted to stay with his mother and his siblings for another couple of weeks, so Joanna traveled home by herself. Had I known this, I would have been in an agony of worries.

We've had lots of moisture this spring, and it has been cool and damp. It's been difficult getting crops in, but in South Dakota, we try not grumble about excesses in either rain or snow.

I'll sign off so Joanna can write her news.

Love, CJ

Dear Mom and Dad Crezner,

The main news I wanted to share with you concerns advice you gave me several years ago about the problems between Ma and me. You said when you were around difficult people, you thought of a couple of verses in Romans 12. I've read that chapter many times. It teaches us to be kindly affectionate to one another, and to live, as much as possible, in peace with each other. As you say, when we ask the Lord for help, He answers in amazing ways. He changed my attitude, not my mother. It made a huge difference during the days we were together.

Shortly after we arrived, Ma was voicing her many physical woes. I mentioned how much she liked her old doctor when she lived on the farm. The next day, she insisted I hitch up the team and buggy and take her to him. When he saw all the potions and pills she was taking, he clucked disapprovingly and took them all away from her. He replaced it with the one heart pill he had prescribed years ago and gave her a good pep talk, saying that nothing was wrong with her and that she best go home and get busy. Only he could talk to her like that!

We saw an improvement immediately. By the following Sunday, when all my siblings gathered together, she was as bossy as ever. And strangely enough, we were glad she was in usual form. I discovered what I used to find so irritating had become rather humorous (a characteristic, I might add, that my siblings did not share, and sister Gertrude worried that I might become just like Ma), but I also recognized that after so many days of being with Ma, even the Lord couldn't prevent my patience from wearing a little thin. It was time to come home. Simon wanted to stay longer, and we decided it was in everyone's best interests if I came home without him.

We always look forward to your wonderful newsy letters. CJ seems to have misplaced your last one, so I can't comment on what you wrote, but I'm sure it will turn up in some unexpected place. It's amazing where men decide to stash things.

The boys say to tell you hello, and that it's only four more months until your visit here!

Love,

Joanna

CJ read the entire letter as the setting sun cast its last glow into the dining room window before it ducked behind the western hills. His world was right again since Joanna was home. The homestead had been forlorn without her bustling activities.

"I wonder why Simon wanted to stay longer. It surprises me," he said, putting the letter down.

Joanna was darning a pair of John's socks and stifled a yawn before answering. "He seemed to have lots of people to see. I was surprised too. But I was too lonesome for you and the boys to stay longer. When he said a couple more weeks, I decided to head out the next day."

"So did your ma want you to stay longer?"

Joanna put the darning needle in the spool of heavy thread and set sock, needle, and thread into her sewing basket. "No. We knew we had reached our limit of being civil to one another. I think we got along better than anyone expected though." She yawned again. "I was happy she was better, and it was good to see everyone. Ma and I are speaking to one another, which is a huge step in the right direction." Joanna stood up and stretched. "I think I'll hit the hay early tonight, CJ. I can't quit yawning."

"You've been sleepy for the past week. Must be the weather," CJ remarked as he got up to stoke the waning fire in the parlor stove.

"Or else it's trying to catch up on sleep I missed while I was gone. I mean to tell you, between Ma and Simon snoring, I don't think I slept a wink for two weeks. Good grief, I could hear them through the walls—Simon on one side, Ma on the other." Joanna stood on tiptoe and kissed him on the cheek. "Did I mention I missed you and the boys something fierce?"

CJ put his arms around her and drew her closer. "You might have said a little something about it," he said and gave her a light whisker rub. "In between planting potatoes, doing laundry, baking, giving the house a serious cleaning, and giving John and Isaac lessons, you might have mentioned it. No wonder you're yawning. Go upstairs and get to bed, woman. I'll finish here."

Even if it was May first, the wind whistling around the corner of the house made CJ shiver. He hoped it wouldn't freeze again, crazy weather anyhow. The air was damp and heavy as he brought in several armloads of wood for the stoves. By the time he was ready for bed, a light rain was falling. In the early dawn, CJ felt Joanna crawl back into bed, and he slowly opened one eye. He noted the sun was hiding behind some clouds, and he also gained a good understanding of his wife's cold feet.

"It's snowing," she whispered and cuddled as close to him as she could.

"It can't be. It's May," he grumbled as he tucked the covers around the two of them. "What did your almanac say about snow?"

Her voice sounded sleepy. "Never looked."

Well. That had to be a first. Joanna always checked and rechecked the old farmer's almanac about everything. He started to tell her she must be slipping in her almanac diligence, but she was already asleep again.

Breakfast that morning was slow and leisurely. It was as if the snow created an unexpected holiday for the household. Chores were kept to a minimum, and Joanna granted the boys extra time to get school assignments done. She fried a pan full of bacon and eggs. Her chokecherry syrup flowed over stacks of pancakes, and the coffee was piping hot.

Even Teddy was quiet while they ate. "You're the bestest cook in the world," he finally said as he chased the last bite around his plate with his fork and finger.

"That's what you told Antonio when you ate her kolaches," John reminded his younger brother. "You can't have two best cooks. One is better, one is best."

"Can too! So there!"

"Boys, stop it. CJ, you spoiled these two while I was gone." Joanna scowled at her sons and gave her husband a light swat on the arm before asking, "Do I know this best cook?"

"She's the best kolache cook, but you're the best everything else cook." Teddy managed to redeem himself while attempting an under-the-table kick at John.

CJ gave Teddy a steady look and an almost imperceptible shake of his head. It was enough of a warning to make his five-year-old son duck his head.

"Antonio and Frank are the little Bohemian couple that live up the valley. She was a cook in the Lake Andes area, and he was a farmhand. They heard about this country opening up for homesteaders and wanted a farm of their own. Just like a lot of others, I guess."

"Oh, sure. I know who you mean. I just didn't know her name. They have the sod house, and she had a baby while I was gone." Joanna laid her napkin beside her plate and rose to get the coffee pot.

"I don't know why she wouldn't let me take him home for a while," Teddy grumbled. "I could learn him American talk."

Isaac and John waited for Joanna's correction of Teddy's grammar, but her mind seemed to be on other matters. CJ watched as they glanced at each other and shrugged.

"What's a kolache?" She wondered as she refilled their cups.

"A sweet roll with filling. She'd made several different kinds, and Teddy especially liked the peach one."

"I ate four."

Joanna looked horrified. "Four! Good heavens, they'll think we don't have any manners at all!" She looked disapprovingly at CJ. "Why didn't you stop him?"

"Well, because." CJ shuffled slightly on his chair. "She was talking and passing the plate around, and Frank was talking and pouring coffee, and I was trying to figure out what they were saying, which ain't easy."

"Daddy said 'ain't'!" Teddy was delighted. "And that's why I kept taking 'em—'cause she kept passing 'em!"

Joanna sank down in her chair. "I leave for two weeks. Two weeks! And father and son have forgotten both manners and grammar. No wonder I'm tired."

"You wouldn't think one man would need a wagon and a buggy plus riders to get his stuff home," Joanna grumbled as they prepared to meet Simon. The middle of May radiated with spring promises. The hills were covered in a carpet of green grass, a refreshing change from the golden hues of late summer and fall. The breeze was fresh with a hint of warmth—a perfect day for Simon's homecoming.

The white ostrich plume that adorned Joanna's black velvet hat waved gallantly as CJ helped her into the buggy. "He could have given us a little more time and a little more information. I don't know what he would have done if his letter hadn't gotten to us. It's a good thing Isaac rode into Belvidere yesterday to get the mail." Joanna settled in the seat before she turned her attention to a pouting Teddy in the back seat. "And you, sir, can wipe that look off your face. Just because you can't ride in the wagon doesn't mean your lip can hang halfway to your chin."

CJ tied two horses behind the buggy before he nodded at Isaac and John in the wagon. At fourteen years of age, Isaac was capable of driving the team, no matter what they were pulling. CJ often wondered what they would do after he started high school in Pierre. He was a gentle-natured boy, serious for his age, and had been CJ's special friend even before CJ and Joanna were married.

CJ stepped from the ground into the buggy with one easy leap. He gave his team a gentle flick with his buggy whip, and with nickers and head bobs, they started up the road. He reached over and squeezed Joanna's knee. She usually gave him a wink and his hand a slap, but this morning, her mind was on other matters.

"Isaac grew up overnight." Joanna's voice had a melancholy ring. "And look at John—almost seven—riding along with him. Time goes too fast, CJ."

"I'm big too. I'm almost as big as Johnny." Theodore Simon thrust his face up and over the buggy seat. "I'm big 'nuff to ride with them too."

"No, you're not. You're your mother's baby boy, and she wanted you to be with her this morning. Now sit back before you crumple my feather." Joanna patted his cheek absently.

"Baby!" Teddy gave an indignant snort. "I'm five. I'm almost growed up!"

Joanna rolled her eyes. "Five." She looked at CJ and shook her head. "Where did the time go? I want it to slow down. I want things to just stay the way they are for a while." She gave a disgruntled sigh.

He patted her knee and put his hand back on the lines. "Well, when you're not here, time drags. I guess when you're visiting and keeping busy, it flies."

She gave a short laugh. "I was definitely busy helping my mother. I cleaned, cooked, sewed, did laundry, and helped her entertain her friends. Once she discovered she was not at death's door, she discovered all sorts of things she wanted to do, places to go, people to see." Joanna leaned more comfortably against the buggy seat. "No wonder I came home bushed."

CJ glanced at her and nodded. She still looked tired with dark circles under her eyes. It wasn't like Joanna to not have worlds of energy.

"What did you enjoy the most while you were there?" He gently pulled back on the lines to slow the team's fast trot.

Joanna wrapped her shawl closer around her. "Well, I enjoyed the Sunday after we got there, when we knew Ma was on the mend, and all my brothers and sisters and some of their kids were there. That was nice." Joanna frowned as a wisp of hair escaped her tightly pinned pompadour. "Except, I almost wore myself out by trying to be agreeable and not arguing with anyone over anything."

CJ chuckled. "I can't imagine my sweet crabby Joanna not arguing with someone."

She smiled at him and lightly swatted his arm. "It's what I love about you, CJ. We can argue so wonderfully together, and you let me be my normal crabby self." They rode in companionable silence with only a meadowlark's song and the clopping of the horse's hooves to break the stillness.

"But," Joanna said, breaking the quiet, "the best time was after Ma's whist party, when her friends left and Simon came. The house was clean, the tea was good, and the three of us enjoyed cake and a good visit."

"Is that when you told her about me and she said Teddy was a grand name?" Teddy had heard part of this story before and loved to have it repeated.

"Yes, but don't let it go to your head," Joanna turned to him and winked.

"Teddy is a good name. But I like Joseph better." Teddy sat back in his seat.

"Joseph?" CJ looked at his son. "Joseph Simon doesn't have the same ring to it as Theodore Simon." He and Joanna exchanged bemused glances. "That must be the time you were telling us it started to rain, and you had a relaxing evening by the parlor stove."

Joanna nodded. "Ma heard some of the ladies ask me about this country, and maybe it dawned on her that she had never asked anything about you or the boys. She was actually interested, and I wasn't so defensive."

"We mature as we get older. I guess that's the advantage of being adults."

"I could be manured too," Teddy said, and frowned at his parents when they started laughing.

Isaac and CJ stopped the wagon and buggy on a hill that afforded them a view of Belvidere. They could see the train pulling into the station and hear the steam and whistle and rumble of the wheels as it ground to a stop. Even coming from that distance, the horses pawed and were nervous. They waited while the steam engines refilled with water and the passengers and cargo were unloaded. Finally the whistle blew again, steam blasted from the sides, and with a great deal of screeching and grumbling, the wheels began to turn. Its next stop would be ten miles down the road at the newly formed town of Kadoka.

The horses were jumpy. This type of noise didn't invade their world often. Once they resumed the last quarter mile, Isaac's team danced sideways until CJ drove beside them with the buggy team. The teams must have felt there was safety in numbers, and in short order, they crossed the tracks without any more fussing.

They found Simon checking several crates on the loading dock. When he looked up and saw them, a huge smile creased his face. In seconds, he was off the dock and headed toward Isaac and the wagon.

"You boys are a sight for sore eyes!" he exclaimed, and bounded up the wagon steps in two big leaps. "I missed all of you!" He enveloped Isaac and John in a bear hug and managed a wave at the rest of them.

After a few minutes of enthusiastic greetings, he took the reins and slowly backed the team to the loading dock. "We'll need some help getting this into the wagon," he said and gave a slightly nervous laugh.

"Which one of these are yours?" CJ eyed the jumble of crates, especially the big one that promised to weigh a ton.

"Ah, I hate to say this, but they're all mine. Well, not exactly all of them are mine." Simon whipped off his hat and ran his hand through his graying brown hair. "Ma insisted on sending some things for Joanna."

"Me?" Joanna's voice held a note of incredulity. "What on earth did she send?"

"Boy howdy, Joanna, you know Ma. She started boxing up things she didn't need or want anymore and sent them all to you. Even her old piano."

"What!" Joanna exploded as she stood up in the buggy. "Her piano? That monstrous beast that's been forever out of tune?" CJ gently pulled her back to the seat. Joanna was still sputtering as he left the buggy and tied up the team. "Just leave it on the dock, and we'll donate it to Belvidere," she hollered at his departing back.

Even with extra manpower, lifting the piano and settling it into the wagon was an awkward and heavy job. Finally, it was positioned where it was hoped it wouldn't tip over, and the rest of the crates were stacked around it. CJ had no idea how they would get it into the house. He shuddered at the thought. Simon lifted a small ornate trunk off the dock and set it in the back seat of the buggy.

"Isn't that Grandma Swanson's box that holds the family Bible?" Joanna asked.

Simon nodded. "Ma sent it to you and said not to tell Gertrude. You know Ma, even when she's trying to be nice, she creates a storm."

Joanna slowly descended the buggy steps and patted Simon's arm as he helped her down. "Gertrude has told us ever since I can remember how much she wanted Grandma's Bible. This is going to be a big bunch of trouble." She sighed in exasperation. She gave her brother a quick hug. "Welcome home. We're glad to see you!"

CJ echoed her sentiments. Simon was an important part of their ranch. He and Joanna had started the Swanson homestead in 1896, with each of them filing on 160 acres. Throughout the years, they had run a good-sized cattle herd on free range and had managed to make a number of improvements on their prairie home. When CJ married Joanna, he was able to add more land. They worked well together, and with CJ's bookkeeping jobs at some of the local businesses, they managed to pay their bills and have a little extra.

"Maybe after you see what else I brought home you won't be so glad to see me," Simon gave another nervous laugh. "Come and see what I bought." He led the way to the stock corrals, and the rest of them filed after him.

Afterward, CJ could never remember what he expected to see, but the sight of ten Guernsey milk cows placidly chewing their cuds and looking at them with bored brown eyes was not on his anticipation list. Milk cows had never been on CJ's list of favorite things. Thick tails with burrs knocking his hat off as he sat on the milk stool, flies, the constant duty of morning and evening milking—to put it in his friend Winn's words, "It ain't purty."

"Oh! Milk cows!" Joanna eyed CJ uncertainly. "My goodness, Simon, where did you get these, ah, these beauties?"

Simon shuffled his feet. "Do you remember little Edith Crawford?" At Joanna's puzzled look, he shook his head and answered his own question. "No, of course you wouldn't. You weren't even born when sister Bertie babysat her. Anyway, she grew up, married, and had a family. Now her husband is ailing, and she needs to sell some of their dairy herd. They live right next to where the folks' place was." Simon seemed to lose track of what he was saying for several seconds as he gazed over the green hills toward their own home.

"And?" Joanna prompted him with a frown.

"To make a long story short, when I saw them, I decided to buy them." Simon let out a quick breath of air, and CJ decided that was definitely making the story short. Very short.

"Ah, well." CJ rubbed his hand over the back of his neck. He tried to think of a positive remark. "When will they come fresh?"

Simon cast him a thoughtful look. "In about four weeks. All ten of them are starting then, so we can expect some nice calves, I hope." Simon leaned against the pole corral and put his arms on the top rail.

"The way I look at it, our days of running on free range are about gone. And I said to myself, we need to figure out some way to make money on this place, and it came to my mind that selling cream might be a good investment." He looked at Joanna and CJ and reached down to tousle Teddy's hair. "The railroad is right here to ship it out."

"We'll need cream cans and a separator and stanchions and," CJ finished lamely, "all that good stuff."

"Yup. I know. That's what's in some of those crates. I thought I could pick it up a lot cheaper in Minnesota than I could here." This time, Simon looked him square in the eye without shuffling his feet. "You folks think about this. In the end, I believe you'll agree with me."

Isaac had untied the two saddle horses and led them to the group. "Guess we better get started chasing 'em home." CJ couldn't tell from the tone of his voice what Isaac's thoughts were.

"The boys and I will get some supplies and head on home ourselves." Joanna seemed to force enthusiasm in her remark.

"I best ride with Uncle Simon," Teddy said and reached for Simon's hand. "I'll be in the wagon if you need me," he informed his mother.

The breeze blew Joanna's feather in a silent dance on top of her hat. She shook her head and gave her youngest son a resigned smile. "Be good for your uncle and don't talk all the way home. " She put her hand on John's shoulder, and the two of them headed toward the buggy.

CJ tightened his cinch and grimly decided it would be a merry ride home chasing ten cows that had no clue what endless prairie was like. He waited until Isaac was in the pen before he reopened the gate. Ten befuddled cows slowly started out of the corral as Isaac whooped softly at them. Once out of the gate, they picked up speed; and in a split second, they turned away from the intended direction and made a dash up the street into the town of Belvidere. CJ knew instantly he was going to hate every last one of them.

2

May 20, 1907

Belvidere, South Dakota

Dear Ma,

I can't begin to tell you all the excitement we had when we discovered you sent your piano home with Simon. It was good you included music books and a hymnbook since it has been years since I have thought of my piano days!

Grandma's trunk with her Bible was also appreciated. I remember how she always sat on her rocking chair and read her Norwegian Bible. I loved to hear her read it out loud, even if I couldn't understand what she said.

The crate full of crocheted doilies and also the handkerchiefs I embroidered for you were a treasure. I didn't realize you had kept them to return to me. The Blue Willow dishes are a treasure. I've always loved the story of the pattern. I didn't remember you had a complete set of them. We will be very fancy now when we have company.

Speaking of company, would you consider a trip this way? You could see the boys and also hear CJ sing. I haven't tried to play a song for him to sing, but we'll get practiced up and see if we can make music together. Ha.

You have been very generous! Thank you.

Love,

Joanna, CJ, John, and Teddy

CJ put Joanna's letter on the table and looked out the window. It was drizzling again this morning, and he came into the house with the idea of coffee and cookies. Neither was made, and Joanna gave every indication of not caring one whit about the situation.

"You didn't mention we about killed ourselves getting the darn thing in the house," he groused, pointing to the huge upright piano in the living room.

"Did you want me to tell your mother-in-law my husband lost his temper and used *very* colorful metaphors to the extent I sent my sons to their room?" Joanna stopped drawing doodles on an old envelope and raised a questioning eyebrow at him.

"Between fighting to get those stupid stubborn milk cows home and then unloading this thing, anyone would have said the same thing." CJ still couldn't find any humor in either instance. Even the rain was beginning to get on his nerves, which Joanna told him was an unheard-of happening in South Dakota.

"At least they didn't break out of the corral last night, which is a first since they came on the place." Joanna resumed her senseless circles. "Where's the boys?" she asked absently, intent on making a whole row of penciled marks.

CJ rose from his chair and headed toward the stove. He guessed if he wanted coffee, he would have to make it himself. "Over at Isaac's." His voice was clipped, and he rattled the coffee pot to show his irritation.

"Mm."

CJ rolled his eyes and reached for the dipper in the water pail. The dipper was where it was supposed to be. The water pail, however, was empty.

By the time he refilled the pail and had coffee brewing, CJ's temper was beginning to climb into the danger zone. It was unreasonable of him, and he told himself that very thing. It was almost childish to dislike God's created beasts to the extent he disliked the milk cows. He would get over it and probably even become fond of them, he consoled himself. But he didn't believe a word of it. It was also unreasonable to be irritated that his usual busy and ambitious wife had taken to wandering through the house without actually doing anything. The cookie tin that always used to be full of the best cookies in the world was pitifully empty.

It was ill timing on Simon's part to choose that moment to come from the cellar. He was whistling a tuneless little song, and he announced cheerfully that he almost had the separator put together.

"We've never had one of those before. How does it work again?" Joanna's voice was muffled. Her head was bent over her paper, and she was intent on her circles. CJ thought it was the fourth time Joanna wondered how a cream separator worked. Maybe Simon should draw a picture on her envelope.

Simon, however, loved talking about his new contraption. He settled himself comfortably on the chair across from Joanna and, with great detail, explained how the large metal bowl on top of the separator had two spigots, one on top and one on the bottom. When he cranked the handle, the milk swirled around the bowl. The lighter cream rose to the top and drained from the top spigot, and the heavier milk settled to the lower spigot and drained into a waiting pail.

"When you get to cranking, it starts to hum. And boy howdy! The longer you crank, the louder it gets! It's quite a deal. You'll have to come and see it!"

"How do you get all the parts clean after you use it?" Joanna had industriously finished all the squiggles, and the whole envelope was covered. CJ looked at it in exasperation. Not only exasperation, but with a small niggle of worry. This was so unlike Joanna.

"It all comes apart so you can clean it." Simon was so enthused over his new gadget that he didn't notice the dismay written on Joanna's face.

She pushed herself away from the table and stood up. "I suppose I should bake something. And think of what to have for dinner. And put Ma's dishes someplace." She looked at the Blue Willow dishes still packed in the crate where Simon had deposited them a week ago. Instead of doing any of those things, she wandered out on the porch and settled herself on the wooden bench.

Simon raised an eyebrow at CJ and shrugged. "I'm heading to the barn to get the rest of those stanchions built. You had a good idea, CJ. The lean-to we added last year is perfect to put our milk cows in." Simon bustled happily out into the gently falling rain, seemingly unaware that CJ hadn't said a word during the whole exchange.

"I think Minnesota made 'em both a little touched," he grumbled as he poured a lone cup of coffee. "Milk cows. Separators. No cookies. This ain't purty."

Lizzie Tinner came to visit the next afternoon. They hadn't seen her since they had buried her father on the Tinner homestead after he was trampled by cattle running across a cellar he was building. CJ and other neighbors had dug him out, but he was badly hurt. Mrs. Tinner seemed quite indifferent to her husband's plight and had the men dig his grave before her husband breathed his last breath.

Lizzie's high-pitched voice could be heard while she was still at the creek crossing. CJ and the boys were getting haying equipment ready and could hear her warning Burr, their dog, to stay away from her horse.

Isaac frowned as she galloped toward them. Lizzie and her spotted horse always seemed to go full speed. The horse came to a stiff-legged, jarring stop and tossed his head within inches of Isaac.

"Back him up!" Isaac was disgusted. "He's slobbering all over me!"

"He is not. He just wants to show you his new bridle." Lizzie slid to the ground and gave Burr a light pat on the head.

CJ looked at the bridle with interest. It was new, and the headstall boasted intricate leather carving. He studied the saddle Lizzie had just vacated and realized with a start that the Tinners always had nice and well-oiled tack.

Isaac traced the fern leaf leather design with his finger. "Who made it for you?"

Lizzie shrugged. She reached over to give Teddy's nose a tweak. "Gotcher nose." She grinned at him and showed him her thumb squeezed between two fingers.

Teddy was immediately concerned he was nose less and ran his hand over his face. He looked relieved when he discovered it was still firmly in place. "Do not," he informed her, and gave his dad a questioning look. "Does she?" He put the index finger of each hand in his nostrils just to double-check.

"She's just teasing," John assured his little brother. "Show him your hand, Lizzie."

Lizzie acted like she flung something away, and then with feigned innocence, she showed Teddy both sides of her hand. "Maybe Burr will find it," she said, not unkindly. When Teddy's eyes widened in disbelief, she laughed and said, "Just kidding, just kidding."

"Your nose is where it always was, Teddy," CJ smiled at his son and patted his back. "And Lizzie, your bridle is pretty fancy. Nice carving on it." He was like Isaac and wanted to ask where she got it, but there was a craftiness in Lizzie's expression that made him hesitate.

"Uh, Ma wanted me to ask you something." She scuffed her feet on the ground before she continued. "She said after you said some words over Pa, that she got to thinking that, well, that maybe she should oughta have some words said over Ben."

CJ remembered well how Mrs. Tinner resisted "words" when her husband was killed. She had informed him that Zed Tinner was not a religious man. He had told her that whether he was or not made no difference. A soul had departed from this world, and he intended to say a prayer over the grave. She grudgingly conceded, but lines of battle were etched across her face.

"Well." He looked at Lizzie Tinner with scrutinizing eyes. She was a little younger than Isaac, but she returned his look with eyes of a young old person. Her mousy brown hair was carelessly pulled back in a straggly ponytail, and her shabby clothes hung on her thin frame. She looked a good deal like her brother Ben, except Ben always had a harassed look on his face whereas Lizzie's demeanor was usually defiant.

"When would she like us to come?"

"She just wants you to come," Lizzie said quickly.

CJ frowned. An unsettled feeling began to sweep over him. He wished fervently that Joanna would come outside and share this visit. She could always discern people's motives much quicker than he could.

"Why don't you boys show Lizzie the new milk cows." It wasn't a question. CJ indicated with a quick jab the small pasture where they had chased the cows this morning. Isaac looked horrified, but John and Teddy were already leading the way.

For a second, he thought Lizzie would refuse to follow. When Isaac started after the younger boys, however, she quickly led her horse and fell in line.

Joanna was taking a batch of cookies out of the oven when he hurried inside.

"Cookies!" He breathed in the fresh-baked aroma. "Joanna, I think I have a problem."

She raised an unsympathetic eyebrow. "That makes two of us. I have a tired problem. What's your big deal?"

He studied her with concern. She looked tired, and he was worried about her. They were going to have to have a discussion about it right after they had the discussion about the Tinners.

"Lizzie Tinner is here. Her Ma wants me to come and say some words over Ben's grave. Alone."

Joanna slid the cookies unceremoniously off the baking sheet onto a clean dish towel. "Alone? Hmm."

"What does 'hmm' mean?"

"Didn't you tell me you and Smokey had a little visit about the Tinners, and he said Sissy Tinner had a huge crush on you?" She put her hand on her hip and glared at him.

"I just repeated what he said, Joanna. Whether she does or not is not even the question here. Why does Ma Tinner want me there alone?"

"Probably because her daughter Sissy has come back home."

CJ looked at her in puzzlement. "Huh? How do you know that?"

"Rumors." Joanna poured herself a cup of coffee. "CJ, you naive silly boy. Some people go to any lengths to get close to a person they're all swarmy over."

"Swarmy? Is that a word I know?"

She handed him an oatmeal raison cookie. "Probably not. I wouldn't go alone if I were you."

"Will you come with me if I decide to go over there?"

"No. Take Simon. I don't feel up to Mrs. Tinner, Sissy, or Lizzie. And take some cookies out to her so she doesn't have to come in."

He hurriedly put some cookies on a plate. "Wife, you and I are going to have a serious discussion tonight when I get back." He didn't know what he expected her to say, but when she sat down next to the table with her coffee cup in hand and nodded, he felt a knot of fear close to his heart.

Lizzie and the boys made short work of the plateful of cookies. CJ told her he would be over later in the afternoon and she better head on out to tell her mother. He didn't think he liked the calculating look that came over her face.

Simon agreed with Joanna's advice, and with a great deal of apprehension, the two men slowly rode to the Tinners.

"With people like them," Simon observed as they crested another rolling hill, "you're never sure where you stand. You want to trust 'em, but you just can't."

CJ let out a pent-up sigh. "I brought along a Bible to give Mrs. Tinner. I doubt she'll take it."

"Yup. It's strange that several months after Ben dies, she thinks she should have a prayer over his body. I sort of heard by the prairie grapevine that some folks thought they'd seen Sissy. If that's the case, what do they think they'll gain if you come?"

"Joanna thinks they have some scheme to get me there alone and then accuse me of flirting with Sissy. I have no idea. In fact, I wonder if we shouldn't just go back home and not even go through with this charade."

"And have them accuse you of breaking your word? No, CJ, I think we better go through with it, but I intend to stay close as glue to you." Simon shook his head. "I don't like it though."

Two mounds of dirt were the only markers for Ben's and Zed Tinner's graves. CJ and Isaac dismounted and waited for Mrs. Tinner to come. Within minutes, a little procession left the tar paper shack that the Tinners called home. Mrs. Tinner strode toward them without smiling. Lizzie followed a short distance behind with a worried look on her face. The third person was nicely dressed and held a handkerchief to her eyes. She was petite with a dainty dimple in her well-formed chin, and walked as if she were listening for inaudible applause.

"Mr. Swanson," Sissy Tinner said, her voice breaking slightly, "how nice of you to come and join us." She patted Simon's arm absently and seemed to dismiss him completely as she held out her hand to CJ. He knew he was obligated to take it, and he felt the hair on the back of his neck stand up.

"And thank you so much for agreeing to do this, Mr. Crezner." Her voice was somewhat breathless and she flashed him a bright smile as she stood uncomfortably close.

CJ nodded. "Your brother Ben deserves a prayer, Miss Tinner." He was aware that she was clinging to his hand with both of hers.

"CJ, do you want my Bible?" Simon was close by CJ's side.

CJ took his cue. He quickly reached toward Simon and dislodged Sissy's grasping fingers. "Thanks. Oh. Well. I guess I have my own." He backed a few steps from the Tinner ladies and reached into his coat pocket. With both hands firmly holding the Word of God, he looked at Mrs. Tinner. Her face was unreadable.

He took a deep breath and began. "Mrs. Tinner, Sissy, Lizzie, I didn't know your son or your brother at all. But that doesn't matter. God knows His children. He knows, the Bible tells us, how many hairs we have on our heads. He knew when Ben was stabbed with a pitchfork in the haystack. God knew the pain, and later, He knew Ben's agony when that same arm froze and had to be amputated."

Lizzie hiccupped nervously, and Sissy dabbed at her eyes delicately with her handkerchief. Mrs. Tinner's eyes never left CJ's face.

"God always knows." CJ met Mrs. Tinner's unblinking gaze. "Whatever we have in our hearts, God knows. He understands, He cares, and His spirit is always calling us to come to Him with our burdens. Ben's life was hard. I think it was very hard." CJ paused and took off his hat. Simon quickly removed his also.

"Let's pray," he said. Mrs. Tinner closed her eyes but didn't bow her head. Lizzie didn't know what to do, but Sissy Tinner did. She knelt on the broken ground, closed her eyes, and bowed her head. CJ wasn't sure if her actions were from a contrite heart or if she thought the world was a stage she should perform upon.

"Our Heavenly Father, You created us from dust. We are nothing, but You chose to love us. Your Word tells us You loved us so much that You gave Your son to bear our sins on His own body. We ask forgiveness, Lord, for the things we have said and done that are wrong. We ask forgiveness for not being better friends to this young boy. We know, Lord, that Ben's body is here, returning to dust, but his soul is free and is in paradise with You. Eternity waits for all of us after we are taken from this world. You have said that if we love You, our eternity will be with You in paradise. If we love Satan, the ruler of this world, our eternity will be in hell. Help us study Your Word and grow in Your wisdom so we can better love and serve You. Help us remember this boy. He tried to please, he was obedient to his parents, and his life was not lived in vain because it was a precious life in Your sight. In Jesus' name we pray. Amen."

CJ glanced at Sissy. She wasn't pretending tears anymore. They were falling rapidly down her cheeks. Lizzie was shifting her weight from leg to leg and twisting her skirt in her hand.

Mrs. Tinner cleared her throat. "Thank you for keeping it short. I was afraid you'd ramble on."

"Would you like this Bible, Mrs. Tinner?" CJ held out the Bible to her. He could see the refusal in her eyes before she spoke.

"No, I have one of my own."

"Then I would suggest you read it and teach it to your daughters."

She took a swift intake of air before she replied. "Unwanted suggestions are seldom heeded, Mr. Crezner."

"I suppose," Joanna said as she folded their bedcovers back, "the God who knew and understood Ben Tinner also knows and understands Mrs. Tinner. Lord knows none of the rest of us understands the woman." She sank onto the bed with a sigh.

"I imagine you're right." CJ dropped his boot on the floor with a thud. "I want to think maybe the girls will—I don't know—maybe get a few things right in their lives." He worked his other boot loose and let it fall beside the first one.

Joanna leaned back on the feather pillow and looked at him. "CJ, how did you put those thoughts together? You hardly had any time at all to come up with anything."

"I prayed." He slid into bed beside her and propped himself on his elbow to look at her. "I also prayed for my wife, whom I'm very worried about."

She reached up to brush his hair off his forehead. "I know." She let her hand drop. "I keep thinking I'll get my energy back but"— she looked at him and shook her head—"it's not there. I suppose I better see a doctor."

He ran his hand over her hair as it fanned out on the pillow. "I think so. We have to get to the bottom of this." He wound his finger through one of her curls and bent to kiss her. It was always a joy to kiss Joanna. She wound her arm around his neck and kissed him back. Not like usual, but with some of her normal affection.

He was relieved that she had mentioned seeing a doctor. It was better if it was her idea rather than his. He had thought it for the past several days and didn't know how to broach the subject. "Joanna"—he propped himself back on his elbow—"when did you start to feel this way?"

She puckered her forehead in thought. "I guess when I got back from Ma's. I thought at first it was just the visit and then catching up on the work around here. But it seems like this last month, I'm just constantly tired." She gave an exasperated shake of her head. "I've never felt this way before. Just so lethargic, and I really don't care if I get anything done. I feel totally lazy, and what's worse, I don't really care." She looked at him and sighed. "Totally unlike myself."

He smiled, hoping to ease her fears as well as his own. "Totally. You've always had energy to burn." He slowly eased himself down on his pillow. The full moon was working its way higher in the eastern sky, and its beams were making magical light in their bedroom.

"Full moon already," he murmured. "You and I have always enjoyed our full moons."

"Yup." Her voice sounded sleepy. "You asked me to marry you under a full moon."

He grinned. "Remember the full moon before you left to go to Minnesota?"

She giggled. "CJ, you are purely wicked. Do you know that?" She reached over and ran her hand over his bare shoulder. He pulled her close to him and kissed her again.

She wriggled close to him and found a comfortable spot in his arms. "That was already, what, two full moons ago?" She sighed and traced his jaw line with her finger. "Time goes so fast, CJ. I wish it would slow down. I wish…" Her voice trailed off.

"What do you wish?" He was in the process of trailing kisses down her lovely throat when she caught her breath.

"Joanna?"

"I said that was two months ago, didn't I? Didn't I say that was two months ago?" She pushed him away and sat up. "That was two months ago!" She grabbed a portion of the sheet and wadded it in a tight ball, and her voice sounded hoarse. "Do you know what that means? Oh horse feathers! Why didn't I think of this before?"

He frowned and watched her sink back into the pillow, not comprehending a thing she said. "Think of what before? What are you talking about?"

She straightened out the crumpled sheet and began to pull it over her head. "I don't like this, oh no! I don't like this at all. I can't believe it!" She was muttering and moaning at the same time, and her voice became muffled under the sheet.

His heart was beginning to thump unpleasantly in his chest. Either Joanna was losing her mind or something was seriously wrong.

He carefully pulled the sheet off her face and tucked it around her shoulders. "What are you saying?" He tried to sound calm.

Her face was pale in the moonlight, and her eyes gazed up at him with a mixture of fear and disbelief. "You're not going to like this either. Even though it's your fault."

"My fault?" he yelped. "Joanna, what are you saying?" He forgot to be calm and gave her shoulder a slight shake.

She took a deep breath before she answered. "I'm saying we're going to have another baby!"

CJ looked at her with incredulity. "What? What? I send you to Minnesota to see your mother, and you come back with a baby?"

Her eyes flashed, and she pulled her hand from underneath the sheet. "That's what riding passenger trains do to young ladies." Her voice oozed with sarcasm.

"I didn't think after five years you could even have another baby." CJ glared at her. "What are you thinking of, Joanna? This isn't good."

"Your darn tootin' it ain't good!" She shoved him away from her and sat up. "You and your blasted full moon. This is all your fault, CJ. I don't want another baby. I don't want to be tired and worn out for the next seven months. I don't want this at all!" She shook her finger at him and then gave him a harder shove away from her. "And for that matter, what's this remark about me going to Minnesota and coming back with a baby? Are you saying I found somebody and had an affair with him in two weeks? Just thanks a lot for that little dig!"

CJ slumped down on his pillow and covered both eyes with his hands. His mind was spinning in several directions at the same time, resulting in a mass confusion that rendered him speechless for several seconds.

"Okay. Okay, Joanna. Just give me a second here. I'm trying to—"

"Shut up, CJ. Right now I don't care one whit what you're trying to do." She slammed back onto her pillow and kicked at the disheveled sheet.

There was silence in the bedroom while CJ pulled his scattered thoughts together and Joanna seethed with her back toward him.

"I'm scared for you, Joanna," he finally said. "I've always been worried about you having another baby and not being able to grow old with me." He turned on his side and reached for her shoulder. He wasn't surprised when she kicked him in the shin.

"And I didn't mean to sound like you had an affair. I know this baby is mine."

"I'm not the one who has swarmy admirers hanging all over them," she muttered and lashed out with her foot again.

He retaliated by putting his leg over hers and pinning it to the bed. "I was just thinking now at least we know why you're tired. I had visions of all sorts of things, and none of them were good. This is a surprise, but when we get used to the idea, we might even like the thought of another baby." He put his arm around her and gave her a gentle hug. Her elbow was wicked as she drove home a swift jab to his unsuspecting stomach.

"And," he continued as he released her and returned to his own side of the bed, "I think the next thing we better do is go to Dr. Riggs in Pierre, so you can have a good checkup. Then we better see about getting someone to come and help you until the baby is born."

"If you so much as think for a *minute* I need my mother here, I'll slap you." Her voice was mutinous, and he knew from long experience that any more talk would lead to heated words. He also knew that if he gave Joanna an inch, she'd take a mile.

"Woman," he said softly. "If you hit me one more time, I'm going to hit you back."

The last of the moonbeams were fading from the room when he heard her say, "Brute. Make me with child and then threaten to beat me."

The room was completely dark when he replied, "I love you, Joanna."

She sniffed and slowly turned to face him. "This ain't gonna be purty, CJ. And I love you too."

3

July 15, 1907

Belvidere, South Dakota

Dear Mom and Dad,

I'm sorry it's been so long since I've written. With our milk cows and the abundant hay crop, we keep busy from dawn to dusk.

The cows are giving lots of milk. I make a trip to Belvidere every week and keep up with the business bookwork at the same time. It works well. John and Teddy had the job of naming the cows, and John wrote all their names on a board in the barn. Good thing, as Simon and I keep forgetting Gloria from Halli and Lulia. We also have Truth, Lilly, Beauty, Trampled. Do you recognize "The Battle Hymn of the Republic" from those words? Joanna found the music in her mother's piano bench, and the boys think it is the most wonderful song they ever heard.

Isaac was hired for the roundup this spring and has just returned after being gone for several weeks. John and Teddy helped Simon and me in the hayfields, but they complain a great deal more about mosquito bites than Isaac ever did. Isaac had high marks on his eighth-grade exam and is officially ready for high school. He has decided to stay with Mrs. Ordin. She offered him room and board in exchange for odd jobs at the boarding house. He was pleased about the offer and took it. We are both excited and apprehensive about his new adventure.

The most amazing news, however, is that we are going to be parents again at the end of the year. Yes, that means you will be grandparents again. Joanna consulted with Dr. Riggs at Pierre and was relieved to hear that both baby and mother will be fine. She has been more tired with this baby than with the boys. I am looking for someone to help her with her household jobs. However, she has refused all of my suggestions.

We have a woman doctor close by. Dr. Sullivan lives about a mile from us, but Joanna says she's heard the good doctor is quite rough and her vocabulary is colorful. The plan is to go to Pierre and wait for the baby to be delivered by Dr. Riggs.

Always glad to hear from you, and we are counting down the days until your visit. Have you considered taking an extra week for vacation now that your associate pastor is helping so much?

Our love,

CJ, Joanna, John, and Teddy

The morning sun had scarcely peeked over the eastern hills by the time CJ finished writing his letter. He and the boys were making an early morning run to Belvidere with the team and wagon to deliver cream to the depot and milk and eggs to some Belvidere residents. So far, Simon's cows had added extra coins to the money box, and even if CJ detested each and every one of them, they probably would pay for themselves in the long run.

"Dad," John whispered as they quietly left the house, "do you think Mom will miss us when she wakes up?"

CJ nodded as he shut the screen door slowly. Left to its own devices, the door slammed closed with a great deal of screeching and banging, thanks to the spring CJ put on it so that it wouldn't stay ajar with their coming and going.

"I think everything's loaded, CJ," Simon spoke quietly also. It was the mission of Joanna's men folk to let her sleep as long as possible in the morning. She grumbled a great deal about them pandering to her, but the usual bustling lady of the house had simply lost most of her energy. Doctor Riggs had reassured them it was a passing phase, and one all of them hoped would pass quickly.

It was completely different for CJ to travel to town from what he had experienced during the first years of his marriage when the prairie was still open and unoccupied. He was beginning to resent the shacks that dotted the landscape as much as Joanna. In fact, this morning, he almost resented his whole lifestyle and was testy with his young boys as they bounced across the prairie. They, in turn, were so surprised at his short and curt replies that they lapsed into hurt silence. The six miles into town were long and quiet.

He was worried. Time and again, he reassured himself and Joanna also, that the baby would come without any problems. Time and again, worry took control and gave him sleepless nights as he pondered what-if scenarios. What if she died in child birth? What if it took away her energy forever? What if she became an invalid? What if…? What if…? The worry had consumed his peace of mind.

CJ had trouble making small talk to his milk and egg customers. When he finished his deliveries, he gave each boy two pennies and told them to spend it wisely while he balanced the scribbled books of his bosses.

To add to his already irritable disposition, the wife of one of his bosses was ensconced in the tiny cramped upstairs office. She was an unsmiling woman and was constantly checking his work. Usually, the issues she debated with him were easily clarified, but it always took more time than he wanted to spend with her. This morning, she was poring over the ledger as he walked in.

"I think you once again have made some mistakes, Mr. Crezner." She greeted him with her usual sour expression.

CJ stopped just inside the door. He knew before she said another word what he was going to do. He also knew he'd regret it later on, but at this moment, he was going to take great pleasure in his next actions.

"A mistake, ma'am?" He made his voice sound mild. "That's terrible. I imagine the best thing for me to do is quit and let you take over." He turned to go before he added, "I'll ask your husband to pay me in full before I leave."

He also took great pleasure in the shocked look she gave him. He thundered down the narrow steps and found the husband stocking shelves.

"Your wife has just gained my job," he said abruptly. "I'll collect my wages for the past month, if you don't mind."

The husband minded a great deal, but there was no dissuading CJ. And when he put the wages in his pocket, he left the store with the sole intention of rounding up his boys and heading home.

Even though it was only midmorning, the sun was unbearably hot. It would be a long, slow, hot ride home. The thought crossed his mind that if he didn't have the two boys along, he'd head into the nearest saloon and have a cold beer. It was a troubling thought, but once it took hold, it wouldn't let go of him.

The boys were sitting in the shade of the wagon with frustration written on their features.

"What's wrong?" CJ wondered.

"Everything we want costs more than what we've got," John said with evident disgust.

"And that, my boys, is the story of life." CJ looked down at their dismal faces. "But I have enough to buy us something cool to drink before we start home. I guess we'll have to be contented with that."

"When I get growed up, I'm gonna have lots of pennies." Teddy stood up and reached for CJ's hand. "And I'm gonna live someplace where it ain't so hot."

Their lemonade at the café was not cool. Their waitress was apologetic, but there was no ice chips to put in it. At least, John observed, it was wet. And that gave CJ the idea to let the boys swim in the Belvidere dam before they headed home.

They stripped down to their shorts after they stopped beside the curve in the road, and the cool water, even if it was a bit mossy, felt refreshing. CJ waded in a big circle to make sure there were no drop-offs and told the boys to stay in that spot. They splashed and shouted, and soon forgot their money woes as they enjoyed and had fun in the water.

CJ looked longingly at the expanse of water and wished that he'd dare leave the boys alone while he swam. He couldn't, of course, as neither boy knew how to swim. And that gave him another idea. He spent the next half hour giving them swimming lessons. They were quick learners, and Teddy boasted he could swim across the dam with just one lesson.

"No, you can't, Theodore Simon, and don't even think about trying to swim unless I'm with you." CJ was firm, and for emphasis, he tweaked Theodore Simon's ear.

"Mr. Crezner! I have to talk to you!" A woman was standing at the edge of the water. It was a tall, gaunt woman, and CJ recognized her immediately as the unsmiling wife of his former boss. Did she know he just had underwear on? What was the woman thinking about anyway?

He waved at her. "I'll come back to the store," he hollered. Surely she would go away.

"You left unfinished business at the store. I need to talk to you right now!"

Bossy woman. First she fussed over his work, then she took his job, and now she wanted to talk to him when he was indecent. He should just wade to shore and stand there in his shorts and see what this was all about. But he was, after all, a preacher's son and a preacher himself—and preachers did not do such things, even if they were extremely irritated. On the other hand, maybe a cattleman might get away with it.

He waved again. "I'm not decent, ma'am. I'll talk to you later."

She waved back. "I'll wait by your wagon. Hurry." He watched her stalk up the grassy bank and head toward his waiting team.

"Daddy! I can too swim! See?"

CJ jerked toward the sound of Teddy's voice, and his heart jumped into his throat. In the few seconds that he had been preoccupied, his youngest son had moved several yards away from him and was now happily flogging away in deeper water.

"John," CJ said softly, "go to the shore and wait."

In a louder voice, he called to Teddy. "Come this way now, Teddy. Swim to me." He moved closer to his errant son as fast as he could. Teddy turned toward him and started to say something more as he moved his arms and kicked his feet. Instead of breathing out to talk, however, he gulped in water, and panic immediately overcame him.

He plunged and coughed and took in more water. "Daddy!" he screamed, and he bobbed under water.

CJ swam as fast and hard as he could and reached his flailing son in seconds. Teddy was terrified and grabbed him around the neck in a death grip. CJ flipped over on his back, and with almost lazy strokes, he made his way into shallower water with Teddy securely in tow.

When the water was waist-deep for CJ, he stood and held Teddy out of the water. His son needed a lesson in minding.

"Ted, I told you not to do what you just did. What almost happened to you?"

"I ate so much water I almost puked!" Teddy blubbered.

"You almost drowned!" CJ yelled and gave Teddy a shake.

"We better go home and see Mama." Teddy looked extremely worried and started to sniffle.

CJ checked to make sure John was on shore. Sure enough, his oldest son was waiting anxiously on dry ground.

"You need a lesson in several areas, Ted. First of all, you need to know more about swimming. I'm going to let go of you. You can swim to shore."

"No! No! Daddy, I can't swim that far!"

"Yes, you can. I'll be right here beside you." CJ lowered him into the water and released him.

Teddy immediately began to howl and started to sink.

"Remember what I taught you! Reach out with your arms! Cup your hands! Scissor kick!"

Teddy bawled and flailed the forty feet to shore. His next lesson began with a good sound spanking because he had disobeyed his father. More tears and sobbing, and while the three of them were getting dressed amidst all this distress, the sharp tone of his former boss's wife rang out.

"Mr. Crezner!"

"What!" CJ roared, and with his pants half-buttoned and his shirt barely thrown over his wet shoulders, he stomped up the bank. "What do you want?" He glared at the woman and didn't care that she was blushing at his appearance.

"I-I..." She turned away from him and looked extremely uncomfortable.

"You boys hurry up and get in this wagon. We're going home!" He finished buttoning his pants and fastened his belt while John helped his heartbroken little brother up the bank. "Ma'am, whatever you have to say to me, spit it out. I'm in no mood to waste time." He lifted Teddy unceremoniously into the wagon while John climbed the steps.

"I had no idea you had such a temper, Mr. Crezner!"

"Well, now you know. Did you come down here to tell me I had a temper?"

"I-I came because I realized, that is, my husband told me…Oh! I'm supposed to ask you if you would come back to work for us." She waved her hands awkwardly.

CJ checked the horses' harnesses before he answered. He knew what he was going to say. He stalled for time so he could answer politely. He slowly climbed into the wagon and sat on the seat before he looked at her.

"No. I'm not working for anyone who questions my honesty. You, ma'am, have checked and double-checked my figures from day one. You never found any mistakes, yet you harassed me about one thing or another. Do the books yourself." He clicked his tongue and flicked the lines over the team and didn't bother to wave goodbye.

They made their way slowly over the dam grade and headed north toward home. Teddy eventually cried himself to sleep, but his sobs continued even as he slept. John sat timidly on the seat next to CJ, and CJ felt a weariness creep into his entire being.

The sun baked the earth, the flies bit the horses, the wind blew hot air all around them, and it was a dismal bunch that followed the dusty prairie trail. Finally, John put his hand on CJ's arm and said haltingly, "Dad, I was thinking about something."

CJ roused himself from his own desolate thoughts and smiled down at his brown-eyed son. "What were you thinking, John?"

"You wouldn't have let Teddy drown. That's why you were right beside him with your hands close by him. I knew that, but it still scared me. I was afraid for him."

CJ gave a pent-up sigh. "I wanted him to know he can swim but that he needs to respect the water. Sometimes, when people get really scared about swimming, they never learn how to enjoy it." CJ sat up a little straighter and gave his son a gentle squeeze on his shoulder. "What about you? Do you like swimming?"

John nodded absently, but it was obvious his mind was on something else. "I was thinking something else. I was thinking maybe God is like you, Dad. Maybe when we think we're in trouble and no one is around to help us, God is right there, with His hands close to keep us out of the water." John looked up at CJ. "Do you think that's right?"

"I think you're a very thoughtful young man. That's a good likeness of our Heavenly Father's love." CJ looked away and found it hard to swallow past the lump in his throat. All the while Teddy was screaming that he would drown, CJ was making sure he wouldn't. All the while CJ was worrying about what might happen to Joanna, God was trying to reassure him that she was in God's hands. He'd take care of her. Simple as that. Where had his faith been? Good thing his seven-year-old son had set him straight.

When he got home, he'd set Joanna straight too. No more moping around for either of them. She would be just fine. The doctor said so. And he was going to find someone to come and help her with all the work. And that was that.

"She did what?" CJ looked at Isaac incredulously while the two of them unharnessed the team and rubbed them down.

"She hired Lizzie Tinner to come and work for her. And the worst of the worst"—Isaac jerked the harness away from the lathered horse—"she's letting Lizzie stay in the old washhouse. That's right behind me and Dad's house. Lizzie Tinner, CJ. Lizzie Tinner living right behind me." Isaac's usual quiet voice had taken on new volume.

"You mean—"

"I mean at this very minute, Lizzie is making herself right at home, and Aunt Jo is bustling around like an old hen. 'Isaac, get the cot out from the cellar. Isaac, check the pump and see that it's primed. Isaac, carry over this bedding. Isaac, get lost for a while. Lizzie is going to take a bath.' I never thought I'd say this, but I'm almost glad

I'm leaving this fall. This is terrible!" To prove his point, Isaac swatted the big rump of the workhorse with his cap and was rewarded with a tail swished in his face.

CJ got some oats from the grain bin and poured it into a wooden trough for his team. He shook his head, muttered unintelligible sounds, and sat down heavily on an upturned keg. "Maybe I better hear this from the beginning. No! Wait! Maybe I better hear this from Joanna." He didn't move, and the only sound was that of the horses crunching their grain. "Maybe I should just sit here and think before I say too much."

"Maybe"—Isaac threw himself on the ground beside CJ's perch—"you better let me tell you what I know."

"Sure. Kill me with information." CJ sighed and put his hands on his knees.

"Well, Dad left to rake up that one creek bottom, and I was cleaning harnesses when Lizzie come riding in. And you know, even though Burr is getting older, she always barks at Lizzie. So here's Burr barking, and Lizzie screeching, and Joanna walks out and tells 'em both to pipe down. Then Lizzie sorta slides off that spotted devil she rides, and I could hear her trying to tell Joanna something, then she ties old Spot up, and she and Joanna go in the house. After a while, Joanna is hollering at me, and the next thing I know, I'm being ordered about like a slave."

CJ shook his head. Isaac never complained about helping Joanna. That was as unusual as Joanna hiring Lizzie. His belly started rumbling, and Isaac looked at him in surprise.

"Been a long time since breakfast." CJ stood up. "Is Simon coming in for dinner?" His question was answered by a horse's whinny and the clatter of the rake.

Isaac jumped to his feet and headed toward the barn door. "I'm gonna fix our own dinner. I will not eat with Lizzie Tinner!"

CJ's hunger pangs growled again. He wondered if there would be anything ready for a meal. Lately, one never knew if Joanna would have cooked plenty or just enough to get by.

Even though it was hot, the cook stove was in full force. Joanna was wiping beads of perspiration off her forehead. Potatoes, gravy, green beans, and fried chicken were on platters, waiting to be carried to the table.

"You've been busy!" He eyed her warily.

"Yes," she snapped. "While you're swimming and cooling off, I'm cooking and getting hotter by the minute!"

He glowered at her and picked up the platters. Anything he would have said was drowned out by running footsteps on the stairway. Lizzie was chasing both boys, and there was a chorus of laughter as they raced to the table. There were two extra plates neatly set with silverware and folded napkins. CJ took them off and shook his head at Joanna and her unspoken question.

Lizzie. CJ looked twice to make sure that it was really Lizzie. Joanna had found a skirt and a waist for her. For once, Lizzie was clean, and her hair was not only combed but also washed and braided neatly.

"I'm working for ya now, Mr. Crezner!" The voice was Lizzie. Loud and screechy. Like an old well pump that needed new leathers.

"Well. Well, I'm sure you'll tell me all about it after we pray." CJ managed a weak smile for her.

"Sure! You want I should get out that fruit you fixed?" At Joanna's nod, Lizzie raced over to the ice box and then slowly, carefully, carried a bowl of canned peaches to the table. She didn't seem to breathe until she had set it down beside Joanna's plate.

CJ thanked the Lord for the food, the safety of the family, the day in general, and lastly, for Lizzie—even though he didn't exactly feel grateful for her being there.

Teddy had become very quiet after his prayer. CJ wondered how much Joanna knew of their swimming episode. When he arrived home, he carried Teddy's sleeping form into the house and upstairs to the bedroom. When he returned downstairs, Joanna had disappeared.

"I guess we were hungry," he said apologetically to Joanna after three helpings of everything. The boys ate almost as much as he did. "And," he added, "everything was very good. So good we forgot to talk while we ate." He pushed his chair back slightly and looked at Lizzie. So far, she had eaten like a bird, taking a few bite of this, a few bites of that, but mostly looking in awe at the way he and the boys were demolishing the platters of food.

"Well. Lizzie, it sounds like you have been hired to help Mrs. Crezner. Why don't you ladies tell me about this?" He smiled at Joanna, who, he noticed, had two little red spots on her cheeks.

"Mrs. Tinner has a job up in the north country herding cattle for the Matador Cattle Co. She couldn't take Lizzie with her, so I have hired her until she can return to her mother." Joanna looked at him steadily, and CJ knew by the expression on her face there was much more to the story.

"I see." He saw very little, he realized, but the rest of the information would come when they were alone. He glanced at Lizzie. "And you're not staying in the house but instead have taken up residence in the washhouse?"

She nodded and stood up slowly. "You want I should clear off the table now, Mizzus Crezner?"

"Yes. Stack everything on the right side of the sink."

CJ watched absently as Lizzie made trips back and forth and put everything on the left side of the sink.

"Daddy, can I be 'scused?" Teddy's voice was subdued.

"No. You cannot be 'scused until I hear about this swimming thing." Joanna was firm.

"We were hot, so we went swimming in the Belvidere dam. Cooled off, came home." CJ looked at Teddy and John. "Or was there more that happened?"

John was not going to be trapped. He shrugged and looked at Teddy. Teddy looked down at his plate.

Joanna looked at all three of them in turn, and then she sat back and folded her arms in front of her. "I'm waiting."

CJ stood and took some dirty dishes to the right side of the sink, and motioned to Lizzie that she needed to move plates from left to right. Then he found two cups and poured both himself and Joanna coffee, which had been kept hot on the back of the stove. He set their cups on the table and opened the dining room window. A blast of hot air came through, and he quickly closed it again.

"You boys are excused, and I think in light of all we've done this morning, you better take a little nap upstairs." Teddy was gone in a flash.

"And since Lizzie is here busily clearing off the table and getting dishes ready to wash, let's go into the other room and have our coffee," he told Joanna, and gently pulled her to a standing position.

He guided her to the old rocker, and she sank gratefully into the worn cushions. Balancing her cup carefully, she put her feet on the footstool and sighed. CJ closed the door between the two rooms and sat down close to her.

"Mizzus Crezner, shall you go first, or shall I?"

Joanna took a slow drink of coffee before she answered. "I know you think I'm crazy, CJ, but where else is she going to go? And I remember needing a home when I was a little older than she was. Mary took me in, rough edges and all. Maybe this is my way of paying Mary back." Whenever Joanna looked at him with her lips in a vulnerable smile and her eyes begging understanding, his heart seemed to have a mind of its own.

"Why the washhouse?"

"That was her idea. She didn't seem to like the thought of being in the house with all of us."

"Will she cause more work, or will she actually help?"

Joanna shrugged. "Time will tell."

He leaned back in the wing chair. "What's her wages?"

"She didn't want wages. Room and board, she said. I think she was quite desperate."

They heard the sound of water being poured into the big tea kettle. Joanna gave no indication she was in a hurry to help her new helper.

"What happened at the dam?"

CJ narrowed his eyes and shook his head. "Our youngest son learned that he pushed his daddy a little too far. I spanked him. He took off in deep water, and I was scared half to death I was going to lose him and also scared that John would try to help and I'd lose him too."

Joanna put her hand to her mouth, and her eyes widened in horror. "I wondered if it was something like that. Teddy has needed a spanking for a long time, and I've been too tired to whop him." She rocked in silence then asked, "How come Isaac and Simon didn't come in for dinner?"

"I believe your favorite nephew is far less than happy to have Lizzie as his new neighbor."

"He should put himself in her place and think what he would do if his only parent left without making any provision for him." Joanna snapped, brushing at a buzzing fly with irritation.

"Ma Tinner has already left?"

"Ma Tinner had her horse saddled at daybreak. She told Lizzie she was leaving, and Lizzie could figure out what she was going to do. She said she was on her own when she was Lizzie's age, and it taught her how to think for herself."

"How old do you think Lizzie is?" CJ sputtered a little laugh. "Lizzie is. That's a mouthful."

Joanna shook her head at him and managed a small smile. "Lizzie is twelve. She knows how to read a little, knows a little ciphering."

"Joanna, I know you want to help her. Sometimes folks like her appreciate it, but sometimes they bite the hand that feeds them. Be very careful how much you feel sorry for her."

They sat in silence while they finished their coffee, and then Joanna asked, "Who was the woman?"

"Woman?"

"The woman who wouldn't let you get dressed before she talked to you." Joanna's voice held an edge.

CJ started to laugh. "Ah yes, Mrs. Prillis. I quit my job at the Prillis store this morning. I got tired of her fussing over the figures. She can do the books herself. Her husband is not sure she can, but I told him I have complete confidence in her. She came to the dam because her husband wanted to hire me back."

Joanna rocked slowly and seemed to be lost in thought. Outside, the wind had picked up, and they could hear the dust particles hit the windows.

"What are you going to do after dinner?" Her head was tilted as she looked at him, and her expression was tender.

He stood and gazed at her, and a smile danced over his face. Bending down, he brushed his lips against hers. "I would love to sit here all afternoon and enjoy my wife, but I suppose I better see what Simon has lined up for us." He studied her profile. "What are you going to do?"

She sighed and slowly took her feet off the footstool."Find jobs for Lizzie Tinner."

4

August 21, 1907

Springfield, Missouri

Dear Joanna, CJ, John, and Teddy,

We've just bought train tickets and will be arriving at Belvidere on Tuesday, September 3! We are so excited to see all of you and to meet Lizzie. Joanna, please don't go to extra bother for us. We're family and want to pitch in and help you when we get there. Save some work for us!

I still can hardly believe we can travel in such luxury on the passenger train. It's truly splendid, and we hope some day, after the baby gets here and can travel easily, you will journey this way.

Missouri is sweltering and humid, as is usual in August. We are looking forward to the 'north' country. John looks tired and *is* tired. We are going to take an extra week of vacation and are hoping he can get revived. Perhaps this time it would be best if he didn't try to do any services while there. I know he will if he is asked, so I am suggesting it might be better to tell folks beforehand. (And he would tell me I'm meddling if he reads this.)

The newspapers talk about extremely dry and hot weather in your area with lots of wind. We are always concerned about fires and pray none get started.

Will save the rest of my chatter for when I see you!

Love in His name,

Mom and Dad Crezner

CJ tapped the letter with his finger after he finished reading it aloud. "I worry about Dad. If even Mom says he looks tired, he must be exhausted. She never exaggerates."

There wasn't a trace of evening breeze on the porch where they sat with the boys and Lizzie. The air was hot and heavy, and faint rumblings of thunder could be heard in the dark blue western sky. Joanna fanned herself with slow, languid waves of her silk-decorated fan, and her bare toes peeked from underneath her skirt. CJ noticed her feet were swollen again and she had kicked off her shoes to get some relief.

"I hope it cools down before they get here, or it won't seem any different than Missouri," Joanna grumbled and kicked at a fly that buzzed around her ankles.

"Fires. Everyone must be worried about 'em. I see a lot of homesteaders plowing firebreaks around their buildings." Isaac was slumped against the porch rail, chewing on a piece of grass.

"Maybe we should do the same." Joanna was ready to argue. They had talked about this before. CJ hated to break up the virgin grass. It usually sprouted weeds unless it was replanted back to grass. On this hot evening, he saw no need to even discuss it.

"Wonder if Ma has saw any fires." Unlike Joanna who kept her bare feet discreetly hid under her skirt, Lizzie stretched thin and scratched bare ankles and bony feet defiantly in front of her.

"'Has saw' ain't good English, Lizzie. Just ask Johnny." Teddy was always quick to point out errors in other folk's speech. No one paid attention to his correction except Lizzie. She stuck her tongue out and looked at him cross-eyed. Teddy moved a little closer to John, even though he always stoutly denied being uneasy with Lizzie's looks.

"Someone said they heard there was a big fire up north a couple of weeks ago. I don't know if a rain put it out or what." CJ folded up his parents' letter and put it back in the envelope. "I suppose if your mother is herding cattle around the Cheyenne River she probably saw it."

Burr erupted from under the porch with growls and frenzied barking. She startled them, and CJ slowly rose to his feet and looked toward the creek in the fading daylight.

"Oh, good grief, someone's walking up from the creek, and they'll catch me without my shoes on." Joanna's voice was low and irritated. "CJ, go talk to 'em before they get any closer!"

CJ eased himself down the porch steps and gave Burr a command to settle down. As usual, she ignored him and barked all the way toward their visitor with bristled hair, showing her displeasure.

"Hey, Burr, it's me. I'm your neighbor, remember?" Nels Christensen's voice held a slight note of intimidation, which pleased Burr greatly, and she barked all the louder.

"Burr! Shut up, you fool dog!" Lizzie and Burr had an active dislike for one another, and her screeched admonition could be heard up and down the creek. CJ wished he could oil her voice like he oiled irritating wheels that made terrible noises.

Even in the twilight, CJ could see the disgusted look on Isaac's face as he bounded toward Burr and gave her quiet instructions to come to him. She, of course, had always adored Isaac. In a flash, she was by his side, tongue lolling around her dog grin and wagging her burr-encrusted tail. Joanna had been too tired this summer to cut them out.

CJ and Isaac met Nels when he was a short distance away, and the three visited about the heat, the drought, rattlesnakes, and life in general. Simon emerged from his house to join them, and when CJ thought Joanna had ample time to get her shoes on, the foursome ambled toward the porch.

"Evening, ma'am." Nels doffed his cap when he saw Joanna sitting in the shadows.

"Mr. Christensen." Joanna smiled and pointed to CJ's vacated chair. "Sit and rest a spell. You've had quite a walk this evening."

"Oh, I suppose it's about a mile. I hear some homesteaders have walked all over the countryside, especially if they don't have a horse."

"I can't imagine not having a horse," Joanna murmured as she resumed her slow fanning.

"The boys and Lizzie must be in the house." CJ could hear Lizzie giving orders to the boys through the open kitchen window.

"They wanted to bring Mr. Christensen cookies and something to drink." Joanna squirmed in her chair and tried to peer through the window. "Maybe you should go supervise, Isaac. Sometimes they all three need a good boss."

Isaac's countenance darkened, but he obediently walked up the porch steps and headed toward the door. "You'd think she could bring out cookies without needing help," he muttered as he brushed past CJ. Isaac and Burr seemed to have the same opinion about Lizzie.

Nels was getting himself comfortably ensconced in CJ's chair. He stuck his folded-up cap in his front pocket and leaned back in his chair far enough so the front legs came up. He teetered on the back legs and rocked back and forth contentedly.

"I was over at the Gardners' for dinner today. You know." He paused and pointed northwest. "They live over there on the hill, maybe a mile or so west of me."

CJ and Simon both nodded their heads.

"Well, sir, we were talking about schools, and Mrs. Gardner said her sister was coming out to homestead and she could teach school. Now that got me to thinking." He rocked some more on the chair's back legs before he went on.

"I said, 'Where's she gonna teach at?' and Mrs. Gardner said she didn't know. And I said, 'How about a claim cabin school? It's not the fanciest, but it could sure do in a pinch. And Mr. Gardner got to counting up how many kids could come, and with their two boys and your kids and I think the Abrahamson kids, it could be a right nice little group."

Joanna stopped fanning herself and leaned forward. "You mean you'd give up your cabin so the kids could have a school house? But where will you go?"

Nels set his chair down with a thud. "I have a job in town, Mrs. Crezner, and I think I'll just take up residence there for a while."

Simon cleared his throat. "I, ah, I believe the government has a stipulation that if a claim shack is used for a school, the homesteader doesn't have to live there to keep his homestead."

Nels looked surprised. "Really? Well, good enough. I won't have to worry about coming out during the wintertime then."

The screen door opened, and Teddy came slowly with a heaping plate full of cookies. Isaac carried a pitcher of lemonade, and behind him, Lizzie and John carried glasses. They carefully served everyone and, finally, themselves, and Lizzie plopped down on the top step with a sigh of relief.

"Whew. We didn't spill a drop. So there, Mr. Grouch Isaac."

"You know, I never thought about it," Nels said between bites of cookie, "but Lizzie could go to school too. I mean," he hastily added, "I mean if you could spare her, of course."

Lizzie looked horrified. Before anyone could answer, a low rumble of thunder grumbled across the western sky.

"I wonder if we'll get any rain tonight," CJ said and set his empty glass down.

"Yeah, it's dry. I worry about fires. Say, I see you don't have a fireguard around your place. Most folks do, you know." Nels brushed crumbs from his hand. When another rumble of thunder was heard, he stood up and handed his glass to John. "I suppose I better head back before it gets plumb dark and rains on me."

CJ stood also. "Thanks for telling us about the school, Nels. I'll talk to Mr. Gardner, and we'll have to figure out teacher wages and so on."

Nels said his goodbyes and thanked Joanna for the home-baked treat. He and Simon left together, and CJ heard Simon offer Nels the use of his lantern as they walked into the deepening twilight.

"Would Mrs. Crezner like a helping hand to get up?" CJ asked as he walked toward Joanna's chair.

"Mrs. Crezner would like to take her puffy bare feet, which will not, and I mean absolutely will not, fit into her shoes, and put her children to bed and also herself to bed. In fact"—Joanna looked at her boys—"Mrs. Crezner has just decided her boys can put themselves to bed. Help me up, CJ. I'm tired and hot beyond belief."

"I'll carry your shoes, Momma," Teddy offered.

"And I ain't going to no school. I ain't sittin' there with a bunch of little kids," Lizzie muttered as she gathered up empty glasses. "And no one can make me go neither. So there."

"Charlotte, you should have heard CJ singing with little Frank and his accordion. The only song they knew together was 'Yankee Doodle'. Young John and I were impressed!"

CJ grinned at his father's words. Finally, after two weeks of cool evenings and beautiful, fresh daytime breezes, his father was beginning to look rested. CJ was more worried than he wanted to admit when his parents got off the train, and John Crezner's slumped shoulders and haggard face drove pangs of fear into his heart.

"We did our best." CJ winked at his mother. "And singing when your tummy is full of kolaches and hot coffee ain't easy."

"Daddy, you shouldn't say ain't." Teddy was sitting on CJ's lap, and his own tummy was very full of Antonio's kolaches. "I wish we could bring baby Joe home," he groused. Teddy always wanted to bring babies home.

Charlotte Crezner smiled, and little beams of sunlight seemed to flash from her eyes. CJ always loved seeing his parents happy, and day by day, he watched them become more lighthearted as they took in the affairs on the ranch and experimented with the chores.

"Antonio wants to have a frame house instead of the sod one, but guess that must have gotten postponed for another year," Joanna murmured from her rocking chair. Her bare feet were propped up on a homemade hassock, and she was once again altering one of her skirts to accommodate her growing waistline.

"How did you know that? I thought you told me once you couldn't understand anything she said." CJ could follow Frank's words with careful attention, but he too was at a loss when Antonio spoke.

"Lizzie told me. She seems to be able to understand Bohemians. Don't ask me how." Joanna closed one eye and held her needle to the light. "I wonder if they could make the eye of a needle any smaller," she muttered as she finally maneuvered the thread into the tiny slot.

"She's always skulking around, listening to everyone's conversation. She should know everything about everyone in Stanley County." Isaac gave a disgusted snort.

Charlotte reached over to rumple Isaac's hair. "I want to hear what classes you'll be taking, Isaac. I'm surprised the school in Pierre doesn't insist you be there since school is in session."

Isaac's scowl left his face, and he gave Charlotte his special grin. "Well, I'm supposed to take Latin. It looks hard." Isaac shook his head. "I can't see why I need it, but the school seems to think it's important."

"I think most schools know the country kids are helping with harvesting now, so they give them leeway." CJ glanced at Isaac before he added, "And we most definitely need his help—"

CJ was interrupted by a frenzied scream and vicious barking. He could hear Lizzie's voice in high screeching form telling Burr to get away and painful yelping from Burr, with more growling and barking.

CJ was on his feet and running to the door in seconds. He had visions of Burr standing over Lizzie with snarling fangs, and he quickly grabbed his pistol that hung in its holster by the door.

"He's been bit! He's been bit!" Lizzie screamed when she saw CJ.

"Get out of the way, Lizzie. Move away!"

A huge rattlesnake was coiled on the path to Simon's house. Burr was in the process of darting in to grab the ugly, hissing reptile. But Burr had age against her, and once again with lightning speed, the snake struck. This time, its fangs sank deep into Burr's shoulder.

"Lizzie, get away!" CJ shouted, and he raced down the path toward the howling dog. He could hear Simon pounding close behind him, and when they reached the frightened dog, Simon took his trusty shovel and slammed it on the snake's flying body. As soon as the snake let go of the dog, CJ fired his pistol. And missed. Once again, he took aim. This time, the snake's head was blown off, and the mass of slithering reptile oozed around the shovel as if loath to admit defeat. Simon pounded its flinching body several more times.

"Are you okay?" CJ asked the sobbing girl.

"Burr's been bit! Twice! She's been bit! Twice! Oh Burr, I'm so sorry! I'm so sorry!" Lizzie flung herself on the ground beside the quivering dog and was rewarded with a gentle slurp.

In a flash, Lizzie jumped up and raced toward the chicken house. "I'll kill a chicken for Burr!" She screeched several more things, but CJ couldn't hear her. Teddy raced after her and hollered that she better not kill any of his chickens and especially not his pet rooster.

Simon and CJ looked at each other in bafflement. CJ took out the remaining bullets in his pistol and tucked it under his belt. Then he bent down to examine his beloved Burr and was sick at the sight of a rapidly swelling lump on Burr's shoulder. A closer examination showed more fang marks slightly below the lump.

"What do we do, Simon?" he asked softly as the rest of the family was hurrying down the path.

Simon shook his head sadly. "I imagine we'll have to…That is, I suppose she's too old to fight off two bites like this. I'm afraid—"

"CJ?" Joanna's voice was tremulous as she bent beside him to pet Burr. "Oh, poor boy. Poor boy."

"Momma, Burr's a girl." John reached out to pat his mother's shoulder.

"I know this will work! I know this will work." Lizzie raced from the chicken house with a wildly flapping and squawking hen.

"Yes." Charlotte's voice was quiet and firm. "CJ, kill the chicken for Lizzie." She turned to her husband. "John, get rags. Hurry." She turned to the sobbing Teddy and hugged him. "Teddy, let's sacrifice this old crippled hen and try to save Burr's life. It might work."

CJ looked from one to the other and did what his mother told him to do.

Several hours later, he sat cramped and huddled under the porch with a trembling and twitching dog and a tearstained young girl who wouldn't leave the dog's side. The dead hen had been plucked and plastered over the cut lump in hopes it would draw out the poison, and rags had been wrapped around the whole mess to keep it in place.

"Couldn't you pray, Mr. Crezner?" Lizzie whispered. Her hair hung in matted disarray around her face, and bloodstains from the chicken was smeared across her cheeks and on her clothes. She had sat with Burr's head on her lap and gave the dog her constant attention for hours.

"I have been praying," CJ said softly. "First of all, I thanked God that it was the dog that was bit and not you." Lizzie sniffed and swiped at her nose with her sleeve.

"And then I thanked God that you knew about this chicken business. And I also thanked God that my mother knew something about it also."

"Your ma is really something."

"Yes, you're right. She really is something very precious."

"My ma learned me about the chicken stuff. She…she…Well, I ain't saying she's precious, but she did learn me that."

"Then we can thank God that she knew about it and told you. Lizzie, we still don't know if it will work or not. Burr—" CJ reached awkwardly to pat Lizzie's thin shoulder. "Burr is an old dog. But if she doesn't live, you'll know you've done everything possible to help her."

Tears flowed down Lizzie's cheeks in rivers. "Don't say she won't live! She might hear you and just give up! Don't say that in front of her!"

CJ took a deep breath. Ruby, Burr's offspring, came bumping under the porch to offer her assistance. Usually, Ruby stayed at the barn to harass the cats. It was rare for her to be at the house, but she seemed to sense the calamity her mother was going through. She whimpered and whined and crawled over to lay close beside Lizzie.

"Shouldn't you pray for Burr to get good again? How come you ain't prayed for that?"

"Well. Well, let's pray that right now." He took Lizzie's cold and dirty hand and held it carefully. "Precious Lord, Burr needs Your healing hands on her. She needs Your touch to make her well, and we ask for You to spare our dog friend because even though she's just a dog, we love her, and we all would miss her. But we know all things are in Your perfect will, and whatever You choose to do is the best. If

Burr can't be made good again, then please take her gently home to be in heaven with You. In Jesus' name, we ask this. Amen."

"I ain't never heard of dogs going to heaven." Lizzie was crying again. "You just made that up."

"I ain't never heard they don't go. So there, Lizzie Tinner. God created animals, and He saved them when He destroyed the world with a flood. What makes you think God doesn't enjoy a whole heavenly palace of pets with gentle souls?"

"I don't know. I don't know," Lizzie wailed. "I don't know nothing, Mr. Crezner. I just knowed that I want Burr to live because I want her to know I'm sorry I yelled at her and called her a stupid dog. That's all I knowed."

"CJ?" Charlotte Crezner was crawling toward them, and it was no easy process, considering she was constantly braking to a stop when her voluminous skirts got under her knees.

"Mom, you don't need to come here," CJ scolded gently.

"Joanna wants you to come in and eat, Lizzie. She's worried about you." Charlotte crawled a little closer. "I told her that I would relieve you for a spell."

"You both scoot on out. I'll stay with Burr." CJ was firm. "Lizzie, go. I'll be right here with her until you get back."

Their vigil lasted two more days and cost two more chickens their lives. On the third day, Burr limply wagged her tail, and by that afternoon, she slowly inched her way from under the porch, drank some milk, and tottered up the steps to find her favorite rug. She heaved a great sigh and slowly began the mammoth job of licking herself clean.

Lizzie, who had stayed under the porch with her day and night, tottered to the little house she called her own and, at Joanna's insistence, took a very necessary and long overdue bath. She tumbled into bed, and Charlotte tucked her in with loving hands and a gentle touch. Several times, Joanna and Charlotte walked over to the little house to check on her. Lizzie never moved, and each time, her snoring seemed a little louder.

When they walked back to the porch, they noted that Burr was stretched out on her rug, snoring with steady volume.

"The sound of tired bodies, I guess," Joanna said. "Charlotte, what will we ever do with Lizzie Tinner?"

Charlotte was thoughtful as they made their way into the house. "I don't know. Only God knows." She patted Joanna's arm. "She needs you. And who knows, maybe all of us need her too."

5

December 8, 1907

Pierre, South Dakota

Dear family,

It sure was good being home over Thanksgiving. And it sure is hard being back at school. I keep thinking of all the things I could be doing at home. Mrs. Ordin tells me I can work all my life and I'll look back at school days and be glad for them. I'm not sure she's right about that.

And, she has two things I'm supposed to tell you. One: "You write to that CJ and tell him I said there ain't no one who filled my wood box as good as he did when he stayed with me in the winter of '98. That is, there weren't no one until Isaac Swanson came." No kidding, that's what she said. Sorry to take over that honor, CJ.

Two: "And tell Joanna that I'm a-fixing up her room to stay while she's a-waitin' for that baby to be born. And you better tell her that she needs to come sooner rather than later 'cause who knows what this crazy weather will do."

I can't get the least little bit excited about Latin, but Reverend Smith and Reverend Drew Wilson both assure me it's important. I finally took their invitation to come over to the Wilsons after school so they could help me figure some of it out, and I guess it might make a little more sense now.

I sure couldn't believe how much John and Teddy grew from September to November. It sure will seem funny for them to start school away from home. I think I heard John say his teacher's name is Miss Noble and she is coming after the first of the year. Imagine Lizzie is still being muleheaded and saying she won't go.

Guess that's all I can think of to write. And I still have some homework to finish. Will be home on December 19. Thanks again, CJ, for giving me the money to come home on the train.

Isaac Swanson

PS: Tell Dad I'll write him next week. And pet Burr and Ruby for me. Burr sure is looking old after that dang snakebite, even if Lizzie does sneak her into her little house every night. (And don't tell Lizzie I told you that.)

CJ finished reading Isaac's letter aloud to Joanna and drummed his fingers on the table. He missed his young friend, and it seemed like Isaac had grown into a young man between September and Thanksgiving. "I imagine by now they've gotten your letter saying we'll be there on the fourteenth," CJ said as he absently scanned Isaac's carefully written note again. "And I wish you would have listened to me, Joanna. I would have felt a whole lot easier in my mind if you were safely tucked away in Pierre."

"This baby isn't even due until the end of December, worrywart. I'll have two weeks to sit and twiddle my thumbs before it comes." Joanna overflowed the old rocking chair and looked the picture of misery with her swollen feet propped on the hassock.

"You will never make two more weeks, Mizzus Crezner. I've looked at too many cows to miss my guess on this." CJ smiled to lighten his remarks.

Just the two of them were in the house this morning. Simon had taken the boys and the cream and eggs into Belvidere. They were experiencing milder temperatures for a couple of days, and if CJ had his way, Joanna and he would have boarded the train in Midland and headed to Mrs. Ordin's while the weather was good.

Joanna waved her hand in irritation. "Let's please stop talking about me. I'm sick of it. I'm sick of being pregnant, and I'm sick of looking pregnant, and I'm sick and tired of being sick and tired."

CJ nodded and slowly stood up. He put Isaac's letter back in the envelope and set it on a bookcase shelf. Joanna had felt better yesterday, and as always when she was even half way feeling good, she had overdone it and paid for it the following day.

Lizzie slammed into the house as she returned from feeding the chickens. Her cheeks were pink-tinged from the fresh air and from running. "Any pains yet, Mizzus Crezner?" Her voice was loud and breathless. Lizzie had asked the same question for the past month. Whenever she left Joanna's side and returned, she was sure she'd find Joanna in the middle of childbirth.

Joanna rolled her eyes and sighed. "No, Lizzie, I'm fine. " She scowled at CJ's bemused smirk. "In fact, I'm so fine that we better go upstairs and start packing. CJ and I leave day after tomorrow. Mustn't keep all the poor people in a dither worrying about me."

She made several attempts to rise and finally took CJ's offered hand and let him pull her to her feet. "And you, sir," she huffed as she caught her breath, "go upstairs in the barn and bring down the little trunk. It'll work perfect to put the baby clothes and blankets in."

"I thought you said everything would fit into the big trunk." CJ wasn't keen on leaving her.

"I changed my mind. I'm going on a shopping spree before I come home. New clothes, Mr. Crezner. Fitted ones. And a new hat. I'll need the extra room to bring it all home."

He stood obstinately in front of her. "I don't have any idea where it is, Joanna. Why don't I wait until the boys come home? They seem to know where everything is in the haymow."

"Just go, CJ." She gave him a shove. "I'll want to get it cleaned before I pack it."

"I'll be sure and tell ya if she has a pain," Lizzie offered as she trailed behind Joanna toward the stairway.

CJ muttered while putting his coat on. Leave it to a woman to think of shopping when she was almost ready to deliver.

The December air felt balmy as he stepped outside. The temperature gauge said thirty-eight degrees, but after the cold snap they'd had, thirty-eight degrees felt warm. He decided to trim his horse's hooves while it was this nice. The next hour was a pleasure as he worked on a job he enjoyed.

"Now to find that blasted trunk," he told Burr as he made his way toward the steep ladder of the haymow. Burr wagged her tail in compassion. "This is from Isaac." CJ patted the old dog and gave her a quick rubdown.

The haymow was cold, and the tiny window lent a pathetic light. He spent considerable time checking all the spots he thought the trunk would be, and finally found it wedged under some harnesses. He wrestled it loose and was carrying it to the haymow opening when he heard Lizzie frantically calling his name.

"Up here! What's wrong?" He hollered back, and leaving the trunk where it was, he hurried down the ladder.

"Pain! She has a pain!" Lizzie shouted from the barn door, and before CJ could stop her, she spun around and raced toward the house.

"Lizzie!" He sprinted after her and managed to catch her halfway to the house. Holding her thin arm so she wouldn't take off, he tried to put a measure of calmness into his voice. "Just settle down. How bad is her pain?"

Lizzie was wild-eyed and gasping. "Really bad pain. She said to get you right away."

"I think, Lizzie, you better...Wait a minute! I'll saddle your horse, and you ride over to Mrs. Anderson's. Come with me!"

He ran to the corral, and while his mind scolded him for taking so long, it was actually just seconds until Lizzie's spotted horse was caught and saddled. All the while, Lizzie was graphically showing and telling him Joanna's reaction to the pains that seemed to have hit without warning.

"Mizzus Anderson ain't home." Lizzie stopped her tirade in midsentence to inform him.

"You don't know that. How do you know that?" CJ yelled in frustration.

"'Cause I just know these things!" She rolled her eyes and shook her head. "Let me think now."

CJ unceremoniously lifted and plopped her onto the saddle. "We don't have time to think, Lizzie! Ride over to Doc Sullivan's! It's closer anyway, and if she's not home, get whoever you can."

"But Mizzus Crezner said she didn't want the doc swearing at her! She ain't gonna like this!" Lizzie gathered the reins and glared at CJ while she scrunched into her saddle.

"Get her!" CJ slapped the spotted horse's rump, and he made several jumps before Lizzie lined him up with Mrs. Sullivan's homestead and raced away. "And hurry!" He knew he didn't have to remind Lizzie. She usually raced her crazy horse anywhere even if it wasn't an emergency.

Like a bad dream, it seemed to take an eternity to get to the house. He heard Joanna call to him as he raced up the steps, and to his chagrin, he stumbled on the last step and sprawled onto the hallway floor.

"CJ!" Joanna's voice was strained. "The baby is coming!"

"No! No, no!" He was breathless as he crawled into their bedroom on all fours. Joanna was lying crossways on their bed, with her head hanging over the edge. Her eyes were screwed shut, and she was gasping for air.

"You've got to help me! Help me, CJ!" She opened her eyes and stared at him in wild disbelief. "I'm having a baby, and you're down on the floor?" She panted for breath while he scrambled to his feet. "You…We…These are pushing pains!" She groaned, and CJ almost collapsed onto the floor again.

"Oh boy, oh boy," he muttered, trying to collect his thoughts. "Oh Lord, have mercy!"

6

December 19, 1907

Belvidere, South Dakota

Dear Mom and Dad,

You will understand why my handwriting is so shaky after you read this letter.

Joanna and I are the proud parents of twin daughters. They are dainty and delicate, and are doing fine, as is Joanna. They came like a whirlwind, and I delivered the first one and thought the job was done. But when Mrs. Sullivan or I should say Dr. Sullivan, arrived, she shooed me out the door and promptly delivered the second one.

Joanna alternated between laughing and crying for the first couple of hours after their delivery, and if it weren't for Simon brewing me several pots of very strong coffee, I think I would have fainted.

We haven't named them yet. No one likes my very biblical suggestion of Tryphena and Tryphosa, which mean delicate and dainty, and I probably don't need to tell you that they are found in Romans 16:12. The boys were astonished when they came home from Belvidere with Simon and found the house in such an uproar. Teddy immediately wanted to exchange both of his sisters for baby Joe over at the neighbor's. John wanted to hold both of them at the same time, and I'm ashamed to say all I could do the first day was repeatedly ask Joanna if she was *sure* she was okay.

Lizzie asked me if she should slap me in the face so I would quit asking the same questions over and over. Her fist was doubled up, so I'm not sure if she meant a slap or a punch. But at any rate, I declined to answer and had another cup of coffee instead.

Joanna slept soundly that first night, and the babies slept like babies—which means they woke up every couple of hours. I had too much caffeine and couldn't seem to settle down, so I became well acquainted with my girls as I gave them each a bottle of milk under Doc's wary gaze.

Simon is going to Midland to meet the train and Isaac this afternoon, and he is waiting patiently for me to get this ready to mail. When we decide on names, I will let you know. They were born on December 12, between ten and eleven in the morning.

Love,

CJ

CJ blotted the ink on his letter and glanced up at his waiting audience before he put the letter in the envelope. He seemed to always have an audience in front of him these past several days since the twins were born.

"I have the stamp, Dad," John said, and carefully glued a two-cent stamp to the envelope.

"I'll be on my way then." Simon took the letter and tucked it into his pocket. "Boy howdy, CJ, you still look pretty peaked. You gonna be okay?"

CJ waved his hand in disgust. Just because a fellow passed out when the doctor says he has two daughters didn't warrant all this unnatural attention from folks. It was just pitiful that he had to have Simon and the boys, plus Lizzie and Doc Sullivan, witness the whole affair. And even more pathetic was the fact that he had hit his head on the corner of the stove when he melted down. He had garnered a nasty cut, which Doc slapped burning iodine onto and about raised him through the roof.

The measured steps of Dr. Sullivan could be heard coming down the stairs. Simon looked like a frighten rabbit and bolted out the door in undue haste. CJ chuckled in spite of himself. For some strange reason, he and the doc understood each other, even though her bark, he decided, was only slightly worse than her unsympathetic care. He wanted to hug her broad shoulders every time he saw her, which made her eyes flash fire, and she would give him a raised fist in warning. What was there, he mused to himself as the doc reached the last step, which made him want to laugh at cranky women?

"And naturally, you're just sitting there doing nothing again." Doc started to add some expletives but abruptly stopped when she noticed two wide-eyed boys staring at her.

"I was waiting for you to come down and have some coffee with me," CJ protested mildly as he pushed his chair back. "And how did you find Joanna this morning?"

"All three of your girls are good, but you need to get them all moved to this downstairs bedroom. Make life a lot easier for everyone." Dr. Sullivan nodded her thanks as CJ set a steaming cup of coffee in front of her.

"Yes, I had my orders the day after the twins were born on how to rearrange our guest room to accommodate two cradles." CJ sat down with his own fresh cup of coffee.

"Don't you boys have something to do?" Doc glared at John and Teddy, and they quickly disappeared into the living room.

"Can't exactly say I like kids," Doc muttered, and she had the grace to look a little sheepish at CJ. "'Course, being married to Denny is a little like having a kid around."

CJ grinned at her. "Doc, I just want to say thanks for coming so quick when we needed you. I don't care whether you like kids or not. You were good to Joanna and the babies. And you've made several trips over here even though it's colder than blue blazes."

"Don't think flattery will lessen the bill any, Crezner. And, besides your wife, I had to tend to you, which was completely disgusting."

He thought he saw a smirk on her face before she lifted her coffee cup to take a drink. He shook his head and threw up his hands in defense. "I've never delivered babies before. Give me credit for getting baby number 1 here. I even cut the cord, so there." Just thinking about it made him squeamish all over again, and he quickly changed the subject.

"Do you know of someone we could hire to come and help Joanna for awhile?"

"What's wrong with Lizzie?"

"Well, she's a little young to help very much with the babies."

"She's a natural-born nurse. Let 'er at 'em."

CJ was shocked. "Let 'er at 'em? Let 'er at 'em? They aren't a couple of puppies, you know?!" He was quite indignant.

"Oh fiddle, CJ, they won't break even if they are little. I'm not saying to be rough with them, of course, but you don't need to act like they're more breakable than fine china, for crying out loud."

"My wife," CJ said coldly, "carried them for nine months with a great deal of difficulty. Now that they're here, we are not, and I repeat, not going to do anything but take the best of care of them."

Dr. Sullivan swore under her breath and placed her empty cup firmly on the table. She leaned a little closer to CJ and said with slow and measured tones, "I heard you had a nasty temper."

"Who told you that?" CJ yelled, forgetting Joanna was trying to rest upstairs.

"The storekeeper's wife. Said you yelled at her too. I'm surprised she lent you the cradle."

"She lent the cradle because she almost caused my youngest son to drown, and she is trying to pacify her guilty conscience. And you, Doc, are trying to wiggle out of making a stupid remark. 'Let 'er at 'em.' You should be ashamed of yourself." CJ wagged a condemning finger in front of the doctor's nose.

"Any more coffee?" Mrs. Sullivan leaned comfortably back into her chair and gave CJ an unabashed grin. "Amazing how you can get color in your face when you have a little temper tantrum."

Joanna's cheeks were flushed with pleasure as the little group gathered around her in the living room. Both babies were in her lap, and she was bursting with maternal pride. Besides all that, she informed them, she had decided on their names.

Isaac shot a surprised glance at CJ. "I thought you told me you couldn't agree on anything," he said in a low tone.

"We couldn't. Whatever Joanna liked, I didn't. And of course, no one liked Tryphena and Tryphosa. I figured she went to all the work of having them, she could choose their names." CJ smiled at his wife. She looked more animated and full of life than she had for months.

"My pick will always be Mary," Simon declared, and he winked at his sister.

"I don't even care." Teddy was still upset they weren't boys.

CJ scowled at his youngest son and shook his head. Teddy looked slightly ashamed and stood a little closer to his mother.

Her arms were full of babies, which meant she couldn't hug him, but she gave him a tender smile.

"And we all know, Teddy, that you wanted to call one of your sisters 'Joey,' but somehow, that didn't fit either one of them." Joanna rocked slowly in the old rocking chair. "John thinks we should call them Faith and Hope, which are lovely names, but..." Joanna shrugged and left her sentence unfinished.

"I've spent a lot of time thinking of names. I really thought we were going to have another boy, so I didn't think much about girl's names. Especially two names!" Joanna's light laugh was music to CJ's ears. It had been a long time since he had heard it.

"This little girl," Joanna said tenderly, looking at the baby in her right arm, "has a fair complexion, with almost violet-colored eyes. I have named her Heather Rose." She looked beseechingly at CJ. "I hope you like that."

"Purely beautiful, Joanna. You did well!" CJ reached over and picked up his newly named daughter. "I'm glad you listened to me and used your middle name for her middle name." Heather snoozed peacefully, and didn't know or care that she had a name.

Everyone nodded their agreement. Each one hoped the second baby would have their favorite name.

"Now," Joanna said briskly, "I wanted to include our mothers' names, but dear me, what do you do with Charlotte Mattie, or Mattie Charlotte? It's very difficult."

"That's why Elizabeth would work," Lizzie declared. "Charlotte Elizabeth—that's my pick."

Isaac visibly shuddered.

"Yes, Charlotte Elizabeth has a certain ring to it." Joanna smiled at Lizzie. "However, this little one is leaner, taller than her sister. Willowy, almost. And that's what I decided to call her. Willow. And then, I combined our mothers' names. *Char* for Charlotte, and *M* for Mattie. And that spells Charm. Willow Charm. Once I thought of that, I couldn't seem to consider any other name. Willow Charm. I-I hope you all like it."

CJ glanced at the others and saw the same skepticism on their faces that he felt. What kind of name was Willow Charm?

"Well." He placed Heather Rose back into her mother's arms and picked up Willow. "Little Miss Charming. Little Willow Charm. A beautiful name for a beautiful baby. You have outdone yourself with this name, Mrs. Crezner. I would have never thought of it." That was a fact, and the world was never going to know that he had doubts about the name Willow Charm for even one second.

"At least you didn't call her Lucky Charm." Isaac's voice cracked slightly.

"I like Lucky better than Willow," Teddy stoutly affirmed. CJ's scowl sent him scurrying over to Simon.

Simon absently patted Teddy's head, and then he slowly rose from the old wing chair and came to stand beside CJ. He gently took the baby into his own arms and peered down at the sleeping infant intently before he spoke.

"Sister, you chose a name that fits this little one like a glove. You put a lot of thought into it. It will be fascinating to watch Heather and Willow grow up on this ranch. Just like John and Teddy. We're blessed to have family growing up here."

CJ thought Joanna's smile was a bit tremulous, and he reached over to pat her shoulder.

"About seven years ago at Christmas, there were just four in our family out here in the middle of nowhere. And now look at us!" CJ caught Lizzie's downcast look and quickly added, "And yes Lizzie, you're a part of this family. I don't know what we would have done without you hurrying to get Doc Sullivan. You didn't waste a second. I'm proud of you."

"I should say!" Joanna spoke fervently. "And you've been a tremendous help to me every since you came. I especially appreciate you helping take care of the babies!"

Lizzie shrugged her thin shoulders and looked embarrassed and pleased at the same time. CJ thought for a moment she would stick her tongue out at Isaac when he gave another visible shudder. But for once, common sense ruled, and she contented herself with a baleful glare in his direction.

"Oh my, Christmas is just a couple of days away. We don't have a tree up yet. CJ, that's the job for you and the boys tomorrow!"

Things were getting back to normal, CJ reasoned, and he felt a surge of elation. Joanna was getting bossy again.

7

January 23, 1908

Pierre, South Dakota

My dear Joanna and CJ and family!

Drew and I are just ecstatic to hear about your wonderful news. Twin daughters! And I love their names. Joanna, I also loved your letter, and I laughed so hard when I read how CJ crawled into the bedroom on all fours! Knowing him like I do, I imagine he was soon able to take control of the situation, but your description of the whole affair really left me in stitches!

And how wonderful that you are feeling so good. Now we all know why you were so miserable all summer. I had trouble with carrying one baby, and I simply can't imagine what I would ever have done if there were two little people involved!

Before I forget, Momma and Daddy say to tell you all they have said many prayers for you! Momma wishes she felt better right now because she would pack her bags and come and stay to lend you a helping hand. She has caught the croup and has been resting quite a bit.

And our beloved Mrs. Ordin says to tell you that she has rented the room she was keeping for you to another young mother-to-be who lives "away out yonder with a no-good husband." I have been to see said young mother-to-be, and she has accompanied Drew and me to church services. Poor little thing, she does have a hard life, but at least her husband rented the room for her before he left to go "away out yonder." Mrs. Ordin made him pay her before he left.

Our Gracie Lynn thinks Isaac is the most wonderful person she has ever met! Whenever he comes to visit, she insists on sitting beside him. He's wonderfully tolerant of her and is so kind and gentle. He tells her all sorts of stories about John and Teddy, and of course, since she is an only child, she thinks it must be wonderful to have siblings!

I do believe Isaac hates being away from his new little cousins almost as much as he hates leaving the farm! But he is studying hard, and with Drew's help, he seems to be getting stronger in his Latin. He is getting well acquainted with Pierre and is often at the O'Reilly's home with all their boys. Can you imagine six boys? I almost want to shudder, but Mrs. O'Reilly takes it all in stride. Of course, Mickey helps his mother all he can, and did I tell you? He had to go back east for more surgery on his feet this fall, but I believe it has helped relieve some of the pain he was dealing with. CJ, he talks so highly of you helping him.

Well! This is turning into an epistle! Forgive me, dear ones, but there is always so much for us to share with one another! Don't be surprised if we catch the train to Midland when the weather is settled and come visit you!

Love to every one of you in Christ's name,

Drew, Deborah Lynn, and Gracie Lynn

CJ shuffled Willow Charm to his other arm and reread Deborah Lynn's last paragraph. A surprise visit from the Reverend Drew Wilson family didn't strike a pleasant chord in his life at the moment.

"You have a sour look on your face, Mr. Crezner." Joanna was folding a mountain of diapers as she sat across from him at the table.

"Do I?" CJ put the letter down and sighed. "Well. I suppose I do. Whenever I read Deborah Lynn's letters, I feel...I don't know. Maybe the word is 'unsettled.'"

Joanna's light laughter floated across the table. "I feel that she has beautiful and sparkling faith, and mine seems rather muddled and dull in comparison."

CJ scowled and drummed the fingers of his free hand on the table while he considered beautiful faith versus muddled. Finally, he shook his head. "Maybe we shouldn't compare faith. Or service. Or each other. I don't know. Maybe you're right."

"That's what I love about you, CJ." Joanna folded another diaper and added it to the stack. "You know your own mind."

"I know that when I continually hear quoted scripture and reminders to pray, pray, and pray, I get aggravated."

"But Deborah didn't do any of that in her letter," Joanna protested. "I think you're in a grouchy state of mind."

He watched as she took more diapers from the clothes basket and smoothed them with her graceful fingers. Joanna's hands were beautiful, he decided for the thousandth time.

"And when did prayers and scripture start to aggravate you?" Joanna's hands suddenly stilled, and she looked at him with her head tilted to one side. "That's odd for you to say!"

Willow Charm had the same look on her tiny face as her mother did. CJ shifted uncomfortably in his chair as he glanced away from their scrutinizing looks.

"Well. Generally she and Drew are quoting Bible verses, and it makes me mad that I didn't think to apply that verse to that situation. I've memorized verses all my life. How come none of them come to mind when I need an answer?"

"Probably because you're trying to think of a solution to the problem rather than a verse to identify the problem." Joanna started folding again. "Or something like that."

CJ decided he'd sort that out when he went outside in the fresh air. He had one more item on his grouch list. "I don't know how Isaac puts up with little Gracie Lynn. She seems like she's always afraid of something."

"She's just timid, CJ. You're used to Lizzie."

CJ wondered to himself if anyone could get used to Lizzie. She had walked the boys to the little claim shack of Nel's this morning. From the expression on her face, one would have thought she was going in front of a firing squad rather than helping the teacher get the little ones settled for school.

Willow was looking at him again with her wise little baby gaze. He smiled down at her, hoping he'd be the first one she'd smile back at. But even though she was over a month old, she steadfastly refused to smile at anyone. Heather, on the other hand, had smiled almost incessantly since the first week.

Joanna folded the last diaper in the pile and stood up to stretch. "I hope they don't dawdle after school. Even if it's only a mile, it gets dark quick, and I want them home."

"You gave them enough instructions this morning to put the fear of death in 'em," CJ observed mildly as he placed Willow in her cradle. "I'm going out to start chores. I suppose Simon has already started milking those blasted milk cows."

"You really hate the old girls, don't you, CJ." It was a flat statement. The more CJ was around Simon's dairy purchase, the less he liked them. And even though it wasn't discussed often, and never in front of the kids, Joanna knew and sympathized with him.

"I hate 'em. I know the cream check is a constant and a good source of money, but I just don't like milk cows." He gave Joanna a light hug before he started putting on his coat. "But with our little herd of kids, it's great to have all the milk we need. And Lizzie can drink a gallon of the stuff in a day. Never saw a kid drink so much milk and stay as thin as a rail."

"She works hard and fast. And she's in constant motion from daylight 'til her head hits the pillow. She earns her keep, CJ, even if you and Isaac fuss about her."

CJ shrugged into his coat. "I know. She's been a blessing. Maybe an irritating blessing most of the time, but still, I don't know what we would have done without her."

Joanna shooed him out the door with a wave of her hand. At least she was back to her sassy form. He felt like he was welcoming a good and trusted friend back into his life again.

The fathers of the school-age children had agreed among themselves to take turns starting the fire in the heating stove at the claim cabin school. If Miss Noble had damped it well in the afternoon, there would still be coals to help get it to flame the following morning. She was proving to be an efficient teacher as well as a fire damper. So much so, to Joanna's dismay, there was little need for Lizzie to help with the little ones. In vain, both Joanna and Miss Noble tried to persuade Lizzie to attend as a student; but Lizzie, with her narrow jaw thrust out in a belligerent manner, refused to consider that possibility.

"It is such a shame!" Miss Noble confided to CJ as he added wood to the stove on a cold and blustery February morning. "Lizzie has potential."

Teddy nodded conspiratorially at John, as if he knew what the word "potential" meant. John scowled at him and shook his head.

"Why don't you boys carry in some wood for Miss Noble before school starts?" CJ saw the slump in the boys' shoulders. It was a damp and raw morning, and they were already cold. He waited until they were out the door before he continued the Lizzie conversation.

"Joanna thinks she's ashamed that she's almost thirteen and still can't read very well. Or for that matter, do her numbers."

"But I could work around that," Miss Noble protested. "We could be discreet in front of the other children. I've told her that."

CJ nodded. Right now, he was more concerned about the small fire taking the chill off the room than Lizzie's education. He was grateful Nels built the claim shack from logs, which provided more insulation than tar paper shacks. Yet, between the chinks, the cold air oozed in, and the child who sat any distance from the stove was going to be cold.

The Claim Cabin School had two south-facing windows which allowed the weak winter sunshine to brighten the room. The door was on the east side, and as yet, the makeshift school yard boasted no flagpole or swings. Standing bravely and bracing itself against the north wind, one lone outhouse reigned supreme on the slope of the hill.

Water from Nel's well had already been drawn for the day, and the dipper, a pail of water, a washbasin, and an only slightly dirty towel all rested on a low table beside the door. CJ noted, with a mental nod to the children's ingenuity, that art reigned in the crude little building with a colorful paper chain. The links had been pasted together and was draped on nails behind Miss Noble's desk.

The commotion at the door caused the teacher to hurriedly open it, and John and Teddy staggered in with huge armloads of wood. CJ helped them unload their burden into the wood box, and while they hung their coats up on the nails, he brought in several more armfuls. By this time, the other students began to arrive, and soon the little room was filled with rosy-cheeked children.

Miss Noble gave him a preoccupied wave as he started out the door. She made do, he mused to himself as he swung into the saddle, with very little. She had books that various people lent to the school, a blackboard of tar paper, and some old calendar backs for extra paper. And she was expected to teach their children for the twenty dollars a month they gave her. Dedicated, he decided, as his horse trotted swiftly home.

Simon was unloading a wagon full of wood that he had scavenged from the creek. With so many settlers across the prairie, wood was a premium. The *Belvidere Times* had run a cheeky little article about someone who said that the west river country boasted fifty miles to water and a hundred miles to wood.

"If they wouldn't have all piled out here on every quarter, there would be water and wood for everyone," CJ muttered to his horse as he started to unsaddle him. "I suppose Drew could find a Bible verse for that problem." He put the saddle and blanket onto the saddle rack and looped the bridle over the saddle horn. His horse shook himself and then looked soulfully at CJ. "Sure, you want oats. Just be glad you're home and not in the schoolhouse barn waiting for kids to get out like your friends are."

"Talking to yourself again?" Simon led the work team into the barn to unharness them out of the wind.

"I'm telling my horse to count his blessings." CJ put a little oats in the wooden box. "What do you think the weather is going to do today?"

"It's spitting a little snow right now."

"Maybe it'll clear up after dinner. I suppose we need to get this cream into town in the next couple of days."

"Yup. Cream, milk, your bookkeeping. I'm glad we've got that extra income. We're pulling ahead, CJ, and that's a plus. Don't mind telling you I worried about buying those milk cows, but I think it was a good investment. We have interest from quite a few folks to buy the calves."

CJ nodded. Even if he didn't agree with Simon about milk cows, the old girls might pay for themselves and give them a weekly check besides.

The weather couldn't seem to decide if the sun should shine or snow should fall. CJ was uneasy. By three o'clock, the warning nagging that had been with him all day refused to settle down, and he saddled his horse and headed for the schoolhouse.

It was considerably colder riding into the wind than it had been in the morning. When he knocked and opened the schoolhouse door, he was struck again at the chilliness of the room.

Miss Noble nodded at him when he entered. She had already dismissed the children, and they were quickly putting on coats and mittens while others brought the horses to the door.

"I decided to send them home early, but I'm glad to see you," she said, tying a little girl's scarf securely around her. "We're all heading in the same direction, except for John and Teddy, so we can keep an eye out for one another. But I was quite concerned about your boys."

CJ helped the smaller ones onto the horses, tucked a few flapping skirts around wool stocking legs, made sure mittens were on, and watched the little procession head into the wind and falling snow. Miss Noble was on foot. She told CJ that a good winter walk cleared her mind. He imagined when she arrived at her sister's homestead a mile away, her mind would be in good shape.

He took his time tending the fire in the stove and finally was ready to leave. Before he mounted his horse, he took one last look to the west. The teacher and her students were halfway to their homes already.

"Daddy, I'm freezing. Can't we run?" Teddy was shivering.

"You boys go ahead. I'm going to ride up the ridge and make sure everyone else made it home."

John nodded, and CJ watched them urge their horses into a stiff-legged trot. He immediately regretted trying to convince his horse to turn to the north and to the top of the ridge. It took swearing and spurs, but finally, he was high enough to see the Gardner homestead on the hill. Squinting through the lightly falling snow, he made out moving figures near the buildings and breathed a sigh of relief.

His horse pawed impatiently, and CJ relaxed the reins. Immediately, his horse turned and headed down the hill, his ears flattened in disgust at this seemingly frivolous waste of time. The boys were a short distance ahead, and CJ soon closed the distance between them.

It was when he was a few yards behind them that the ground exploded with a covey of grouse. Whirring wings and startled clucks made the horses jump. Teddy's gentle horse snorted in fright and uncharacteristically bolted into wild flight.

"Pull him up, Teddy!" CJ's voice was lost in the wind as he thundered after him. To his horror, he saw that Teddy had lost both reins and was clutching the saddle horn. In a second, he had to decide if he should put himself between the runaway horse and the creek or on the side of the open prairie. With trees flying by, he made an instant decision to get between Teddy and the creek.

He spurred his own horse unmercifully, and the distance between the two quickly evaporated. Winter-dead tree branches slapped him across the face as he neared Teddy's horse and grabbed the flyaway reins.

"Whoa! Whoa, boys!" The horses tossed their heads and came to a lurching stop. He could see Teddy's horse trembling, and he could feel the tremors of his own mount.

Teddy wanted to cry. His lip trembled, and the wind made tears stream down his face. Somewhere on his wild ride, his cap had fallen off, and he only had one mitten.

"Well. Teddy Boy." CJ was breathing hard himself. "You made quite a ride for a five-year-old." He gave his son a reassuring grin.

Teddy took a swipe at his runny nose. "Daddy, your face is all bleeding!"

"Just a tree branch. Nothing to worry about." CJ dismounted and looked anxiously behind them to make sure John was coming. He stifled an oath when he saw John's horse without a rider.

He patted Teddy's leg, and then to his relief, he saw John walking toward his horse with Teddy's cap and mitten in hand.

After Teddy was bundled up again, they rode slowly to the barn. CJ sent both boys to the house to warm up, and he slowly unsaddled the horses. Simon was getting ready to start milking chores, so CJ settled onto the milking stool and leaned into Gloria's warm side. Alleluia was next, and it wasn't until he reached Truth that Simon saw his face.

"Boy howdy, CJ!" Simon's eyes were wide. "What happened to you?"

Willow Charm started crying while Joanna fussed over CJ's face. He interrupted her rather rough nursing tactics and picked up his unhappy little daughter from her cradle. As usual, she looked at him with sober eyes and no smile.

"The boys said you ran into a tree branch, but good grief, CJ, you should have come in and had it taken care of before you milked the cows." Joanna scolded and dabbed at the dried blood.

"Didn't want to take off all my coats and then have to put them all back on," CJ grumbled. He thought to himself it would be easier just to let nature take its course and leave the scabs on, but Joanna had other ideas.

When she had finally softened them up to her satisfaction, she began to wipe the right side of his face with a damp cloth.

"You're going to make it bleed all over again," he muttered, and gave Willow a slight smile.

No response from his daughter or his wife.

"Looks bad!" Lizzie rolled her eyes and watched Joanna's work intently.

"It can't be bad. It was just a tree branch." CJ was embarrassed at all the unwanted attention.

"Daddy saved my life!" Teddy had knelt down at his feet and also watched the whole proceeding with great interest.

"I just stopped your horse. He would have eventually quit running on his own."

"Sure, after he dumped Teddy off," Lizzie said, her eyes never leaving CJ's face.

"John, hand me that stuff on the table." Joanna stood back and admired her handiwork.

"Wait a minute. What's in that 'stuff'?" CJ had experience with Joanna's concoctions before, and it usually wasn't pleasant.

"Healing things." Joanna took the cup of 'stuff' from John and took another clean cloth to dab it on.

"Joanna, darn it all, if this burns like the last time—"

It burned like the last time. It made his eyes water and took his breath away, and in the midst of his pain and agony, he squinted a downward glance at Willow Charm.

She was grinning a toothless grin from ear to ear.

8

June 8, 1908

Mankato, Minnesota

Western Union Telegram

Arriving 6–9 at 2. Meet us. Mother

CJ removed his dusty hat and slapped it against his leg. He had just returned from taking Isaac to the spring roundup crew and found Joanna in an uncommon dither. She shoved the crumpled piece of paper at him, and he read, and reread, the short message.

"Your mother—" He looked at her. She nodded her head bleakly.

"The ninth is—"

"Tomorrow."

"And she and someone—like your sister Bertie, maybe? Are coming for a visit. Tomorrow."

"Tomorrow. Ma is going to be here tomorrow. I'm in the middle of washing clothes, I've been planting the garden, the house is a mess, I'm a mess, the kids are a mess, the yard is a mess— everything is a mess! CJ," she wailed, "what are we going to do?" Joanna sat on the porch bench and put her head in her hands. "She *would* do it this way. Just up and out of the blue. Here she is. No warning or nothing. I feel like screaming!"

"Does Simon know?"

She shook her head. "He and the boys are working on the chicken house. Some guy rode in this morning from Belvidere and handed this to me while I was hanging up clothes."

"Well. Well, she can't expect things to be picture-perfect when she doesn't give any warning." He patted her shoulder and put his hat back on. "Joanna, just sit for a minute. I'll bring us out some coffee, and we'll get a plan worked out."

She looked at him with grim determination, and he gently pulled at an escaping strand of hair from her braided bun.

"Sit woman. Ten minutes isn't going to make or break anything."

Returning to the porch seconds later with two steaming cups of coffee, he discovered, as he figured he would, an empty bench. Joanna was on her hands and knees pulling weeds from the iris bed near the porch steps.

"We better take a few minutes to enjoy a June morning." He joined her at the flower bed and set both coffee cups on the porch step before he sat down.

It was a rare moment for them to be alone. He fervently wished they could enjoy it without thinking of her mother's visit. The bird songs from the creek filled the air, and the pleasant balminess of the spring morning surrounded the place with promises of sweet contentment.

"There's a million things to do and we're sitting here drinking coffee." Joanna plopped herself beside him on the step.

"Joanna, my love." He raised his coffee cup to her. "Here's to a few minutes of worship and praise, and then we'll get down to planning."

She leaned against the top step. "Are we worshiping and praising each other, or are you suggesting we give a few moments to God?" Her eyebrow was raised, and he noticed a smile for the first time since he'd returned.

He gave her a lazy grin. "Well. Only God can create a morning like this, so I would imagine He'd appreciate it if we took a few minutes to enjoy it."

"I *was* enjoying it until I got that blamed telegram."

"Yeah." A meadowlark sang his song from a nearby fence post.

"Ma always told me they were singing "I'm prettier than you." It made me mad to think a dumb bird was so egotistical. But Mary said, "No, they are saying, 'I'm singing for you.'" Then I was mad at Ma for telling me such nonsense." Joanna sighed and took another drink of coffee.

In an unusually meek voice, she continued, "I wish I could feel happy she was coming, but all I can think of is how she'll criticize everything and everybody. And how mad I'll be when she does."

"If she's going to do that, there's no point in all of us working around the clock to make things perfect." He patted Joanna's knee. "Let's just pretend that she loves you, and she wants to make this one trip out to see you and your family, and let it go at that. Finish your washing, and the boys and I can work on the yard. Then we'll get their rooms ready. We'll all pitch in, but let's work because we want to and not because we have to impress her."

She took a sip of coffee and tilted her head back. For several seconds, she gazed into the deep blue of the sky as if she was gathering serenity from it. Finally, she looked at him and smiled. "Easy for you to say, Mr. CJ Crezner. And for your information, I know you're right." She stood up and took his empty cup. "But as your friend Winn says, 'It ain't gonna be purty.'"

It had been decided that Simon would fetch Mrs. Swanson from the train. That would give the rest of them time to finish up the last-minute details Joanna insisted needed to be done.

John saw the buggy crest the hill to the south in the late afternoon and gave the warning to the rest of them. By the time Simon pulled into the yard, everyone except the twins had gathered on the porch.

Joanna and CJ both hurried down the porch steps, and when Simon brought the team to a halt, they were by the buggy to help Mrs. Swanson out.

"I never thought you would come west! Did you have a good trip?"

Mrs. Swanson waited until she was firmly on the ground to answer Joanna's question. "I never thought I would either. And yes, Joanna, the trip was, shall we say, interesting."

The two women hugged briefly. "And actually, I may never have come except for Sissy." Mrs. Swanson patted her hat a little more securely on her head.

CJ looked into the buggy to see who Sissy was and caught a glimpse of a young woman hurriedly descending the buggy steps on the other side.

"Sissy?" Joanna glanced in the same direction CJ had.

"Mmm uhmm. Sissy. I hired her awhile back. I thought I told you that. Simon says he didn't know about it either." Mrs. Swanson waved her hand in a dismissive gesture. "Sissy Tinner works for me."

Joanna and CJ exchanged incredulous looks with Simon, who shrugged and shook his head.

"How...?" Joanna's question was interrupted by Lizzie's ear-piercing scream.

"Sissy? Sissy?" Lizzie bounded off the porch in one leap and raced toward her sister with howls of joy. "Is it really you?" Lizzie could hardly contain herself and made several wild hops before she threw herself at Sissy and wrapped her arms around the older girl's neck in a bear hug. Sissy laughed and scolded her at the same time, and she begged Lizzie to let loose before she choked the life out of her.

The two girls were undeniably excited to see each other. It occurred to those watching them that even a dysfunctional family was still a familiar and welcoming sight when you're all alone.

"Ma, let me introduce you to CJ." Joanna's voice never wavered even if her thoughts were in turmoil concerning Sissy Tinner.

CJ took the offered gloved hand and gave a gentle squeeze. "Mrs. Swanson, I'm glad to finally meet you." Then forgetting his carefully rehearsed speech, he blurted out, "And now I know where Joanna's good looks come from."

"She'll tell you it's from her father." Mrs. Swanson used her other hand to tap CJ in the chest. "But now you know," she emphasized while her index finger stabbed him a few more times, "the whole blamed truth." She nodded emphatically, and the ostrich plumes on her hat waved wildly. With a conspiratorial wink at CJ, she turned her attention back to her disbelieving daughter.

For a woman who had been at death's door a year ago, Mrs. Swanson, in her early seventies, seemed to have plenty of vim, vinegar, and vigor. Her sharp comments were often made without any pretense of tact; and yet, CJ decided, she cared for both her son and daughter——as long as they understood things were to be done her way.

For some reason, it took several days before they could get the full story of how Sissy Tinner came to work for Mattie Swanson. After the sketchy details Mrs. Swanson provided, CJ and Joanna quizzed Simon to see what he knew.

They finally pieced together the fact that Mrs. Swanson had decided that she needed a "domestic," as she put it, as well as a cook. On the advice of her whist club friends, she placed an ad in the paper, and who should apply but Sissy Tinner? On the how or why Miss

Tinner was very conveniently in Mankato when the ad appeared was never fully understood.

Mrs. Swanson seemed very pleased with the arrangement, and, so she claimed, it wasn't until Miss Tinner had been there for a couple of weeks that the two ladies realized Sissy knew Mrs. Swanson's South Dakota family.

That knowledge prompted the two of them to make plans for a visit. Sissy seemed to know Lizzie worked for Joanna, although how she knew it was also a mystery.

At any rate, Lizzie was beside herself with excitement and scarcely let Sissy out of her sight. Heather and Willow lost their vigilant caregiver, and other than taking a few moments to show them to a very disinterested Sissy, she became so rattle headed that Joanna dismissed her from all household duties while they had visitors.

Mrs. Swanson's first introduction to her granddaughters was thought to be a success, as babies and grandmother smiled and cooed at each other. However, Willow Charm soon decided the dancing plumes on Grandma's hat could be better examined in her little hand. With a swift yank that practically pulled off the silk-and-chiffon creation on Mrs. Swanson's head, the bonding moment ended rather abruptly.

The boys fared better. Mrs. Swanson preferred older children, and she asked them about their school and their teacher. She immediately became intrigued when John mentioned their bachelor neighbor, Otis Addison, seemed to be at the schoolhouse often to help Miss Noble—especially after the little school hosted a Valentine's Day box social and he bought Miss Noble's fine food basket. Miss Noble had blushingly sat beside him after he insisted she should eat with him.

She seemed glad to see her piano and admired the Blue Willow dishes in the oak china cabinet. She clucked with displeasure when she found out the cost of the cabinet and that CJ had ordered it from the Sears catalog.

"Eight dollars and seventy-five cents? CJ, are you made of money? And that wouldn't even include the shipping price. You young people don't have any sense when it comes to money! What is this world coming to?"

CJ grinned at her. "When a certain woman, who has a certain daughter, sends said daughter certain dishes, would you expect the fine young husband to store them in boxes? I bet not." He delighted in saying outrageous things to her. Even with her shocked reactions, he knew she enjoyed a good battle with him, and while Joanna and Simon became exasperated with her critiques, he looked forward to a lively debate. Of course, when Mrs. Swanson was losing said debate, she would look into space and laugh a queer little laugh and claim he didn't know what he was talking about. CJ soon learned that was a sign to back off. The game was over, and Mrs. Swanson wasn't a gracious loser.

Both ladies expressed keen disappointment that Isaac was at the spring roundup and wouldn't be back during their visit. They lamented daily on not being able to see him until finally, Simon offered to take them early the following morning to where he hoped the cattle and men would be. Joanna packed a lunch for them, and she and CJ breathed a sigh of relief when the buggy disappeared over the big hill before the first morning light brightened the world.

"What are you going to do today?" Joanna put her arm through CJ's as they walked toward the house.

"I'm going to rake the hay bottom I cut yesterday. What are you going to do?"

Joanna's mind was far away, he decided, when she didn't answer. She was looking over her shoulder toward the big hill with a frown tweaking her lips. He stopped and looked in the same direction and then turned her to look at him.

"What's wrong?"

"I don't know. Something. But I can't put my finger on it. I don't like Sissy working for Ma, for starters." Joanna looked troubled and started to say more. But she gave herself a mental shake and didn't continue.

"It does seem odd she would just happen to be in the same town as your mother. I wouldn't know of any reason for her to be in Mankato, do you?"

"I don't know. But she hates me, CJ. I can feel it whenever she's around me. "

CJ wanted to scoff and reassure her she was mistaken—except he remembered all too well the first evening at supper when he glanced at Sissy and seen the malevolent look she directed at Joanna. It quickly disappeared and was replaced with artificial sweetness, but it startled him.

CJ gave her a light hug. "Why would she hate you? You took in her sister and gave her a home, and your mother gave her a job. What could she possibly have to hate you about?"

Joanna smiled and rested her head on his chest. He put his arms around her. For once, there was no one around to snicker and fuss at them.

"I'm sure it's a revelation to you, CJ, that I'm not the most likable or lovable woman in the world." Joanna's voice held a hint of laughter.

He held her, relishing the smell of her hair and the feel of her against him. She was his world, and it made knots in his stomach to think of anyone with a vendetta against her. He kissed her long and slow while the sun broke from behind the morning clouds. And Joanna kissed him back.

Mrs. Swanson dabbed her cheek with Joanna's linen napkin. "You're a good cook, like your grandmother Swanson. I wonder if you have any kind of life beyond cooking and cleaning and gardening and working. Do you play any kind of cards with the neighbor ladies?"

"No, Ma. Some of the homesteaders get together though. Actually, I think some of them get together quite a bit. But I never go to the neighbors to play cards."

"Do you neighbor with anyone?" Mrs. Swanson sat back in her chair as if to settle into a long debate.

"Ma," Simon said, joining the fray, "Joanna and all of us help each other out. We work cattle together, and we get together for church when a minister comes. But the homesteaders have their 160 acres, and some of us who have been here longer have more land, more cattle, and more farm work. We're busy."

"Oh, phooey. You sound like your dad. People shouldn't be so busy they don't have fun."

"You're right." CJ was emphatic. The silence was immediate, and CJ grinned at his surprised mother-in-law. "In fact, tomorrow afternoon, we should go visiting our neighbors. Frank and Antonio have a new baby boy that we've been wanting to see."

"Can I go too?" Teddy was up and off his chair, ready for his important mission.

"Yes, Mr. Teddy. And be sure and remember to take your present to them." CJ and Joanna exchanged glances. Teddy had determinedly saved every scrap of material Joanna had so she could use it to make a baby quilt.

"Is it very far?" Mrs. Swanson asked cautiously. She still was feeling the effects of the long journey to find Isaac. Even the comfort of the buggy didn't lessen her complaints about South Dakota being an endless odyssey of hills and draws and shacks.

"It's just up the little valley." Joanna pointed to the west.

"And I think it's high time Lizzie and Sissy had an afternoon to themselves." Mrs. Swanson smiled thinly at the two sisters. "Perhaps you should visit your old homestead."

The girls exchanged glances, and Sissy murmured, "That's a good suggestion."

After the table was cleared off and the dishes were done, Mrs. Swanson settled herself comfortably in the old rocker and requested, in the form of a demand, a song from CJ.

"I came all the way out to this country to hear you sing, and you've been as silent as a mute sparrow," she groused.

John and Teddy both looked at her in surprise. "We've never seen a mute sparrow," John ventured, rather timidly.

"That's my whole point. Someone who can sing should be singing."

"Come with me at four in the morning and you can hear me 'sing' to the milk cows." CJ was very comfortable in the wing chair, and didn't relish getting up to serenade anyone.

"Have you ever gotten the piano tuned?"

"No, but it isn't too bad. Come on, CJ. I'll play the one song I can play, and you can sing." Joanna sat down at the piano and played a few chords of "Amazing Grace." She roundly vetoed his suggestion that he could sing from the chair, and with a mock groan, he rose and stood by her while she played an introduction.

Mrs. Swanson sat a little straighter and looked surprised when he started singing. The twins, who had been fussing from their blanket on the floor, gave him their usual toothless smile of approval and clasped their tiny hands together. He had lullabied them into dreamland more than once, sometimes with one on each arm and a slow promenade around the house.

He was on the last verse when he glanced again at Mrs. Swanson. Oddly enough, she had fixated her gaze on Sissy, and when he glanced in Sissy's direction, his voice faltered for a second. He quickly looked away and finished the song with his eyes on his baby daughters.

"That was wonderful, CJ." Mrs. Swanson stood abruptly. "But I know you must be tired, and come to think of it, so am I." She dusted her hands together and made a shooing motion. "Enough for one day. And tomorrow we'll go visiting."

CJ nodded and patted Joanna's shoulder. He knew why Mrs. Swanson ended the evening. She had seen the same malicious look on Sissy's face that he had. And it was directed at Joanna.

The sod house Frank had built for his bustling little wife was snug and cozy. She had hung crisp white curtains on the windows, and a cheerful potted geranium waved merrily on a bench beside the door.

"Yak se mas? —How are you?" They both seemed to be delighted to see their Sunday afternoon visitors, and with hand gestures and smiles, they soon had everyone seated. Coffee was almost immediately served in handsome Blue Fjord cups with saucers, and it was plain to see Antonio loved company. Her smile and broken English was continuous while she passed a heaping platter of kolaches to her guests while admiring the twins at the same time.

Joanna, in turn, was captivated by Antonio's two little boys, and Teddy was almost beside himself with importance as he gave Antonio the baby quilt. She was delighted with it and insisted on giving him a peck on the cheek along with a hug. Even though Teddy squirmed at such an affectionate display, he hugged the little woman back.

In short order, toddler Joe followed John and Teddy outside to play in the June sunshine. Baby James lay contentedly on his new quilt, and the adults tried to communicate without totally understanding what the other was trying to say.

Suddenly, Frank held up his hand, and the rest of them fell quiet. "CJ, music. Frank"—he pointed to himself—"music." From the corner of the room, he opened a black case and pulled out an accordion. "I play, you sing."

After several attempts, the two men found a song they both knew. Mrs. Swanson nodded her head in approval, and as one song progressed into another, the minutes flew into hours. Suddenly, everyone realized it was time for evening chores to begin.

"Perfectly delightful!" Mrs. Swanson said as they clipped home in the buggy. "CJ, I meant to tell you and Joanna last night that your song was wonderful. I somehow, ah, was distracted." She was sitting beside him in the buggy seat, and when he turned to look at her with a quizzical glance, he met her raised eyebrow and worried eyes with a barely perceptible nod. He and his mother-in-law were on the same page when it came to Sissy Tinner.

9

February 9, 1911

Mankato, Minnesota

Dear Simon, Joanna, and families,

Ma passed away in her sleep on the morning of the third. We went ahead and had her funeral like she wanted and didn't write quicker 'cause you remember how she fussed at all of us about not making a fuss for her funeral. It's a good thing we had the reunion and birthday party for Ma last summer, and she really enjoyed it. I think. You know Ma.

Anyways, wanted to let you know that she had sealed letters for all of us, but we couldn't find yours. Finally, Mrs. Dawes, Ma's housekeeper and cook, thought she remembered Ma giving it to Simon when he was back again this fall. I stayed awake a couple nights worrying about it until she told us that. Write me and let me know. If you don't have it, we'll look some more in Ma's house.

Joanna, she got your last letter, and it was lying by the stand by her chair with her reading glasses beside it. Guess she got it the day before she died, and couldn't make up her mind whether to read it that evening or wait until morning. But Mrs. Dawes said Ma could never wait for anything, so she sure enough read it and laughed out loud. Mrs. Dawes said Ma read her the part about the twins playing the piano and pretending they were in church. Hope you don't mind that we all read your letter too. It was pretty funny.

And I guess everything had already been sorta divided up, except no one can find the little trunk with Grandma Swanson's Norwegian Bible, but I kinda thought maybe Ma gave it to you. Let us know if you have it so as we don't have to keep looking for it.

Guess we must all be getting older and mellower because none of us fought over Ma's stuff. Actually, we were kinda surprised that there was so little there. Gertie would have liked Grandma Swanson's Bible, but if you have it, I say keep it.

I'm sure glad you folks could all come last summer. I know it was a lot of work with the little gals, but it sure was good to all get together. I just can't believe how Joanna and Ma got along. Gertie wouldn't like for me to say this, but I kinda think these past years, Ma sorta favored Joanna more than the rest of us. And Joanna, I think that CJ has had a lot to do with diluting the vinegar you used to sass Ma with. You sure did good with her last summer.

One last thing. That old neighbor girl of yours, that Sissy whatever-her-name-is, came to the funeral. Ma was always pretty closemouthed about why they parted ways so quick after their trip out to South Dakota in '08, but even if that girl is sorta purty, I just don't like her. Too sweet or something. She wanted to know if Isaac was graduating from high school this year. Guess her sister, Lizzie, is studying to be a nurse. Ma always said she was surprised Lizzie came with them when they left your place, and she said she didn't know how you ever stood that squawking voice. We ain't none of us seen either one of them for a couple of years.

This is getting real long, and my hand is tired. Ma was lucky she could just go to sleep and wake up dead.

Love to all,

Your oldest sister, Bertie, and family

"'Wake up dead.' Well. That sounds like a Bertie saying," CJ mused as he quickly scanned the letter a second time. Joanna had said little since he and Simon came in for coffee, other than to inform them about the letter and Mrs. Swanson's death.

"Boy howdy. I thought maybe last fall it might be the last time I saw her. She just acted tired." Simon reached across the table and patted Joanna's hand. "I have our letters, Joanna. Ma was pretty insistent that I take them."

Joanna nodded absently and took another sip of coffee.

CJ studied her and tried to think of an appropriate comment. Joanna and her mother had many ups and downs. In the early years of their marriage, it had seemed mostly downs. But the last couple of years were different. After Mrs. Swanson's visit, they wrote more to each other, and Joanna looked forward to hearing her mother's news. She even seemed to take pleasure in writing her mother about the kids and the happenings on the place.

When 1910 refused to rain and give them crops to harvest, they had decided to take a long-delayed trip to Missouri to see his parents. And then, they decided to add a loop into Minnesota and visited Joanna's family. It had made a long, hot and dry summer more enjoyable.

Mrs. Swanson had all sorts of things packed for Joanna to bring back to South Dakota. Amazingly, she was quite secretive about it. Or maybe, CJ reflected, knowing Mrs. Swanson, it shouldn't have been amazing at all. She often done things without bothering to inform anyone else and was usually quite surprised at the uproar it caused. At any rate, when the train pulled out of the Mankato station, there were crates and boxes and trunks that had been instructed to go with the Crezners.

Joanna had laughed and cried as she unpacked everything. In her letter to her mother, she had chided some and praised more because of the many useful articles. "But really, Ma, what am I to do with six brand-new decks of cards?" Her mother promptly wrote back, "Invite your neighbors over for some whist!"

When Joanna had a New Year's Eve party and invited some neighbors over for cards, she wrote her mother a long and detailed account of how folks enjoyed it and what dishes of her mother's she used to serve lunch on. Her mother's last letter was brief. "I told you so. Love, your mother."

"Bertie is right. Your mother is lucky to have passed away in her sleep. Last summer, she told me she had made peace with the Lord and was ready to go. Except she wanted to be sure and get in on the whist party some of her friends were planning for her birthday after the family all left."

Joanna laughed out loud at CJ's remark. "Sounds like Ma."

"Ma. She sure was hard to figure out sometimes. I sometimes think she fought a lot of dragons none of the rest of us knew about or could even understand." Simon scratched his chin thoughtfully. "Sometimes I think God has a special understanding for folks like Ma who sort of struggle with their faith."

Joanna nodded in agreement. "Did she ever say anything to you about Sissy Tinner or Lizzie?" Joanna's train of thought had shifted to their former neighbors.

Simon frowned and studied the cup he was holding. "Ma seemed to think it was odd that Lizzie left with her and Sissy. And she seemed to have something against Sissy, but she never said exactly what." Simon shrugged. "You know Ma."

CJ leaned back in his chair and stretched out his legs. "I haven't thought of Lizzie for quite a while. Seems like we were all too busy to give her much thought after she left. I can't quite figure out how she can go into nursing when she isn't old enough to be done with school. They must make exceptions."

"In Lizzie's case, they could probably tell she has a talent for it. She really did, despite what you and Ma thought. And even if her voice was rough and scratchy and got on all our nerves, she had a good heart." Joanna looked at him with raised eyebrows. "I'm sure *she* has a good heart. I've never been sure of what kind of heart her sister has."

"Well. I doubt we'll ever know because it's unlikely either one of them will come back. There's nothing much left on their homestead except the old barn. I don't even think the taxes have been paid." CJ got up to refill his coffee cup and poured Simon and Joanna another cup while he was at it.

"Ah, yeah. Yeah. Speaking of taxes, ah, I better make a confession." Simon put both hands around his cup and looked uncomfortable.

CJ and Joanna exchanged glances.

"I suppose this isn't the best time, on account of hearing Ma's news, but well, you know I've always kinda wanted our folk's homestead in Minnesota that Ma sold. And it was getting more and more run-down, and I found out last fall that the taxes hadn't been paid on it for a year. So, well, to make a long story real short, I paid the taxes, and well, now I guess it's back in the family. So to speak. Well, it is back in the family."

Simon looked sheepishly at them. "I told Ma, but I never told anyone else. Because, well, because you know that ever since Edith Crawford's husband died, I've been going back there every fall to get more bred heifers for our dairy herd. And well, she has all those little kids and the rent to pay on their farm and..." A slow flush crept across Simon's cheeks.

"Simon Swanson!" Joanna's eyes were round with wonder. "Do you mean to say that all those trips you were making back home weren't only to see Ma but to court Edith?"

"Boy howdy, Joanna!" Simon took a nervous gulp of coffee. "Leave it to you to put it on the table plain and blunt!"

"I think it's plain and wonderful, big brother!" Joanna was grinning from ear to ear. "It's wonderful to hear you have someone special in your life!"

CJ was slower than Joanna to figure out what Simon had been trying to say. In fact, he still wasn't too sure he knew what they were talking about.

"Now wait a minute. Spell this out for me." He smiled at his uncomfortable brother-in-law. "I'm slow on these matters."

Simon shook his head. "I guess this is what I need to say. Isaac is graduating from high school this spring, and I'm proud of him. He's a young man now and will have a life of his own. Edith has all those little kids. Five of them. She needs a husband, and they need a dad."

Simon raised his cup and took another drink of coffee before he continued. "We've talked a lot about this, and we decided we'd get married this year. Well, actually, this August. I, ah, I'll moving back to Minnesota and the home place."

CJ and Joanna were speechless. There was no sound in the kitchen except the ticking of the clock. Finally, CJ cleared his throat a couple of times.

"Well. Boy howdy, Simon. I can't imagine this place without you. I...well..."

Joanna had tears in her eyes. "We're happy for you Simon. It's such a surprise, is all." She sniffed and brushed her fingers across her eyes. "Happy for you, and sad for us."

Nels Christiansen came to visit them a couple of weeks later. Young bachelors often made the rounds throughout the neighborhood at mealtimes. It was actually expected by the ladies in the community to see hungry and somewhat lonesome young fellows ride into the yard just as everyone was getting settled to eat their meal.

He offered Joanna sympathy about her mother. He was a kind young man and had a caring nature. He also enjoyed Joanna's cooking, and during the summer when school was out and he could reclaim his cabin, he often dropped by.

It was unusual, however, for him to come from Belvidere in the middle of the week. He joined them for dinner and, as usual, took several helpings of everything before finally settling back in his chair with happy satisfaction.

"That was delicious, Joanna. I'm going to miss your good cooking."

"Are you leaving us or getting married or what Nels?" Joanna poured everyone a final round of coffee.

"I'm going back to my old home. I've sold my land to O. R. Gardner, but I made a stipulation that I think you might be interested in, CJ."

"Wait a minute. I didn't know you were selling." CJ wouldn't have minded being told there was some land available to buy. Although now with Simon leaving, maybe he didn't need more of a workload. He could hardly bring himself to think of the time when his brother-in-law wouldn't be there with his quiet good sense and advice.

"Yup. Last year was so dang hot and dry, and this year is starting out just as bad. I am getting out. Lots of folks are leaving before we have an even worse drought. At least there's a little money to be had, and if I wait another year, there probably won't be anyone in the country left to buy anything."

"Well, I'm leaving myself." Simon grinned at him. "I'm going back to Minnesota, and I'm getting married to a fine woman. You should do the same, Nels."

Nels sputtered in his coffee. "How about that! I sure didn't know anything at all about you getting married!"

"I hope it hasn't forgotten how to rain in Minnesota. I'm taking some of our stock back there in hopes we can keep our herd going here."

Nels reached over to shake Simon's hand. "I forgot my manners! Congratulations!"

"But what's the stipulation you were talking about?" Joanna wondered.

Nels was delighted she asked. "I decided a church was needed. Right up there on the hilltop. Right where you can see St. Peter's Church clear across the hills. A United Norwegian Lutheran Church. And you, CJ, can be the pastor!"

10

March 15, 1911

Belvidere, South Dakota

Dear Mom and Dad,

We always enjoy your wonderful long and newsy letters. Joanna especially looks forward to them, and now that she has been to Missouri and has seen the house you live in and the church, streets, and town, she has a new appreciation for your reports.

We learned the sad news that Joanna's mother passed away in her sleep last month. Joanna said she was grateful her mother's death was quick, but she mourns they only had a short time in this life to really know and love each other. She has mentioned many times how glad she was that she listened to your wisdom about reconciliation. I think she offered the olive branch of peace to her mother, and her mother took it. It blessed both of them.

We have another sad/glad situation. Simon is leaving this summer and going back to Minnesota. He has purchased his parent's homestead, and the happy part of it all is that he plans to marry a young widow with five children. She is the same lady he has been buying the milk cows from, and now we know why we have so many of them! But we are going to be lost without him. I wonder and worry how I'll manage the place when I don't have him to guide and direct me. He has been a port in the storm ever since Joanna and I were married. He wondered the other day if I'd get rid of the milk cows. I would truly love to see them all leave with him, but they have been a good and steady source of income. I know I'll keep them because we can't afford to not have them.

And more things to ponder. Our neighbor who has lent his claim shack for the school house has decided to sell his homestead. He has given a small piece of land to the community to have a church built there. He wants it to be the United Norwegian Lutheran Church. It's a nice gesture, but in these hard times with another drought looking at us, I don't know how we'll afford to buy building material. I'm most troubled, however, at his insistence that I be the minister. I've never understood how a Christian man, and one who comes from a line of ministers and who studied for the ministry, could have such a dread of being a minister. If you have any advice, I'd appreciate hearing it. I'm afraid I was rather abrupt (at least that's what Joanna told me) in my refusal. He, however, seemed sure that I would capitulate and left in as merry a mood as when he arrived.

And isn't that how life goes? Things move along smoothly and uneventfully, and suddenly, there is one thing after another that demands us to change our passive thinking. Joanna and I have both prayed for answers. She seems quite troubled by several things. I would imagine with her mother passing, Simon leaving, and Isaac on the brink of manhood, she has quite enough on her plate. That, coupled with my own doubts and worries about the church offer and running the place on my own, has put quite a strain on both of us.

But enough gloom. We are delighted that you are planning to come for Isaac's graduation! That is the sunshine of our life right now. Joanna, Deborah Lynn, and Mrs. Ordin have been busy planning for a reception after the ceremony. It will be good to be with loved ones and friends for this happy occasion.

Willow and Heather send kisses. John and Teddy send hellos, and we all send our love.

CJ, Joanna, and family

CJ sat in silent contemplation after he sealed his letter to his parents. Of all the things he wrote about, the offer to pastor the new church bothered him the most. He woke up dreading the thought of it, and he went to sleep feeling sinful because he dreaded it so much. It was a vicious cycle that left him irritable and unable to settle into his normal routine.

To top matters off, it was the driest spring he could ever remember. Simon and Joanna agreed it looked ominous. Already, the ceaseless prairie winds whipped the fields of the homesteaders, and there was a constant haze of dust in the air. There was also a constant migration of homesteaders across the region heading back east. Folks were leaving because they couldn't make a living without money from their crops. Others, like Nels, were disillusioned with prairie life in the Dakotas. "I'm hungry and thirsty and hot, and I'm sick of the country and sick of my lot." Teddy had read that someplace and continually quoted it.

I can handle drought. I can even handle Simon leaving. But Lord, when I think of preaching sermons and being a pastor, my belly tightens up and I feel trapped. And I'm ashamed of it. I'm ashamed to write it to my dad who has given his life to be a minister. I'm ashamed to tell my wife and my kids how much I dread—yes, dread—the very thought of it. I must be a hypocrite or a coward or...I don't know what. I pray for Your wisdom, Your guidance, Your will. I know I've prayed this constantly the past month. So far, Lord, I can't seem to hear anything You're telling me.

"Oh! I didn't know you were still up." Joanna had a Wednesday evening ritual. After the household was in bed, she enjoyed a leisurely bath in her pride and joy—her enameled tub. The family learned in short order it was not wise to disturb her or trouble her with anything while she relished her solitude and her soak.

She looked at him questioningly as she neared the table. She was wearing the long kimono he had bought for her after she had the twins. Somehow, she managed to make the flounce on the bottom of the full skirt billow and glide as she walked noiselessly into the dining room.

The soft glow of the oil lamp gave her features a gentleness he didn't often take time to appreciate. He smiled slowly at her and patted the chair next to him.

"I'm contemplating our life, Joanna."

She sighed and settled in beside him. "And what did you decide, Mr. Crezner?"

"I haven't decided what I decided. Except..." He leaned over and slowly kissed her. "Except I do know I married a particularly handsome and wonderful woman."

"Mmm." Joanna, as always, kissed him back.

"So, woman"—he drew back and ran his hand down her arm—"tell me what you decided in your solitary soak."

"The skin on my belly has finally shrunk back to almost normal since I had the twins."

Her remark was not at all what he expected, and after his initial astonishment, he threw back his head and guffawed.

"That is serious stuff, Joanna," he choked out when he caught his breath. "How long did it take you to figure that out?"

"Well, the twins are a little over three years old. It's taken that long to get back into shape, so it's taken me that long to figure it out."

He raised his eyebrows at her. "You're a brilliant woman. You know that, don't you?"

She ran her long slender fingers over his hand. "I know that you are worried about many things, CJ, especially being a preacher. But the church won't be built for awhile. Why don't you give your troubled mind a break and think of more pleasant things?"

He took his free hand and raised her fingers to his lips. "Why don't I? I'm thinking of something very pleasant right now. And Joanna, it's a full moon."

The June graduation and the reception afterward was an award-winning South Dakota day. A light balmy breeze whispered through the overhead leaves of the cottonwood trees, adding melodious music as the guests gathered for food and festivities to honor young Mr. Isaac Swanson.

Joanna and Mrs. Ordin planned the menu, and Deborah Lynn and her mother masterminded the other details. Mrs. Smith insisted the affair be in her yard, and the location was perfect, giving the guests a picturesque view of the Missouri River with the added advantage of the new state capitol building.

People had come and gone for a couple of hours, and now a scattered handful was visiting in shady areas. CJ let his gaze and thoughts drift as he stood on the porch, slightly apart from the assembled group. His parents and the Smiths were seated around a table, having an amiable visit. Drew, Deborah Lynn, and Joanna were laughing at something as they stood beside the depleted serving tables. Isaac, looking handsome and grown-up in his suit, was in deep conversation with Mickey O'Reilly. Mickey's cane was close beside him, but he looked healthier and happier than CJ had ever seen him. Grace Lynn had a twin on each side of her. She held their little hands in her bigger ten-year-old hands, and the three girls were the essence of charm in their long dresses with bows.

John hadn't left Isaac's side since the reception started, and Teddy, suddenly bereft of his constant companion, had wandered forlornly over to Mr. Ordin. From the looks of the hand gestures, the two were discussing fishing stories.

"Come and sit a spell, CJ. My feet told me it was time to enjoy this wicker chair." Mrs. Ordin was rocking and fanning her flushed face.

CJ glanced behind him. He hadn't noticed her sitting on the porch chair. With a sudden grin, he joined her and, before he sat down, he kissed her cheek. "You've been working too hard again," he scolded her lightly.

"I know it. But I wanted to be part of this. Ain't it just grand, CJ?" She gave a satisfied nod that sent her earrings bobbing and dancing. "These four years Isaac has spent with us has been a study, I can tell you. He went from a shy young boy into a confident young fella. Danged if it hasn't been fun to have his friends come by. And look at all the folks that stopped in today to wish him well. I'm proud. Proud as an old mama bear."

CJ nodded. "Me too. Proud of all of you. He wouldn't be here if it weren't for you, and the Smiths, and Reverend and Mrs. Drew Wilson. You all helped."

Mrs. Ordin cocked her head to one side while her earrings twirled merrily. "You know what I'm a-thinkin'? I'm a-thinkin' ain't none of us would be gathered here today if it weren't for that darned handsome Missouri boy that wandered into our midst several years ago. Good-lookin' and with a voice like an angel." She swatted his arm affectionately.

CJ sat back in his chair and stretched his legs. "You're a sweet lady, Mrs. Ordin." He grinned at her. "Maybe a little untruthful, but very sweet."

"Honey, I don't think 'sweet' is on my list of virtues. But say"—she leaned a little closer to him and lowered her voice—"what's on Joanna's mind? She seems a little, you know, kinda in a world of her own."

"I was hoping you could tell me. I don't know. When I ask, she just shakes her head and laughs a little. Tells me it's nothing."

"Hmm. Do you think it's her ma dying that's a-botherin' her?"

CJ glanced in Joanna's direction. As if she could feel his gaze upon her, she half-turned toward him and raised her hand in a gracious wave. He returned a salute and a smile and gave his attention back to Mrs. Ordin.

"Well. No. She mourns her mother, but I think it's something else."

Mrs. Ordin shook her head and frowned. "And what's a-botherin' you, CJ?"

"How is it you can always read me like a book? I thought I was being a cheerful fellow, and here you ask me what's a-botherin' me." He gave her a wry smile and patted her hand that rested on his arm.

"Honey, I'm a meddlin' old woman. And us meddlin' old women have a sixth sense when something ain't quite right."

"Ain't quite right probably describes me. I've been asked to be a pastor of the church they want to build near us."

"Ain't that a good thing?"

If his father had asked the same question to CJ, he would have hedged and made a careful reply. With Mrs. Ordin, he was painfully blunt.

"No." He shook his head and repeated himself. "No. it's not a good thing at all. I feel like I'm fighting the same war I fought thirteen years ago when I first came up here." He raised his eyebrow at her and was pinned by her piercing blue eyes. "I'm not preacher material."

"Says who?"

"Says me. Look at my dad and Reverend Smith and Drew Wilson. They've got the conviction and the powerful messages and—"

"And fiddle, CJ Crezner." Mrs. Ordin's earrings bobbed in annoyance. "Listen to me. They all preach. But you, CJ, are a teacher. You can say more in a few words than most preachers do in an hour. I mean, they're very good, but sometimes, when I just want to know what a verse means without a sermon, I know I can ask you. Isaac has nothing but praise for what you've taught him about the Bible, and I say, you don't have to be a blood-and-thunder preacher to your friends and neighbors. Just get up there and talk like you were a-sittin' around your kitchen table." Mrs. Ordin fanned her flushed face a little more vigorously.

CJ opened his mouth to protest and then clamped it shut again and contemplated her words.

"I declare, you two look like you've been in an argument! Now, say that isn't so, CJ and Mrs. Ordin!" Deborah Lynn's light laughter settled over them like a gossamer veil.

"It isn't so. Mrs. Ordin was just a-tellin' me a few things I was unaware of." CJ reached over to pat the red cheek of his old counselor and friend.

"What do you three have up your sleeves?" Mrs. Ordin's blue eyes flashed him a look that said she could tell him more things he was unaware of if they hadn't been interrupted.

Drew gave his hearty laugh. "We are conspiring against this man." He pointed at CJ. "These lovely ladies believe the two of us should sing at church on Sunday. And I gave my ready consent! What about it, CJ?"

Singing, yes. He could sing without fear of failure. Maybe he could even teach. Maybe. He had never thought about being an unassuming teacher, but at least it didn't hold the nightmare of preaching.

He gave Joanna a sudden smile. "What did our lovely ladies have in mind for us to sing?" His question seemed to take the lovely ladies by surprise. They gave each other a blank look.

"'His Eye Is on the Sparrow.' I love that song." Mrs. Ordin took matters into her own hands, and after a short pause, the others nodded in agreement.

After a few minutes of small talk, the trio moved on. CJ rocked in silence with his hands clasped together. Finally, he stole a look at

Mrs. Ordin. She had quit fanning herself and was sitting motionless in her chair. Her gaze never left his face.

"Well." CJ cleared his throat. "Knowing you, and I think I know you quite well, I imagine you want me to pay attention to the words of the song."

She nodded, and her earrings once again bobbed in crazy circles. "Honey," she said softly, "you're discouraged, troubled, and a-seein' shadows. You're forgetting Jesus is your fortress."

"Portion, sweet lady. The verse says, 'Jesus is my portion,'" CJ corrected her mildly.

"Fiddle. If I was a-writin' the song, I'd say fortress. Mainly 'cause I don't know what 'portion' means."

"'Portion' means fate. When Jesus is my fate, my all in all, my destiny. You know."

"What's the next line?"

"''A constant Friend is He.'"

"That's right. 'His eye is on the sparrow, and I know He watches me.'" She gave him her special smile that made her eyes twinkle. "And I want you to sing because you're happy!"

He unclasped his hands and gave a slight chuckle. "Well. You preach a mighty good sermon, Mrs. Ordin. We could be a team. You preach, and I'll happily sing."

Isaac sat spellbound on the oak pew. His two mentors, CJ and Drew Wilson, had just walked up to the podium and were getting ready to sing. CJ looked as comfortable as if he were riding the range with Isaac and the boys. Drew smiled at the congregation and nodded at Mrs. Smith. She began her piano introduction, and the two blended voices caressed the listening flock like a summer breeze.

"Why should I feel discouraged, why should the shadows come?"

An unplanned sigh escaped Isaac. Since Simon had told him gently that he would be returning to Minnesota and a new life, he had felt the shadow of forlornness pass over him. Not that he didn't want his dad to marry again, but it seemed like nothing was the same anymore. Aunt Jo and CJ were preoccupied with their own thoughts, and judging from the grim look they usually wore, their thoughts were troubling.

The shadow of the drought seemed to hover threateningly over everyone. Isaac would only be home a short time before he joined the neighbors and trailed cattle to their leased land on the Indian reservation. It would be a long summer in the saddle, but maybe it would give him time to think of what he wanted to do with his life.

CJ was looking at Aunt Jo, and Isaac noticed that the special little smile she used just for CJ was hovering on her lips.

"I sing because I'm happy, I sing because I'm free."

How the guy could hit the high note and hold it effortlessly was a puzzle. In fact, CJ's singing was a mystery to Isaac. He might go for weeks and never utter a note. And when the family least expected it, they would hear him singing as he milked cows or saddled his horse or just out of the blue for no reason at all.

"Let not your heart be troubled,' His tender word I hear, and resting on His goodness I lose my doubts and fear."

Was that a little tear racing down Aunt Jo's cheek? Without staring, Isaac couldn't be sure. She had mellowed in the last couple of years, he decided. But ever since Grandma Swanson had passed away, she'd had this little worried pucker on her forehead, especially when she saw him. Once he had asked her what was wrong, but she had just smiled and then unexpectedly gave him a quick hug before she told him nothing was the matter. She gave a forced laugh and said he was growing up much too fast and hurried outside to hang laundry on the line.

Drew's harmony was subdued, which was rather odd for that boisterous fellow. Drew had a powerful preaching voice, and he belted out hymns with joyous elation. Usually, Drew took the melody when he and CJ sang, but this song was all CJ's, and Drew gave him full benefit of his supporting role.

"Whenever I am tempted, whenever clouds arise, when songs give place to sighing, when hope within me dies."

Isaac shuddered. For some reason, Ben Tinner's thin face flashed into his mind. Poor Ben. One time, Isaac had come across Lizzie crying at Ben's grave. He had swung off his horse and had stood awkwardly beside her, trying to think of something to say. "Ben just gave up. He hurt so bad all the time. He just wanted out of life. His hope died." Tears had raced down her red cheeks, and she had used the corner of her dress to wipe her nose. "How come nobody helped him?" She had screamed the accusation at Isaac, and he had no answer.

What would it be like to have hope die? Isaac thought of the life he wanted and the people he wanted in his life. No hope for a better tomorrow would be the epitome of despair.

"I draw the closer to Him, from care He sets me free."

Isaac sat back in the hard pew and let the music speak to him. If Christ's eye was on the inconsequential sparrow, it was a sure fact His eye was also on Isaac Swanson, and Isaac agreed with the song.

"I know He cares for me."

11

October 5, 1911

Springfield, Missouri

Dear CJ and Joanna,

I thought I would be modern and use this typewriter, but after several attempts at it, I decided to go back to pen and paper. I think I will send the thing to you, CJ. Maybe Isaac can use it if you can't.

And so it is. A modern age has come, and I feel rusty and behind. And tired. Last month I gave notice to the elders I would resign the first of the year. I think our growing church needs a new and invigorated pastor to meet the challenges of our time. Our associate pastor is a godly man, and I had informed him before the meeting of my plans. He was supportive and prayerful.

Your mother and I had discussed this, as you know, for almost a year. When we were with you at Isaac's graduation, we both knew we wanted to be able to spend more time with our family. We are thinking of taking a house in Belvidere to reside in for part of the year. Now that you have a chance to pastor a church, I thought maybe I could be of some help to you.

I read where South Dakota is experiencing the worst drought in state history. As you say, you live in "next-year land." Thankfully, the milk cows are bringing in some money, and I hope and pray you have enough feed to keep them going.

Imagine the boys are back at school, and Isaac is on the fall roundup. After hearing about his wagon boss, Mr. Jones, for so many years, I was delighted to meet your neighbor at the graduation.

One more piece of news. Doc Regis has offered us the cottage his mother used to live in. He has no use for it, he says (knowing Doc like we do, I would imagine he has all sorts of uses for it), and we can live there and pay the taxes. We are very thankful for his kind and generous offer. Your mother has made plans to enjoy a smaller home rather than the work of caring for the manse.

In His name,

Love,

Dad

CJ sat on his horse in the October sunshine. As far as he could see, the prairie was brown and brittle. An August gully washer had filled the water holes, but the ground was so parched and baked that the water had quickly disappeared.

As his father said, he hoped he had enough feed to last throughout the winter. But finding water was more challenging, he decided. Even Bad River had dried up during the summer. He took off his hat and ran his sleeve over his forehead and groused to himself about homesteaders. If they hadn't all piled into the country and plowed up the grass, cut the trees, and scavenged for water, which, he sighed wearily as he dismounted, was all the things the government bureaucrats ordered them to do, if the country was still grass... "If horses could fly," he muttered to himself and looked at the stakes in the hard ground that marked the outline of the new church.

"I hope, Dad, that you will come and do what your son doesn't want to do. I hope you can fill this building with needy folks who want to hear a message and hear it delivered with assurance. Because I can tell you, I have no heart for it. Even after Mrs. Ordin's speech."

His horse put his head down and started cropping the short grass even shorter. CJ looked at the hills all around him. It was a peaceful spot, though probably not the best place to build a church.

But still, it was on a serene hill with Brave Bull Creek meandering below, and the view of endless prairie hills gave one a sense of peace.

He wasn't surprised at his father's news. He knew when his parents left in June that they were in prayer over the future. He could tell his mother was worried about his dad's health; and in truth, he was relieved the decision had been made and a home was being made ready for them. And he knew they wanted to be closer to their grandkids. He and Joanna had looked for a house in Belvidere but could find none they thought would work for his parents.

A distant sound floated over the prairie and wafted to the hilltop where CJ stood. His horse stopped chewing and put his ears up.

"Little Frank and his accordion." CJ's horse resumed eating. Little Frank. Playing his accordion to his houseful of growing children. Joe, Jim, Aldrich, Alyse, and baby number 5, who was due in March, Antonio had confided to Joanna. Each baby seemed to bring them happiness, and somehow, the sod house accommodated all of them.

"He makes me ashamed of myself." CJ's horse snorted and kept eating, unmindful his owner was confiding his woes to him.

CJ gazed up the little valley where Frank's homestead could easily be seen. "Actually, Lord, he makes me really ashamed of myself." CJ recognized "Baruska," a Bohemian polka Frank belted out with energy. "Just became a citizen, has two mortgages on his 160 acres, a houseful of little blond kids, just a little shaver of a fellow, and he puts a big oaf like me to shame. Pathetic.

"I don't know why Your servant isn't more enthused about serving You as pastor, Lord. Joanna called me a Jonah a long time ago, and it still describes me. To admit the truth, which I'm sure You already know, if I could run away today, I would. If I were younger and didn't have a wife and kids and a ranch..." He gave an exasperated sigh. Life would be wretched if that were the case, he finally decided. He gave himself a mental shake as he walked the perimeters of what would be the United Norwegian Lutheran Church.

It wasn't going to be a big church. In fact, as some of the homesteaders said when they came to inspect what Nels had given them, a country church might not survive if the drought didn't end. People were leaving. Yet there were enough of them left who seemed excited to have a place to meet and worship.

CJ mounted his horse and headed home over the short and crunchy grass. "I know I'm blessed, Lord. I just don't understand why I can't be excited about preaching for You."

The middle of October proved to be as hot and windy as the first part. CJ clamped his hat down on his head a little tighter as he rode the breaks of White River behind the roundup herd from the reservation. There were many cowboys and cattlemen pushing the cattle they had left onto the south flat by Belvidere. The railroad had proved to be a bonus in shipping cattle out, and the stockyards beside the train would be full while the cattle were loaded into the rail cars.

Finally, the sorting was finished. The small herds the cattlemen were desperate to keep for another year were headed to home range, but the bulk of them were in the corrals and would be sold.

"This ain't purty."

CJ turned to the speaker and thrust out his hand to shake the offered hand. "Winn! You took the words right out of my mouth. How are you?"

The blue eyes of the older cattleman were as clear and twinkling as they had been the first time CJ met him. They had driven cattle from Fort Robinson to Bad River in 1898 and had become fast friends. CJ hadn't seen Winn for a couple of years. He was so glad to see him he would have given the man a bear hug if he hadn't been sure Winn would have knocked him off the saddle for such unmanly conduct.

"Well, sir, I must be getting old. They tell me the young man over there who sure enough knows how to drive cattle is young Isaac.

And the two young lads trying to keep up with him are your boys. Dang! Makes me feel old."

"This drought is enough to make us all old. I hope the train gets in here soon. Those cattle won't even make it to market if they can't drink somewhere."

Winn shook his head. "I ain't never seen the country looking so bad, and I've been around a few years. No water. No water nowhere. What are you doing with your herd, CJ?"

CJ's spirits sagged clear down to his toes. "Most of them are in the corrals. They'll all be on the train headed for Sioux City. I'm keeping milk cows for the cream check and a handful of my range cows."

Winn nodded. "And that ain't purty. I'm here as rep for some of the big herds. They're doing the same. Get some cash while you can, I guess. I'm only keeping a small herd myself. We can't raise cattle without water or grass, and these past two years showed us we ain't got neither."

The conversation changed as Isaac and the boys rode toward them. Isaac seemed as glad to see Winn as CJ had been, and of course, John and Teddy had heard enough stories of Winn, Joker, and Smokey to be fascinated at finally meeting him. Teddy declared that his mom would love to cook for them all; that is, all except Isaac. He was riding the rails with the cattle, and it was on his newly responsible shoulders to bring home the money from the buyer.

The train's whistle coming from the west alerted everyone to get busy. When the train huffed into Belvidere and the railcars were in position, the hopes and dreams of many cattlemen were pushed without ceremony into the cars. And equally without ceremony, the herds that had been built over the years with a discerning eye for improved genetics were on their way to butcher shops. Such is the story of droughts. *No water, no feed, no cattle*, CJ mused.

CJ gave Isaac last-minute warnings and instructions. He finally squeezed the young man's shoulder and grinned. "Have a good time," he said and ducked out of the car with John and Teddy following close behind him.

Winn accepted Teddy's invitation and, as usual, was an appreciative supper guest, spinning tale after tale of early range days and interspersing them with flattery for Joanna and her cooking.

When he stopped for seconds of dessert, Joanna quizzed him about his present day life.

His blue eyes began twinkling, and he sighed contentedly. "Well now, I can tell you that Mary and I have a mighty rambunctious two-year-old."

CJ and Joanna looked at each other with raised eyebrows, and CJ sputtered somewhat before the question came out. "Did we know you were married, Winn?"

"By golly, by the look on your face, you didn't even know this old bachelor tied the knot! Yessir! Married a fine woman with four young 'uns, and now we have one of our own. Lots happening on White Willow Creek. Even have a school a couple miles away with about thirty-two kids. Imagine that! Thirty-two kids, and ten years ago, there wasn't that many kids in an entire community."

"Did you know Joker also has a family?" CJ asked as he sat back in his chair with a fresh cup of coffee.

"Two or three, last I heard," Winn answered. "I reckon he loves 'em all, but his daughter Little Sparrow is the apple of his eye." And Winn was off again recalling earlier-day stories about Joker and Smokey and telling tales to CJ's wide-eyed children about their father.

CJ shook his head and helped Joanna gather dishes off the table. In fact, he even dried as she washed; and for once, Willow and Heather were allowed to listen and not help with kitchen cleanup.

Winn opted to spend the night in Simon and Isaac's house and graciously insisted that he would head out early in the morning so

Joanna wouldn't have to cook his breakfast. Of course, he knew she would refuse such an offer.

The sun was barely peeking over the brown hills the next morning when CJ walked his old friend to the corrals and helped him catch his horse.

Winn mounted slowly. His full belly of pancakes and chokecherry syrup made moving at any speed slightly uncomfortable.

"Thanks, CJ. I sure enjoyed this. It's good to talk about old times, ain't it?"

CJ nodded. "We've got some good memories together. Tell your wife and son hello for us."

Winn peered down at him, and there was a question in his blue eyes. "Now, CJ, this ain't none of my business, but I just can't help but wonder what's troubling Joanna. She sure seems like, well, like she's got a problem she's trying to work out."

CJ stepped back from Winn's horse and expelled a troubled sigh. "You're not the first one to notice or ask me. And I have to tell you what I tell everyone. Whatever it is, she keeps it to herself."

Winn looked toward the house and nodded. "What man ever understood a woman's mind anyway? They just think different than we do." He raised his fingers to the brim of his hat. "Take care, CJ. Come to White Willow Creek and visit Mary and me sometime."

For some time, CJ leaned against the corral fence as he watched Winn's disappearing figure. The old days Winn talked about the previous evening caused certain nostalgia, and with remembering, he recalled the Joanna of old. Laughing, scolding, always busy. When had she started changing? He couldn't pinpoint a time. She was still busy, and she still scolded all of them—but absently, like her heart wasn't in it. And when was the last time he'd seen her laugh—really laugh—with merriment in her eyes? And why wouldn't she tell him what the problem was?

"Things change, Lord. People change. All the time." He ambled to the barn and coaxed one of the milk cows into a stanchion. "Except You probably already know I'll never change and love these milk cows." He grumbled softly as he put his head against the soft flank of Glory.

He thought of the time, work, and patience he had put into building his range herd. It had been enjoyable. With Simon gone, he'd have to put his mind on keeping a decent dairy herd. "And that ain't purty," he muttered as Glory switched her tail across his back and mooed for her calf.

12

November 1, 1911

Sioux City, Iowa

Dear CJ, Aunt Jo, and cousins,

The cattle stood the trip in fair shape. I think I got a good price for them; at least that's what the neighbors seemed to think. I'm mailing the check to you like you suggested. Took out the amount you told me to for Dad and myself.

Almost got lost in the stockyards. Prefer green pastures and grass to this setup, but guess they do what they have to with this many cattle rolling through every day.

I'm heading to Dad's tomorrow. Think I'll stay there until after Christmas. His last letter sounded like he could use a little help, even with all his new step kids! Plus, I'm sure lonesome for him as I haven't seen him since he and Edith were married in August. Lots of changes this year.

John and Teddy, wish you were here to see all these pens and all the cattle. Plus all the other sights in Sioux City. I picked up some souvenirs for you boys and Heather and Willow. I even saw a telephone. Watched some guy talk in it, and then he listened to a little black thing he held to his hear. I know they have 'em in Pierre too, but it's always fun to watch people talk to a box.

I better close now. Most of the neighbors plan to head back home, and I'm heading toward Minnesota. See you in January.

Love,

Isaac

CJ rocked back in his chair and reached for his coffee cup. "I was sure hoping he'd be home for Christmas."

Joanna barely looked up from her ironing. She was working on a frilly little sleeve that seemed to defy any attempt to lay the way it should. "I was too," she finally muttered, taking Willow's dress and giving it a shake.

CJ set his chair back on its four legs with a noticeable thud. "I don't know why women waste hours trying to get some darn fool sleeve on a kid's dress perfect. The minute she puts it on, it's going to wrinkle anyway." The subject was a constant source of irritation between the two of them.

Joanna looked at him with narrowed eyes and walked over to the stove to get a different-sized sadiron. Her next ironing project was his shirt, and judging from the way she was unrolling it over the ironing board, she was going to tackle it with vengeance.

"I thought you came in here with a sweet frame of mind and intentions of reading Isaac's letter to me," she answered mildly enough and put the shirtsleeve over the pointed end of her ironing board. "Who asked you to criticize the way I iron?" She shook the heavy iron at him in mock anger.

He grinned at her and shook his head. "I'm just making a point about—"

"I don't need any ironing pointers from you, Mr. Crezner. What I need is for you to run upstairs and check the girls and make sure they're still napping. Then you could bring us both back some hot coffee. I'm ready for a little break. Oh, and was there any other mail?"

CJ groused under his breath as he stood up. "Yeah, I left it all on the table."

Heather Rose was sleeping peaceably, covered up nicely with her dimpled hands folded under her cheek. Willow Charm had flung off her cover and was scrunched up in the middle of the bed with one arm trailing over the edge. CJ marveled at how his twins could have such opposite personalities. He covered Willow with the blanket that had fallen to the floor and hurriedly tiptoed out of their room. She was a light sleeper, and he wanted to be gone before she realized he was there.

He thought Joanna would be done with his shirt by the time he returned, but she was still working on the sleeve. He set her cup of coffee on a table beside her ironing board and took his own cup and himself back to the chair. He wanted to tell her she didn't even need to iron his work shirts, but there was something in her demeanor that told him it would be best to drop the subject.

"Both girls sleeping," he reported. "I'm glad Isaac's letter was in the mail this morning. With the cattle check he sent and the cream check, we should have enough to pay our bills and still carry over for the winter. I sure hope I can keep some money back to buy more range cattle this spring."

"Who will have any that you can even buy? And what kind of shape will they be in by spring with so little hay?" Her voice was uncharacteristically bitter. "It would have been nice if Isaac had come home to at least help you with the milking this winter. He's been gone all summer with those stupid cattle down on the reservation."

CJ looked at her in exasperation. Stupid cattle? They paid the bills on the place. What did she want to raise, tumbleweeds and sheep? He took another sip of coffee and debated whether to get up and leave like he usually did when her temper turned ugly or try again to discover what was really bothering her.

As if reading his mind, her expression softened. "Maybe you better go and start the milking. I'm in a bad mood right now."

He wanted to say he was sick and tired of her bad moods. He stood up and slammed his cup on the table before he stalked out the door. For spite, he slammed it shut behind him and didn't care if he woke up the girls or not.

The months that followed brought a change on the landscape. The United Norwegian Lutheran Church that Nels Christianson envisioned was taking shape. Lumber arrived, and the community rallied together to construct the small building. A stove was brought in, chopped wood appeared, and homemade benches and a pulpit were added to the interior. To be sure, it was not anything fancy, but it was a church with a steeple and (surprisingly, in CJ's mind) a nice-sized congregation of Bohemians, Norwegians, and other homesteaders. He was amazed that the little building was crowded every Sunday.

He needn't have worried about the absence of a piano to lead the singing. There was always someone who just happened to bring a violin, an accordion, or a guitar to help with the hymns. Sometimes he listened in disbelief to the mixture of languages that rose up in worship, but he supposed that to God, who understands all things, a little thing like several different languages being sung at the same time was a small matter.

A church board was quickly organized, and to no one's surprise, least of all CJ's, he was formally asked to be the minister. He politely declined.

Mrs. Deborah Lynn Wilson, wife of Reverend Drew Wilson, sank into her mother's tufted wing chair in disbelief.

"Carl John Crezner. You simply never cease to amaze me." Her blue eyes were reproachful.

CJ looked from her to her husband and then to her parents. All were studying him with various stages of doubt and dismay written on their faces.

Drew cleared his throat and tried to keep his booming voice soft. "CJ, you tell us that you're sure God has no plans for you to preach His Word. I, uh, I assume…but of course I know you have…but I assume you've been in prayer about this."

CJ sighed. He slowly rose from the uncomfortable chair and walked over to the parlor window. He knew it was going to be difficult to tell the reverends and their wives that he had no plans to preach. He also knew they deserved to hear his reasons from him personally. From the window's viewpoint, he could see the new state capitol's copper dome shimmering in the January sunshine.

"Yes, Drew." He tried unsuccessfully to keep the edge from his voice as he turned to face them. "There is no calling for me to preach. There's...nothing. I'll tell you what I told the board. I love the Lord, I want to serve Him, but it's settled in my heart that He has other things for me to do than to preach."

Deborah Lynn stirred restlessly. "What does Joanna have to say about this?"

"Joanna has said from the beginning that she would make a terrible preacher's wife. She's too argumentative and outspoken." He threw up his hands at their dismayed reaction. "Those are her words, not mine."

"Well, CJ, I was wondering what your father thinks? I know he had plans to come to Belvidere to help you with the church." Reverend Smith's compassion almost broke CJ's composure.

"My parents are in the process right now of moving out of the manse, and I decided to wait until they were settled in their new home to tell them." CJ knew his voice sounded stiff and heavy. His heart, to be truthful, was stiff and heavy with dread at telling his parents that their only son was still not going to follow the Crezner line of ministers. He knew they thought if he had enough time to study the Bible and live the Christian life, he would eventually be led to the pulpit. They were so excited to hear about the church and the plan for him to be the minister. He was filled with remorse to disappoint them again.

Mrs. Smith rattled cups while she poured coffee. Rising gracefully, she carried a dainty cup and saucer to CJ and patted his arm as he awkwardly tried to balance it with his calloused hands.

"They'll understand. Parents understand more than we give them credit for," she said soothingly. "And for what it's worth, young friend, *I* understand. We were, of course, quite shocked to hear that you turned down the pastorate." She gave the rest of her family a look that said she wanted their agreement on what she was going to say next. "But who's to say what God's will is for someone else's life? And if you have prayed for wisdom and guidance, and this is what you feel the answer is, then praise God! And who knows what your next adventure for the Lord might be?"

CJ carefully set his china cup and saucer on the small table beside the window. "Thank you," he told Mrs. Smith warmly and gave the dear woman a gentle hug. He would have liked to give her one of his bear hugs in appreciation for her comforting words; but somehow, today, she seemed rather fragile to him.

"Oh, Momma!" Deborah Lynn's laughter always seemed to float up and down a musical scale. "You always know the right thing to say!" She was at her mother's side in a flash. "Of course, I can't say I understand. But if Momma says she does, that's good enough for me!"

Her glance at CJ, however, left no doubt in his mind as to how very disappointed she was in him. He sighed inwardly. *This must be how a germ feels under a microscope. Examined and found wanting.*

He knew he would have to make the same arguments to a number of people, including his parents. And then...there was Joanna.

"Horsefeathers!" Mrs. Ordin slapped the table with her hand and glared at CJ. "I know Joanna better than that."

"Well, what else could it be? She's getting letters from somebody, her mind is a million miles away from me all the time, and she's as nervous as a cat." CJ glared right back at his former landlady.

"She's got something on her mind, but it ain't another man. I know about these things, CJ."

CJ drummed his fingers on the table with quick staccato beats. "When I told her I was going to take the train to Pierre today, she was relieved I was going to be gone. No, my dear Mrs. Ordin. You can defend her all you want to, but she's been hiding something for quite a while."

"Did she say that she was glad you were going to be gone?" Mrs. Ordin quizzed, and for once, her dancing earrings were perfectly still.

"She didn't have to *say* anything," CJ snorted. "The expression on her face said it for her."

In Mrs. Ordin's homespun kitchen, he finally spoke the words he'd been hiding in a secret place of his heart. There could be no other explanation for Joanna's behavior. There must be someone else in her life. It was grim relief to say it out loud instead of having the whispered dread sifting through his mind all the time.

Mrs. Ordin would have none of it. "Pure nonsense. Pure nonsense." However, even Mrs. Ordin admitted that there was *something*. She hugged him as he was leaving. "Honey, you just keep the faith in her. It'll work out. I know it will."

13

February 28, 1912

Springfield, Missouri

Dear CJ,

I received your letter about the pastorate. You said the church board formally offered you the position of being pastor for their church, and you refused it. I read with interest how you prayed for God's will and how it dawned on you the morning you were offered the position that God had continually been giving the answer but you didn't recognize it because you were sure He wanted you to become the minister. You wrote how you wondered if you would ever learn to quit second-guessing God's will.

Well, you are your father's son. And I confess, CJ, that I'm guilty of the same thing. I presumed that a church on the Dakota prairie, just a quick ride from your own place, with a congregation of your friends and neighbors was an opportunity God was providing for you. I quickly made my own plans to move to Belvidere to help and rejoiced (and even felt quite smug) that I had retired at a most opportune time.

Doc Regis and I were fishing and discussing your letter. I was quite disappointed in your refusal to serve and voiced my frustrations to my good friend. He listened and smoked his pipe, and he finally asked me in his gruff manner if I had ever heard a resounding heavenly yes to my plans to move up north and help you.

I was stunned by the question. In fact, I was so lost in contemplation that Doc had to remind me I had a fish on the line. The answer to Doc's query was a definite no. Like you, I was so sure of what I thought God's will was for both our lives that I wasn't listening closely to what the Spirit was trying to tell me.

When your mother and I had an honest discussion, we realized we loved Missouri, our friends, and fellow church members and were quite content to live right here. The joy of being retired is that we can visit our family often and for as long as you can stand us!

You didn't mention Joanna's reaction to your decision. I know last spring she said she was leaving the matter in your hands.

When it warms up in your country, we will plan a visit. In the meantime, both your mother and myself have found ourselves enjoying being extremely lazy. Doc and I head to the fishing spot often. Your mother can be found with her feet up, a good cup of tea by her side, and one of her many books in hand. The Lord knew we were more tired than we wanted to admit.

We are very proud of you, CJ. When you realized what the Spirit was trying to tell you, you chose to obey rather than please the rest of us. That takes courage. In the end, your pleasing God also pleases the rest of us who love and serve Him.

Our prayer is God's continued guidance for all of us. We serve an awesome and wonderful Lord!

Love,

Dad

CJ read and reread his father's letter while standing outside the small wooden building that constituted Belvidere's post office. It was a relief to finally hear from him. The mind can work up quite an argument when it's dealing with the unknown, he decided.

He disagreed with his father's declaration that he was courageous. He considered himself a chief coward, always whining to God about how he had no enthusiasm for the Lord's work. He slowly folded the letter up and placed it inside its envelope.

And finally, he released the pent-up sigh that seemed to continually hover inside him. Even a grown man with kids likes to have his parent's approval, he decided, as he squinted down the dusty street. He quickly placed the letter in his inside jacket pocket and looked toward the little café where late-morning coffee drinkers sometimes gathered.

He was getting ready to step off the plank steps when a young woman hurried toward him carrying a new-looking leather satchel.

"CJ! Oh, I can hardly believe it's you!" She arrived at his side breathlessly and looked up at him with doting eyes. "Now don't you dare tell me you don't recognize me!" She gave a forced tinkling laugh and grasped his arm with her free gloved hand.

"Well. Ma'am—" He got no further than that when she reached higher, to his shoulder, and gave him an exasperated tap and then patted his cheek tenderly.

"You sang to me a couple of years ago," she chided with a saucy smile. CJ was becoming uncomfortably aware of the interest this little exchange was causing in the doorway of the post office.

Recognition finally came. And it wasn't purty. "Ah, oh." CJ gave her a grim smile. "Sissy Tinner. I believe you accompanied my mother-in-law when she came to see Joanna."

"Yes!" She bobbed her elaborate hatted head with an enthusiasm that sent all the ribbons, rosettes and fake cherries into a bouncing fit. She seemed unaware of his own reticence.

"Ah, how is Lizzie?" He backed away a couple of steps to rid himself of her patting hand.

"Oh, fine. Just fine. Of course, she's so busy being a good little nurse that I never see her." She flashed him another smile accompanied by her carefully orchestrated tinkling laugh. "CJ, walk me to the hotel and carry this heavy bag for me, will you?" She thrust the satchel at him and twined her arm around his. "My goodness, Belvidere needs to greet her paying guests with a more level walkway! I'm practically exhausted from slipping and sliding up that hill!"

The Simek brothers were stifling amused grins as they walked out of the post office and climbed into their freight wagons. CJ gave them a tight smile. Next time, he vowed to himself, he would wait until he got home to read his letters.

She pressed herself against him as they walked. "You must tell Joanna that I work for Parker Vinue and his wife now. He's such a charming man and often asks about her."

CJ paid scant attention to Sissy's remarks and started walking at a faster pace. He was uncomfortably aware of her closeness.

Sissy Tinner was not about to be hurried. She chatted aimlessly but coyly evaded answering any question CJ asked her. She stopped repeatedly to comment about Belvidere's changes. She waved to people who didn't have a clue who she was. When they finally reached the hotel, CJ was ready to forget his mother's lessons on how gentlemen act.

"I must run. Here's your bag, and have a good day ma'am." He placed the bag inside the hotel door and made his escape with scarcely a glance at her. Had he taken the time, he would have been mortified to see her cat-that-ate-the-canary smirk.

"So she did come," Joanna murmured absently as they sat down to their late dinner.

CJ looked at her in surprise. "You were expecting her?"

She nodded and then bowed her head, the signal for him to pray before they ate. She busied herself afterward with dishing up the twins' meal, and Sissy Tinner was not discussed again at the table.

There was the usual mail that CJ sorted through after they ate. It was then that he discovered an official-looking letter in a monogrammed envelope for Isaac.

"Whoa! Something here for you, Isaac. Fancy, fancy envelope with some initials on it. Looks like PV or some such thing."

A pan slipped out of Joanna's hand and clattered noisily on the floor. She had her back turned to him and was kneeling on the floor scraping the contents back into the container.

"What could it be?" Isaac wondered. There was no return address.

"Pitch it," Joanna said. "It's probably junk stuff." She still had her back toward them, and her voice sounded muffled.

Isaac grinned and winked at CJ. He took his time slitting the envelope open and carefully withdrew the typed page of stationery.

"Hmm. Says it's from a bank." Isaac looked puzzled. "Who the heck would I know from a bank in Mankato?"

Joanna left with the pan and its flyaway contents. CJ could hear the porch door closing.

Isaac skimmed through it and frowned. He read it again and handed the letter to CJ. "What do you make of this?"

"Willow, don't sit on Tulip. You'll hurt him." CJ took the letter and shook his head at his little daughter.

After he read it, he sat back in his chair and looked at Isaac speculatively. "It seems like this man, this Parker Vinue, met you at Simon's during your stay there and now wants to offer you a job at his bank. Is that what you get from this?"

"Yeah." Isaac scratched his head. "But I can't remember him. He says he knows both Simon and Aunt Jo. I guess I'll have to ask her when she comes back in."

"Do you want to work at a bank, Isaac?" CJ had never heard him express such a desire.

"If I did, I'd ask L. A. Pier for some work at the Belvidere bank and not traipse off to Mankato. Even if Dad is there."

Willow Charm let out a piercing scream and ran to her dad with blood dripping from her finger. CJ lifted her onto his lap and made his usual assessment. "Did Tulip scratch you again?"

"I hates him!" She sobbed while tears cascaded down her cheeks.

Heather Rose sat on the floor and watched with interest. Even though the same scene was repeated day after day, she still seemed to find the whole episode fascinating.

Isaac glanced out the door, and with no sign of Joanna returning, he slowly got up and found a rag to tie around the little wounded finger.

CJ, as usual, kissed it well several times, and Willow finally scooted off his lap. CJ knew that tomorrow she would try sitting on the cat all over again with the same results.

The next day, Isaac sent a polite note thanking Mr. Vinue for the kind offer of a job. However, Isaac wrote, he felt he was probably not suited for this opportunity and respectfully declined the offer.

He and CJ both thought that would end the matter. They were very wrong.

14

May 5, 1912

Belvidere, South Dakota

Dear Mom and Dad,

We are excited you are going to be with us in a couple of weeks! Isaac has been cleaning up his bachelor's quarters in Simon's house and announced the other day that he wanted you folks to stay there. He said you could have privacy and yet be close to all the family doings. He will bunk with John and Teddy for a while, but he plans on being with the roundup crew for most of the spring and summer.

John and Teddy are anxious to show you their "new" school. It's actually not new at all, but since the little claim cabin school closed, the kids on this end of the district have attended the Highland Center school district on the north side. It's a farther ride for them, but the boys haven't seemed to mind.

There are Bohemian kids attending, and their teachers have their hands full teaching them English. Teddy seems to come home with more knowledge about their language than our own. In fact, he loved a certain word so much that he was constantly shouting it out— to us, to the milk cow, to his sisters. I quizzed him on the meaning, but he didn't seem to know or else pretended he didn't. I finally asked Little Frank what it meant. He sort of stammered and stuttered and for a while was at a loss for words. He had me repeat it. Then, looking off in the distance, with a funny little twitch to his mouth, he gave me the English translation. Quite a raunchy swearword. Teddy is forbidden to ever say it again. He was quite forlorn for several days. He's lucky his mother or I didn't take him out to the woodshed. Again.

Our little church is doing well. The minister preaches from the Word, and he has quite a circuit of Lutheran churches to shepherd. I do what I can to help him, and we seem to be working well together. We had a sad occasion when two homestead children died of scarlet fever. Digging those little graves in the prairie sod was a poignant reminder on how fleeting life can be.

I hate to keep whining about having so few range cattle, but it has seemed a dismal spring to not be riding and checking on newborn calves. I hope this year will be better and we can increase the herd again. Sometimes I get tired of the newspaper articles ranting about those who left because of the drought. This country was not created to have lovely little farms on each quarter. I say the ones who left recognized that fact and dealt with the problem.

Joanna is reading over my shoulder and told me not to get started on my soapbox subject.

We are counting the days until we see you!

Love,

CJ, Joanna, and kids

"I don't know why I didn't think of your folks staying at Simon's house. Or maybe I should say, Isaac's house." Joanna picked up the letter and folded it to place inside the envelope. "They'll have their own space and schedule, and yet, they'll be close to us."

"You've had other things on your mind," CJ answered abruptly, and he didn't miss the wary look that came across her face.

She didn't say any more. A stamp was found, the letter was put in the letter rack, and Joanna found other business to attend to in a different room.

"Dad." John's voice was barely above a whisper. "Dad, there's something funny going on outside."

CJ awoke with a start. He could barely make out John's form bending over him. "What is it?" He kept his voice low.

"I don't know. I hear sounds. And there's...It looks like—"

Teddy interrupted with an excited whisper. "It's Indians! A whole reservation of Indians all around the house!"

CJ was out of bed and stumbling into his clothes as fast as he could in the dark.

"What's going on?" Joanna mumbled sleepily.

"Shhh!" All three of her men scolded her.

CJ crept to the window and, without moving the curtain aside, peered into the early dawn. A light fog draped over trees and buildings, shrouding them in mystic secrecy. As CJ's eyes became accustomed to the scene below, the hairs on the back of his neck stood up. Around the house and in front of the barn were figures on horseback that resembled immobile statues. He could only guess at the number of them, but in the eerie light, there seemed to be hundreds.

He quickly made his way back to the bed. "Take your pistol and check on the girls. We've got company," he whispered to Joanna. "I don't think they mean us harm, but who would know?"

She was gone before he pulled his boots on.

"You boys stay with your mother. Teddy, don't argue." He knew his youngest son well.

The question racing through his mind as he hurried down the stairs was whether to grab his pistol or leave it hanging on its peg in the porch. For a brief second, he looked at it in indecision.

Leave it.

He listened to the internal voice and, taking a deep breath, opened the door and walked as casually as he could out the door.

"What's going on?" His tone was pleasant, as if he were accustomed to visiting with a yard full of Indians in the early morning hours.

"White man always asks questions." Joker and a woman were sitting on the bench seat of a wagon. At the sound of his voice, the team tossed their heads and snorted.

CJ walked down the steps toward his old friend. "Joker! What can I do for you?"

"Little Sparrow wants you to sing her song for her." Joker looked straight ahead with chiseled features.

The words caused a chill to start a downward spiral on his spine. CJ hesitated and cast a glance into the back of the wagon. A blanketed form resting on more blankets could barely be made out in the weak light of dawn.

"When would she like to hear her song?"

"She loves sunrise." Joker's bronze face showed no emotion, but when he spoke again, there was a slight tremor in his voice. "Does God and your white church care if an Indian is buried there?"

"God and the church are not concerned about skin color. It's what's inside the heart that matters."

Joker shook his head and finally looked at CJ. "My heart, white man, is empty."

The woman beside him spoke abruptly in Lakota. There was silence when she finished, and finally, CJ asked for a translation.

"She say I'm in danger. When nothing in heart, demons move in."

"You listen to your woman, Joker. She's right. Let me get my Bible. We need to get going if we're going to meet the sunrise." CJ said the last words over his shoulder as he hastened into the house.

Joanna already had his Bible ready and was holding his suit jacket. He quickly shrugged it on, and she handed him a pint jar full of lethal-looking liquid. "Drink this before you sing. The kids and I will get up there as quick as we can."

He nodded his appreciation and hurried out the door. When he started toward the back of the wagon to jump in, he was surprised to see the woman already seated beside Little Sparrow's body. She pointed to the wagon seat, and without wasting time to argue the improprieties of her humble action, he climbed up the wheel to sit beside Joker.

They were alone. Where the others had vanished to could only be speculated. With the fog, it was difficult to see any distance.

They were halfway up the hill before Joker broke the silence. "She was special to me."

"I was thinking she was probably about nine or ten years old."

Joker nodded. "She go in early morning and sit below riverbank to watch sun come up. She said she pray then. Not to sun, but to your God."

Another interruption in Lakota from Joker's wife. When CJ looked at him with raised eyebrows, Joker said, "She say God is my God too. She go all time to church. She take Little Sparrow." Joker gave a barely perceptible shake of his head. "She make me promise to bury..." Joker compressed his lips and looked away.

"The bank buried her once. I not want to bury her again," he finally muttered.

"We just buried two young homesteader children by the church. They died of scarlet fever. It never seems right to put those little bodies in a grave." CJ gave his friend's tense shoulder a gentle squeeze before he continued. "But I can promise you this, Joker. The body is there, but the spirit of those kids and Little Sparrow is with God. No doubt. They are running across paradise this second in complete joy."

They had reached the top of the hill, and the church was barely discernible. CJ squinted to see better and finally noticed the other wagons and horses of his early morning visitors.

Joker's voice was heavy when he spoke again. "Maybe. But why should God take her when He has so many others?" Joker's wife started to talk in the Lakota language, but Joker waved her silent. "You tell me why, White Man."

His eyes bored into CJ as they pulled in front of the church.

Please grant me wisdom to answer this. CJ's prayer was fleeting. He met Joker's challenging eyes with a quietness that suddenly welled from within him.

"If I could answer your question, I could sit on the left side of God and help Him rule the universe." He rubbed the back of his neck and gave the other man a rueful smile. "I don't know, Joker, why God takes some and why He leaves others. But I trust that God knows, and when we get to heaven, we'll understand."

The grave had been dug. Beside the open hole was a casket made for a child. Inside the casket, cedar boughs nestled a quilted blanket. Tucked into the blanket was a doll.

Before the men could get down from the wagon, several women climbed into the wagon box to help Joker's wife lift Little Sparrow. They carried the blanketed form tenderly to the waiting casket and soon had arranged blankets, body, and doll to their satisfaction.

One of the women turned to scan the group before her and, finding who she was looking for, gave a slight nod. A red haired man approached CJ. He was attempting to roll his sleeves down over powerful arms, and by the time he reached CJ's side, CJ recognized him as J. E. Utterbach, a cattle rancher near the White River not far from Belvidere. Winn had told him many stories of the black smith from Fort Robinson who had married one of the beautiful French and Indian Larabee sisters and branded his cattle with the mark of an anvil.

"Good, you came." He squeezed CJ's hand in a grip of iron. "They've had a wake service for a couple of days. Joker's wife was beside herself thinking they would put Little Sparrow in a tree. It's their custom, you know."

CJ knew. He had been with Joker once when they rode upon an Indian body wrapped in blankets and resting on cedar boughs. He also knew the sun would be breaking over the hill and through the fog in a few minutes. "I'm sure glad you're here. I suppose we better begin. Joker wanted this to be at sunrise."

Mr. Utterbach stepped back to stand beside his wife, and CJ threw a desperate glance heavenward. *Oh, Lord, never have I been asked to say something so important with so little time to think of what to say. Help me! Help me to glorify You. Help me to sing to glorify You.*

He remembered Joanna's drink then, and he quickly reached under the wagon seat for it. Several swigs of it burned a lucid path clear down to his toes. He should be able to sing an entire opera with a drink like that!

They were hushed, waiting for him to begin. He stepped closer to the open casket and looked at the little form beside the doll.

Slowly, he looked up at them, his eyes traveling from one to another.

"I...I told Joker on the way up here that it never seems right to bury a child. Even when we know her spirit has left this earth, and even though we know she's in the arms of God, we mourn our own loss. And that's the way it should be. We can have joy that she's in heaven, and we can also have sorrow that she's not with us."

CJ took a deep breath and stood a little taller. He needed all the lung power he could get to sing this. And he needed all the help the Holy Spirit would give him to sing it for God's glory.

He noticed his own team and buggy by the church. Joanna, Teddy, and the girls were here, but his hurried glance didn't find John.

"Joker named Little Sparrow after this song. 'His Eye Is on the Sparrow.' God's eye has always been on Little Sparrow. His eye is also on each one of us. The song says 'I sing because I'm happy.' Little Sparrow was happy because she knew Jesus. And she's happy now because she's in paradise with Him. Once when a great king lost his child, he wept. Then he dried his tears and said, 'He can't return to me, but someday, I will go to him.' That's the joy we have because we trust God that what He tells us in His Word is true. Someday, as believers in Christ, we will all be together."

On the prairie hillside, with May wildflowers blooming in soft profusion and with the morning sun dawning through a light fog, a strong but tender voice echoed over and around those listening. And in the surrounding hills, from homestead shack to soddy, snatches of song caused the listener to pause and strain to hear more.

Why should I be discouraged?

Why should the shadows come?

Why should my heart be lonely and long for heaven and home?

When Jesus is my portion, my constant friend is He.
His eye is on the sparrow and I know He watches me.

I sing because I'm happy. I sing because I'm free. For
His eye is one the sparrow, and I know He watches me.

CJ knew and loved all three verses. He sang them all. He repeated the chorus and, in abandonment, hit the high note with more power than he thought he possessed. He doubted, when he finished, if he would ever be able to sing this song as tremendously as he had for Little Sparrow. It was God's moment.

He sought to make eye contact with Joker and his wife. "Little Sparrow is free from earthly cares and woes. She's free to soar beyond us. She would want us to be happy with her."

CJ took a deep breath and bowed his head for prayer. He was startled to hear resounding amens when he finished.

Slowly, the pine box was lowered into the ground. Shovels were produced, and dirt was carefully packed around and over it. Little Sparrow was laid to rest.

Joanna came and laid her head on his shoulder for a brief moment. "I'm so proud of you," she whispered. Then, hastily wiping an escaping tear, she informed him that John was telling the neighbors what had happened. She wouldn't be surprised, she said, if some of them came with coffee and rolls. In fact, as she spoke, they could see several buggies heading in the church's direction.

Death can be a great equalizer. No matter if language was a barrier, the folks who came and the Indians who stayed grieved together. Grief intermingled with food and then a quiet laugh or two, and by the time the sun was midway in the morning sky, fellowship and goodwill had joined hand in hand. As wagons and buggies were getting ready to leave, Teddy gave a whopping shout and pointed to the sky.

High above, soaring gracefully on air vapors, an eagle slowly circled. With everyone craning their necks to watch, he spiraled upward and out of sight.

15

July 2, 1912

Mankato, Minnesota

Dear CJ, Joanna, and family,

First of all, please tell Joker for me when you see him again how sorry we are to hear about Little Sparrow's death. You said there were already three graves at the churchyard and all of them children. So heartbreaking.

I do have some news from here that is actually quite good. I wish I could see you in person to tell you. However, we won't be doing any traveling because we are going to increase our family come February of 1913. I told Edith it's nice to own my grandparents' homestead and know another Swanson will be born here. Raising Isaac was such a joy, and I always enjoyed my nieces and nephews. Edith's youngsters are also a blessing, and now we are adding another joy to our lives.

Was sorry to hear your dog Ruby died. Guess she was older than I realized, but she was always such a goer that she seemed younger. Joanna, I know you will especially miss her when you go walking. She loved to race along beside you. It's a blessing when our old dogs can peacefully die in their sleep like Ruby did.

Looks like we're going to have a good crop of corn, and the beans seem to be doing good. Tried twenty acres of flax, and so far, so good. Sows farrowed good this spring, and the piglets are about ready to go to market.

I guess I sound like a farmer. Edith tells me that anyway. She has a huge garden and a lot of little hands to help her weed and water. She will be forever grateful to Isaac for all the help last winter while he was here. I was so blamed busy trying to get the barns and sheds ready for winter that I had no time to help with the house. He took over the outside jobs so I could work on house projects. Joanna, you would love the way the old place looks. Hope you can come and visit us soon.

And boy howdy! That Parker Vinue can't quit talking about how impressed he was with Isaac. Said he was going to keep after that boy until he wore him down because he needs young fellows with Isaac's work ethic working for him. I told him Isaac was a country boy, but Vinue says he can tell just by visiting with him that Isaac would be perfect for the job Vinue has in mind for him. Isaac said he can't remember meeting him, but I think it was one time when we were in Mankato.

I can't figure out how Sissy Tinner got the job as Mrs. Vinue's secretary. Maybe since Mrs. Vinue is so plain of looks and speech, she thought she'd class up her act a little. Don't know if Sissy fills that bill, but it seems to work for them. Mrs. Vinue loves her father's money. Sometimes I think she makes Parker dance a merry dance because of it. I said that once to Ma, and she said she hoped so, that it would serve old Parker right. I don't know why Ma turned against him. She used to think he was the best lawyer/banker in the country.

Enough for now. Miss all of you and wished we lived closer together.

Simon and Edith and family

Isaac sauntered into the kitchen while CJ finished reading Simon's letter. He had been with the neighbors and the roundup crew on the reservation during most of the spring and summer. During that time, he had grown and filled out and also sprouted a beard. He looked, CJ mused, every inch a cowboy, even down to the rolling gait acquired by hours in the saddle.

"I'm glad you picked up the mail before you headed out here." CJ tapped Simon's letter on the table. "Sounds like you're going to be a big brother."

Isaac found a glass and dipped some water into it before he sat down. "Dad's happy. I could tell that this winter." He took a long draught of water. "Where is everyone? I thought you were all out in the hayfield."

"The boys and I were. We finished one field, and it was too late to start another, so Teddy talked his mother into taking all of them over to Antonio's. Mrs. Utterbach gave Joanna some dolls for the girls, and Antonio wanted to take a look to see how they were made. She said that since she has a couple of little girls, she better start thinking girl things."

Isaac's eyes crinkled at their corners while he grinned. "Teddy's always got plans. How are you coming with haying?"

"If we hit it a good lick this week, we can have the biggest field done. I guess this is the little breather before we work our tails off the next few days."

They discussed machinery and horses and haying items in the quiet of the kitchen before CJ asked if he had seen Joker on his way home.

Isaac nodded. "Joker was in a rare talkative mood. He showed me where the bank caved in on Little Sparrow."

CJ felt the weight of his friend's loss steal over him again and looked down.

"And he talked about how everyone came to help dig. He said they had to go slow because they were hoping she had found a pocket to survive in and they didn't want to hit her with their shovels. It must have been a nightmare." Isaac put both hands around his glass.

"He also said his wife had wanted a Christian burial and wanted it off the reservation. She was afraid Joker's family would want the traditional ceremonies and put Little Sparrow's body on a tree, and she couldn't bear that. So during the wake when there was a full moon, she convinced him that they better bring Little Sparrow to you. I think he's glad he did."

Isaac spun his glass a few times before he looked at CJ. "I wished I could have heard your message and song. It seemed to have made quite an impression on a lot of folks."

CJ absently tapped his fingers on the table. "Sometimes God works through us in ways I can't even begin to explain." He sighed and pushed his chair away from the table. "I guess I better get the milk cows in."

"The text for today's message comes from John 8:31–32. And let me read the words of Jesus to you. "If ye continue in My word, then are ye My disciples indeed. And ye shall know the truth, and the truth will make you free."

The minister at the little church spent the next thirty minutes expounding on this thought, finding verses in other books of the Bible to support it. It was a good sermon, well prepared and well delivered. Joanna listened intently, but for some reason, CJ's mind wanted to wander. More than once, he dragged his thoughts from their scattered directions to focus on the message. But before he could keep them in a tight rein, they had fled onto another dim trail.

The children's graves outside the window gathered one thought. The prairie flowers that decorated them were wilted now. It made him sad. Joanna was stealing another thought. Would she ever be his companion of old with her spunk and bounce and unfettered passion? She had changed. If it was another man, he wished she'd tell him and get it over with. He worried their old life together would disappear forever.

His folks seemed in command of another thought. They had spent a month living in Simon's house, and the time had flown. But he sensed the questions they wanted to discuss and cautiously avoided.

When they boarded the train to go back to Missouri, he felt he should have tried to answer what was never asked.

If that parade of thoughts weren't enough, the pace of the past week had worn all of them to a frazzle. They worked from dawn to dusk getting the biggest field cut, raked, and stacked. He was grateful that Isaac was there. He was also grateful that there was actually a crop. The rains had been sparse, but they were enough to grow what was planted. Every stack of hay meant one less they'd need to buy in the fall.

Finally, the last hymn was sung, the benediction said, and the church was emptied of its congregation. Usually, they visited and someone had coffee and cookies, but this July Sunday found most of them exchanging only a few words as they headed toward horses and buggies. Antonio had left most of her family home and was scurrying to her buggy to get back and put dinner on the table for them. CJ noted she was talking to Teddy as she placed baby Helen on the seat.

Teddy ran toward them with excited sparks emitting from his eyes. "Dad! Dad! Antonio says if me and John and the girls want to come over this afternoon, she has a surprise for us! Can we go? Can we?"

Before CJ could say no, Joanna said yes. Teddy spun a quick turnaround to tell Antonio before his mother changed her mind.

The mail that had been neglected all week was finally brought to the table for sorting and reading over Sunday afternoon coffee. Once again, there was a letter from Mankato addressed to Isaac.

Isaac frowned and skimmed through the contents. "The guy is persistent. I think this is the third or fourth letter he's sent me about a job."

CJ was absorbed in the *Belvidere Times* and scarcely looked up.

"Who is this Parker Vinue anyway?" Isaac stroked his beard absently.

"He's your father," Joanna said, taking a sip of coffee.

CJ rattled his paper and thought it was unlike Joanna to make a tasteless joke.

Isaac frowned and tilted his head to one side. "What did you just say?" Both he and CJ looked at her incredulously.

Joanna set her cup down. "You asked who Parker Vinue is. He's your father, Isaac."

CJ folded the paper noisily and frowned at her. What in the world was she talking about? "Ah, Joanna, maybe this conversation should be between Simon and Isaac."

"No, this is my story, not Simon's." She seemed absorbed in her cup as she moved it in tiny circles on the table. Finally, she sighed and looked up and began speaking quietly. "When my father died, I was sixteen. The executor of Pa's will was Parker Vinue. He was at our place quite a bit."

Joanna gave CJ a lingering look before she glanced back at Isaac. "He came one rainy afternoon when Ma was gone. I was alone. And I was crying. Ma and I had fought like cats and dogs that morning. He was an older, unhappily married man." She pressed her lips together and looked down. "His comforting turned into an altogether ugly seduction." She struggled to gain her composure, but when she spoke again, her voice was firm. "When he left, I hated him beyond anything you could ever imagine. If I'd had a gun, I'd have killed him."

CJ unknowingly clenched his fist.

"The only thing good about that, Isaac, is that you were conceived. But of course, when you're sixteen, unmarried, and you're carrying an illegitimate child..." Joanna shook her head. "Simon and Mary came to visit. Mary knew how unhappy I was, but of course, she didn't know the reason. No one did. Anyway, I left with them, and when Mary discovered what had happened, she spent a lot of time in prayer for me. And we decided that the best we could do for you, Isaac, was to say you were Mary and Simon's child. They lived in an isolated part of Minnesota with very few neighbors. We put up an elaborate facade, and you were born at home with only Mary attending. "

Isaac had covered his face with his hands. CJ could only stare at her in disbelief.

Once again, Joanna's look lingered on CJ. "Simon wanted me to tell you the whole story when you and I got married. And I was going to, but then I reasoned it was pointless to burden you with my secret. And it was just that. A secret only Simon and I knew, and not even Simon knew who the biological father was. At least that's what I thought. But I didn't reckon on another woman that carried another child of Parker Vinue's. She had followed him out to the farm that day and knew what he done. She has blackmailed him for years, not for a lot of money, but enough to help her out when she needed cash. But when she saw you, Isaac, she decided she could get more money from him."

Joanna rubbed her forehead and seemed unsure how to continue. Finally, she straightened her shoulders and took a deep breath. "Ma had a letter for each of her kids when she died. Mine said some very tender things, and she ended by saying she knew Isaac was Parker's son and she was extremely sorry for___everything. She also warned me about this lady and her child. So when I started getting letters from Parker demanding that I tell him the truth, I wasn't surprised. I destroyed every one and never answered. I thought he would let it go. I didn't take into account that now he's older and without legitimate children. He wants an heir. He wants you, Isaac."

"Oh boy." Isaac groaned and propped both arms on the table with his head sunk down. "I can't believe this." His voice was muffled. "I think I'm going to be sick."

CJ tapped his fingers together and studied his wife. "You could have shared this with me, Joanna, rather than have me think you were having an affair with someone."

"What!" She half rose from her chair. "CJ Crezner, how could you think such a thing!" Suddenly, her expression softened, and she dropped slowly down to her chair. "It never occurred to me that you would think that. I've been caught up in this nightmare that seems to have no end, and today when the minister said the truth will make you free, I decided I would tell both of you. I...I just cannot fight it alone anymore."

She looked pleadingly at CJ and then at Isaac's suffering frame. "I'm so sorry, guys. I'm so sorry."

The only sound was the soft ticking of the clock. Joanna moistened her lips and drew out an envelope from her pocket. "Here is the last letter I have from Vinue." She handed it to CJ.

It was typewritten and very brief. CJ read it out loud, and it made his blood boil.

Joanna, work with me on this. If you play your cards right, Isaac will be a very wealthy young man. I'm coming to see you soon. PV

CJ met Isaac's angry look with one of equal force. He wasn't surprised when Isaac cursed and stumbled to his feet. "I need fresh air!" The whole house seemed to shake from the after effects of the slammed door.

CJ was also on his feet. He paced across the room and back, waving the sheet of paper. "'If you play your cards right.' What is *that* supposed to mean? And if he even looks at you again, I'll kill him myself!"

He straightened the chairs around the table while he fumed. "A yellow-bellied coward! Taking advantage of a young girl. Killing would be too good for him! And now—" CJ let out a line of cuss words he didn't even realized he knew. He thought about repeating the whole mess of them, but he stopped when he saw Joanna's face.

155

She looked as astonished at what he was saying as he was at saying it. "I didn't know you knew words like that." She blinked a few times.

"If he's *coming soon*, like he says, he'll get to hear those words and more!" CJ was shouting and didn't care. Vinue was a creep who stalked young innocent girls and, to top it off, was a no-good blackmailer.

He stopped abruptly. "How many letters did he write? What did the others say?"

Joanna slowly left her chair and came to stand beside him. She took the note from his hand and started toward the stove.

"The first one was several months after Ma died. Flowery-sounding. He begged my forgiveness, and I was to write to him." She took a match from the box and struck it on the stove. A tiny flame flared up instantly. "I burned it. I was furious he would think I was dumb enough to answer him."

She placed the flaming match to the note and watched it blaze before she dropped it into the firebox. "The second one was scolding. He was in agony, he wrote, not knowing if I received his first letter, and if I had gotten it, why I was so coldhearted that I wouldn't forgive him." She spun around to look at CJ, and there was fire in her eyes. "He must have forgotten that I wasn't a sixteen-year-old girl that could be taken in by such stupidity!"

CJ was unaware that his fists were clenched.

"It was probably nine months later that I received another one. I thought maybe he had dropped the whole mess, but he was just collecting more ammunition to use against me." Suddenly, she looked exhausted, as if the weight of the past two years had finally drained her completely.

CJ walked toward her slowly and gathered her into his arms. "You should have told me," he whispered as she melted against him. "You didn't need to keep it from me."

Her shoulders convulsed, and a wrenching cry escaped her. "I was so ashamed! And I was so scared you'd walk away." Tears streamed down her face as she looked up at him. "I couldn't bear living if you left me, CJ. I just couldn't bear it."

She buried her face on his chest. He felt her trembling as he ran his hands over her back and hugged her even closer to himself. His anger flared all over again, but he didn't curse this time. Instead, his mind became cold and detached. Parker Vinue would pay for this. He didn't know how or when, but it would happen—even if it took CJ's lifetime.

She pulled slightly away from him and searched her pockets for her handkerchief.

He handed her one from his back pocket and then ran his hand over her hair and pale cheeks. "Joanna, you should have known I would never even consider leaving you. But I could get darn mad at you for not telling me." He smiled into her tear-streaked face and waited while she dabbed her eyes and blew her nose. "Now," he said when she handed him back his handkerchief, "I want to hear about the other letters. And in case you're wondering, I'm still madly in love with you."

She gave him a wry grin. "'Madly' being the key word?"

He looked away and then glanced back at her with a smile. "Key word, Mrs. Crezner, is love. I love you."

"I'll start bawling all over again if you keep looking at me that way." She took a deep breath and squared her shoulders. "Now, Mr. Crezner. The third letter came after he saw Isaac in Mankato. He was positive Isaac was his son. He had no legitimate kids, he wanted to work Isaac into a good position in the bank, and he wanted to make sure I wouldn't cause any trouble. He knew a lot of things about us. I suppose with Sissy Tinner working for his wife, he had unlimited information." She shrugged and walked over to the window. "I was to say nothing to you or Isaac. I was supposed to let the charade continue and convince Isaac to take the job, and all would go well. If I upset the apple cart, there would be consequences."

An even colder chill sped through CJ's mind.

"I suppose that's what he meant when he said he was coming to see me." Joanna peered out the window, and the sound of a team and buggy could be heard. She patted her hair and swiped at her eyes. "Our children are returning home." Quickly, she turned to him and gave a semblance of a smile. "CJ, please. We must act as if all was normal around the kids."

The excited laughter and chatter of four happy children filled the air as they poured out of the buggy and came running into the house.

"I get to tell her first!" Teddy came bursting into the kitchen with importance

"No! No, you don't. We do!" Willow was right behind him and tried to grab onto his shirt.

It only took a second for Joanna's demeanor to change from distraught to composed. She had, after all, a couple of years to practice. CJ had to take several breaths before he could appear calm.

"Tell me what?" Joanna glanced at CJ.

Heather ran to her mother with arms outstretched.

"You should see what Antonio and Frank gave us!" She was breathless with excitement.

Joanna knelt down and gave her a hug and was almost knocked over by both Teddy and Willow trying to get into the circle of her arms.

"I get to show her!" Teddy made a quick dive at John, who had followed them in with a wide grin on his face. He carried a wooden crate and set it down carefully beside his mother.

"For you, Mom!" John pulled off the old towel that covered the crate.

At once, a brown bundle of fur scrambled against the slatted sides. There was a whine and a slight howl, and with a lot of scratching and whimpering, a puppy with one brown ear and one black ear tumbled into Joanna's lap. He was as excited as the children, and jumped into her arms with his tongue wildly licking her face.

16

July 18, 1912

Belvidere, South Dakota

Dear Edith, Dad, and family,

Congratulations on your news. I know from experience that Simon Swanson is a good dad.

I'm heading out again to the reservation where our neighbors have their cattle on lease land. I plan to be there the rest of the summer and into the fall. Mr. Jones has hired me full time.

Need to pack and run.

Later,

Isaac

PS

I'm not interested in Vinue's job offer. He doesn't need to contact me again.

CJ read the terse note Isaac handed him. "Well, it's short. I guess, after what we heard yesterday, it has a double meaning to it." He watched Isaac throw his saddle on his horse and adjust it. The barn in the early morning was still warm after the sun's heat from the day before.

Isaac grunted and reached under his horse's belly for the saddle cinch. "I need to be alone. I'm sorry if I hurt Aunt Jo's feelings, but I just have to leave." He gave a derisive snort and added, "Aunt Jo, or whatever she is to me."

"It's probably good for a troubled feller to head out by himself." CJ tucked the letter into his shirt pocket. "We'll write Simon and send this with it."

He took saddlebags off the stall fence and secured them to the back of Isaac's saddle. "If I were you, until you get a better grip on yourself, I'd call Simon 'Dad.' I'd call the woman who prayed for you and Joanna even before you were born, 'Mom.' Don't confuse yourself with changing people's titles."

"And that's what you'd do if you were me." Isaac's voice was filled with sarcasm.

"Yup." CJ ignored the slur. "And I'd probably head out of here, mad and confused and sarcastic, just like you're doing." He grinned and clapped Isaac on the shoulder when Isaac threw him an irritated glance.

"It's hell when you don't know who to be mad at," Isaac muttered, slapping the latigo into place and giving the saddle fender a final tug.

"Here's your slicker." CJ handed the rolled-up raincoat to him. "What else do you need?"

"I don't know. A different life, I guess."

"Yeah, well, I can't help you there."

"What about you? What are you going to do about all this?" Isaac checked his saddlebags and paused when he saw the food supplies CJ had tucked into them.

"I don't know yet." CJ rubbed the back of his neck. "After you left yesterday, Joanna told me some of the things he wrote her. You should know that he basically threatened her if she told you or me anything." CJ felt the cold hit him once again, and he looked unseeingly into the distance. Finally, he glanced back at Isaac and added softly, "No one threatens my wife, Isaac. No one."

Isaac gave a swift intake of air and whistled softly. Neither said anything, and the silence was broken only by the horse's snort and stomp. Finally, Isaac cleared his throat. "Don't do anything stupid, CJ." He tilted back his hat and rubbed his beard.

CJ remembered something else. "Joanna said you best keep your beard. Your cleft chin resembles Parker Vinue's."

Isaac's hand froze on his beard. "That's how he knew? Because of my chin? That's slim evidence!"

"He must think he has a good case." CJ thrust out his hand. "Isaac, you're a good man. Remember that. Good men take hard knocks and get down on their knees to ask God what He wants them to learn from being flattened. It's a better feeling than drowning your sorrows in booze and having a hangover the next day." *Or having a cold rage that makes you afraid you really might do something stupid.*

Isaac gave him a grim smile as he shook his hand. When he was astride his horse, he looked down at CJ and shook his head. "Why aren't you a preacher, CJ?"

CJ's slow smile reached his eyes as he tapped Isaac on the knee. "Maybe God thinks He can use me in the barn rather than the pulpit."

"Sure. When He hears you cussing the milk cows, He probably wonders if He can even use you in the barn." A boyish grin lightened his face.

CJ slapped the horse's rump, and it made a couple of jumps in the yard before Isaac reined him in the right direction. "Don't forget to come home!" CJ yelled as the horse began to work its way into a mile-eating trot.

Isaac's wave was his answer. CJ watched until he crested the hill, and even then, he stood by the corral watching. The dawn was spreading over the eastern sky, the robin was making his queries, and in the distance, a meadowlark trilled. While God's world was waking up, a young man was in an agony of hurt. Isaac was the innocent victim. CJ fervently prayed his young friend had the strength and faith to help him through these troubled waters.

"And these peoples gave Antonio two puppies and Antonio said 'Dva loutka' and—"

"Wait a minute." CJ shifted Heather on his lap. "What does 'Dva loutka' mean?"

"Daaaady." Willow hated for their stories to be interrupted. "It means 'two puppies.'" She was comfortably situated beside him in the old rocking chair.

"Well. I see. Go ahead, Heather."

"Where were I?" Heather looked at Willow. "Oh, I know. And then Frank said, 'Why don't you give Joanna one of those puppies?' And Antonio said, 'That's a good idea, Frank.' And Frank said, 'She's all sad because Ruby done died.' And Antonio said—"

"Heather," CJ interrupted again, "I think I understand that part of the story. And now you want to name the puppy something Bohemian and you were thinking of the real live Bohemian Princess Sophia. But we have a little problem because—"

"Because," Willow chimed in, "he's a boy dog, and boy dogs can't be princesses, and we don't want to name him Prince Ferdinand."

"And thank God for that!" Joanna stated emphatically. "I will not stand on the step and holler 'Prince Ferdinand'!"

"But," Heather sighed, "what can we name him?"

"Well. How about—"

"Oh! Oh! I know!" Willow stood up on the chair and looked dramatically at Heather. "Ferd! We'll call him Ferd!"

Heather looked skeptical, and Joanna didn't mince words. "No."

Willow gave her mother a reproachful gaze and plopped down beside CJ again.

"Since this is supposed to be my puppy," Joanna said, "I'll name him. And it was very nice of Frank to think of me."

"Hey! Call him Frank!" Willow was extremely proud of herself for thinking of that.

"No!" CJ and Joanna were agreed.

Joanna scratched the soft little black ear, tickled the brown ear, and lifted the puppy closer to her face to scrutinize him carefully. "I think you are a prince of a dog," she crooned as his little pink tongue found her cheek.

"There. That's decided." CJ lifted Heather off his lap and stood up. "Call him Prince."

CJ felt that he had spent most of August watching the road leading into the ranch. Wait. Watch. He could have added worry to the mix. It was a relief when they received a telegram from Simon the first part of September asking them to meet him at Belvidere.

Joanna took the buggy into town by herself. CJ thought it would be best if she told Simon in private who Isaac's biological father was. The expression on Simon's face when he and Joanna pulled into the yard was a mixture of disbelief and rage.

"Boy howdy, CJ. Had I known all of this earlier, I wouldn't have allowed that man to speak to Isaac."

The two men were alone as they rode Brave Bull Creek to hunt for milk cows. "I ain't in any way saying anything against Joanna. She was right in never telling anyone who Isaac's real father was, but I'm saying, *had* I known, the scum bag wouldn't have set foot on my place." Simon reined in his horse and looked back to see if they had missed anything.

"Now we know what was bothering Joanna. I sure have wondered about it," Simon continued as the horses picked up their pace again. "Always kinda worried about that Sissy Tinner. Somehow, she's mixed up in all this. I feel certain about it."

CJ squinted his eyes and looked up a small wooded draw. No milk cows hiding there. He could feel the cold of his anger creeping into his inward being. When he looked back at Simon, the older man gave a low whistle.

"Don't do anything stupid, CJ."

CJ smiled grimly. "Vinue may be Isaac's biological father, but you're the man he takes after. He even whistles like you do and says the same dang thing."

"I love that boy. Mary and I seemed to forget almost immediately that he wasn't our own. If you'll let me borrow old Buck, I'll head down to the reservation tomorrow and try to find him. I need to talk to him."

CJ nodded. His prayers had been somewhat garbled the past weeks, but there was one thing he had asked for consistently. He prayed that Simon would come and find Isaac. He also prayed that the Lord would prevent him from doing "something stupid." But when he thought of Vinue and Joanna, there was no denying that a cold and deadly feeling of vengeance crept over him.

Simon was gone for ten days. When he returned, he looked saddle-weary but far less anxious than when he left.

"He's hurting, and he sure didn't know how to react when I rode up," Simon told CJ and Joanna as they talked late into the evening. "I didn't rush things, but I think I finally got across to him that he and I had a bond stronger than many men and their sons."

Joanna walked over to the stairway and looked up again. It was her unspoken fear that one of the kids would be listening from above. Satisfied that all of them were in their beds, she hastened back to the table where the two men were seated beside a low glowing lamp.

"That's good," she said. "I'm glad your relationship is back on track. Did he say anything--?" She paused and looked at Simon.

He shook his head. "I told him a lot of things. How young you were, how desperate for him to have a good home. I told him the stigma a young kid would have growing up with just his mother but no father. I told him you could have been totally selfish and thought only about yourself and how you wanted to keep him, but you chose to let Mary and I be his parents." Simon looked at her kindly. "He'll understand some day, Joanna, but he feels deceived right now. Sort of like we lied to him, even though a part of him knows why it had to be that way."

CJ sat back in his chair and stretched his legs in front of him. Something was niggling his mind, and he couldn't put his finger on it. He put his hands behind his head and stared into space, trying to remember what it was that made him think he was missing an important part of the puzzle. Something---there was something, but he just couldn't find the loose end that would tie the knot.

17

October 16, 1912

Elko, Nevada

Dear family,

I didn't intend to come this far west, but once I got on the train at Merriman, I kept traveling. I had summer wages in my pocket and decided I may as well see a bit of the country. I'm going to be here for a while working on a ranch, so you can send mail to Elko if you want to.

Hope everyone is doing fine.

Isaac

CJ watched Joanna read the brief note. She read it twice before she carefully laid it down on the table.

"At least we know where he is," she said softly. If words could sob, hers would have rented the air with wailing.

"Yeah. We already knew he headed west after the roundup crew loaded the cattle at Nebraska rather than trail them back to Belvidere." Somehow, CJ thought Isaac would be back with them this winter. He smiled wryly. "Now I have a little taste of what my folks thought when I didn't come home."

Joanna bustled to the desk and soon was back at the table with pencil and paper. "I'm going to start a letter right now. When the boys get home from school, they can add to it."

Several minutes later, she was still staring at the paper with pencil in hand. Finally, she got up and wandered into the living room.

When CJ walked out the door, she was aimlessly picking up clutter and setting it back down in the same place.

He was halfway to the barn when he heard the cranes making their whirring call overhead. When he looked skyward, he soon made out the *V* high above him. They seemed to be changing leaders, and the birds drifted back and forth.

"Joanna! Come and see this!" he hollered. She must have been looking for an excuse to come outside, he decided. She and the girls were out the door in a flash.

For some time, they watched as the birds regrouped; and finally, the *V* became an orderly flying formation and headed south once again.

"Oh, I love seeing that!" Joanna reached for his hand. "Thank you, Mr. Crezner. Sometimes I get so housebound that I forget to enjoy what we have."

"I know." He grinned at her. "Mrs. Crezner, why don't we play hooky this afternoon? I'll hitch up the buggy, and you and me and these young ladies will go for a drive."

The girls jumped up and down with excitement and were screaming yes at the top of their voices.

"Do we dare leave Prince alone?" Joanna's eyes were shining.

"No. We'll take him with us so he doesn't get lonesome. Girls, go get his leash that John made. Wife, be ready in ten minutes."

"Oh pooh, you can't catch the team and hitch them in ten minutes." Joanna tossed her head and started to the house.

"Just watch me!"

Twenty minutes later, they moseyed across the dry creek bed and headed north. "Remember when you homesteaded there?" Joanna pointed to the spot where CJ and Simon had built a small shack.

"How come Daddy didn't live with you?" Willow looked puzzled.

"We weren't married. Daddy lived on this side of the creek, and Simon and Isaac lived in a little house on the other side of the creek, and I lived where Simon and Isaac live now. I mean, where they used to live."

"Oh." Clearly she was still confused, but she shrugged and leaned back into the buggy seat. Prince sat between Heather and Willow, making sure he didn't neglect either one. In the past months, he had grown considerably and still didn't think of himself as a dog.

"When is Isaac coming back? I wished he would have said goodbye to us." Heather asked the same question many times. The answer was always the same. "Soon."

Many of the trees along the creek had already lost their leaves, but a few elm trees seemed reluctant to admit October was ending. The air was warm, but when the sun went down, it would have a surprising chill to it.

"I never can remember. With the fencing law they just passed, are we supposed to fence to keep our livestock in or to keep the neighbor's livestock out?" Joanna studied the fields and pastures of the homesteaders that were in the process of getting barbed wire and fence posts.

"I understand it to mean that if you don't want the neighbor's livestock in your grass, you fence to keep them out. Which is why we put a fence around some of our land. It's just two wires, but it helps until we can get the third one up."

"But I hate the looks of it." Joanna shook her head as they trotted along the section line. "All boxed in. I guess I might as well get used to it. I doubt life will ever go back to the way it was."

CJ squeezed her knee. "Progress, my dear. Even when we don't want it." He slowed the team and turned west on another section line. "Guess where we're going."

She smiled and patted his arm. "I had a feeling you were going to take us to Frank and Antonio's. I brought them their housewarming gift."

"I figured that was the package you put in. She'll like it. Antonio appreciates pretty things."

It wasn't long before they turned again, and the modest two-storied home appeared against the brown of the prairie. A long shed that doubled as a barn was behind the house, and several other buildings dotted the yard.

CJ's intentions were to only stop for a short while, but before he and Joanna knew it, they were ushered inside for a quick tour. Even though Antonio had only been in her new home for a short while, she had curtains on the windows, and a sense of hominess pervaded.

"And no rattlesnakes," she repeated several times. Both she and Frank went into detail about the rattlesnake in the sod house. "I say to Frank, 'We move!' or big trouble come!" Antonio grinned at them. It was hard to believe this good-natured little woman would ever cause any trouble. She was delighted with the crystal dish Joanna gave her and showed them some Bohemian crystal she had brought to America from "the old country."

Before they left, Frank had one more thing to show them. He set a bottle on the table and urged them to take a closer look. Inside the bottle was an intricate windmill. Every detail was minute and perfect.

"Where did you get that?" CJ wondered.

"My friend Vaclav. Yes, he made this for us!"

CJ pointed to the west. "Vaclav Drabeck?"

"Yes, yes! How does he do it? Look at every tiny piece! Good, yes?"

"Good, yes!" CJ answered and bent over again to study it.

When they finally loaded daughters, dog, and cookies for the boys into the buggy, the sun was midway in the western sky. The team was anxious to get home, and when they started back down the section line, they met the boys riding their horses home from the Highland Center school.

When Teddy heard about the cookies, he was sure he might be in danger of starving before he reached home. He and John loaded up their pockets and took a short cut across the prairie and homesteader's quarters.

"Well, Mr. Crezner, this was lovely." Joanna tucked her hand into his.

"I don't know why we think we need to work every day except Sunday." CJ squeezed her hand gently. "With just the milk cows and those few range cows, I shouldn't have so much to do. How come I'm always busy, anyway?"

"Because you have a family to feed and you are missing a couple of people who use to help you with all the chores. I wonder if Isaac plans on coming back this summer?"

"Well. Yes, I would imagine by then the novelty of seeing the world will have worn off." At least, CJ hoped that would be the case.

The winter of 1913 blew in with a vengeance. Storm followed storm, and the prairie was covered with snow. Blizzards raged, and for the first time, CJ was grateful that he only had a small herd to worry about. He put most of the critters in the barn and then worried that they would get too warm. He needn't have worried. Temperatures plummeted.

Word passed through the school district for students to stay home. The teacher wasn't able to get to the schoolhouse, and conventional wisdom was to err on the side of safety for both teacher and kids.

Joanna dusted off her homeschooling skills, and lessons continued for the boys. Heather and Willow gathered around the table and began learning numbers and letters. It kept them well occupied as Joanna was still a hard taskmaster who tolerated no sass or whining.

The few trips to Belvidere that winter were harrowing ordeals. Cream froze before CJ could deliver it, as well as milk and eggs. Groceries froze before he could get home. He took his clients' bookwork back to the ranch rather than waste precious time at their stores. The cold seemed to seep into his bones on the trips back and forth, even with his old and dependable buffalo coat.

Even the little church on the hill stood cold and empty for the greater part of the winter. The homesteaders and cattlemen fought with deep snow, thick ice, and the ever-present howling north wind. By Sunday, they were content to stay by the fire and look out their windows.

It sometimes seemed to CJ that the whole world was irritated as it waited for spring. The papers that would pile up for days at the post office told grim tales of local hardships. The national news harked on political issues, and world news constantly centered on the bickering the Europeans harbored. Those faraway countries all seemed to be waiting for peace, yet ironically, they were waiting for war to settle boundary disputes so peace could come.

"I'd like to read some good news for a change!" Joanna slapped the paper on the table one evening after an hour of reading one dismal editorial after another.

"I know." CJ paused from rummaging through a pile of books that his folks had sent the family for Christmas. "We might as well get started on our Bible reading for tonight."

"Sometimes that gets frustrating too," Joanna grumbled as she reached for her sewing basket. "You'd think somewhere along the line the 'chosen people' would stop their nonsense and listen to God."

"Ain't gonna happen, Mizzus Crezner." CJ smiled at her as he settled into the rocking chair with his Bible. "We try, but our minds aren't stayed on the things of the Lord, and we drift into trouble."

"My mind is stayed on Mom's raisin cookies. I think I could listen better if I ate one." Teddy looked wistfully at Joanna.

"We'll all have one after your father is finished reading." Joanna threaded her needle and gave her youngest son a slight nudge with her foot. For all of Teddy's bluster, he loved to sit on the floor next to Joanna and lean against her legs while he listened to CJ read. It wasn't uncommon for her to reach out and tousle his hair occasionally.

All the kids had their favorite spots. Heather cuddled beside CJ. She could sit still as a mouse while he read until he wondered if she would be forever frozen into permanent disability from being scrunched by his side.

Willow wanted to be on the other side, but her restless nature found her back on the floor beside Prince. She was very seldom still, but at least her constant patting and scratching the dog kept them both settled.

John lounged on the davenport. After helping CJ with chores when he wasn't doing his mother's required lessons, he often fell asleep, only to be tapped on his unsuspecting chest by the ever-vigilant Willow.

CJ had started reading from the beginning of Genesis over a year ago. He would read several chapters and then try to explain it to them in simple language. It was a slow progression, but he hoped they could finish the entire Bible in time.

John had put together a crude map, and they traced the journeys of Abraham, Isaac, and Jacob. They followed the wilderness journeys of Moses and the children of Israel. They put dots where the battles of Joshua were fought, and they drew rough outlines where the twelve tribes settled in the land flowing with milk and honey. They glued another sheet of paper to expand it so they could see where Israel was taken captive by the Assyrians, and then they followed Judah's trail of tears to Babylon.

Now they were on the rather daunting books of both major and minor prophets, interspersed with short readings of Psalms and Proverbs. Tonight, CJ was going to close with a thought from Charles Spurgeon. His dad had sent him the compiled morning and evening devotions from the British minister, and he hoped it would be a good way to see how to apply Scripture to everyday living.

"Willow, what book of the Bible are we reading from?"

"Isaiah, and I can even spell it! I-S-A-I-A-H!"

"I can spell it too," Teddy muttered disgustedly.

Willow threw him a pitying glance. Teddy's spelling was quite atrocious.

"Heather, next question. We're reading Isaiah 53, and Isaiah is describing someone who had no special beauty. He was hated and rejected, had pain and suffering, and was wounded for the wrong things we did. He was like a lamb being led to be killed. Who did we say Isaiah was talking about?"

Heather looked at him with her grey-green eyes and smiled. "Jesus."

"Can you spell it?" Willow had cushioned her head on Prince's sleeping form, but her legs were kicking the air with gusto.

Heather started to shake her head, but a motion from John on the davenport caught her attention. He was making a crude *J* with his thumb and index finger. She squinted and slowly said. "Ah, *J*..." She paused, and John mouthed *e*. "Ah, *e, s*," she continued as she studied her brother carefully.

Willow's legs kicked even faster, and Joanna put her sewing down and gave Heather a surprised glance.

John held up his fingers to make a *u*. Heather misinterpreted it and said, "*V*." At John's scowl and headshake, she amended it. "Ah, let me think. It must be *u*, and now it's...it's *s*?" John wiped his brow in imaginary relief, and Heather giggled.

CJ grinned at Willow. "Did she spell it right?"

"I think so, but I'm only five years old, so I'm not sure." Willow's legs hit the floor with a thud.

"There's no *v* in Jesus. She sorta spelled it right." Teddy gave his grudging approval.

Joanna looked at Heather and at John with raised eyebrows. "Hmm. Interesting. Now I have a question for Teddy. When Isaiah wrote these things about Jesus, had they already happened, or was he talking about something that was going to happen in the future?"

Teddy puffed up importantly. "Mom, Jesus happened in the New Testament, and Isaiah wrote this in the Old Testament. He was, you know, that big *p* word."

"And, John, the big *p* word is what?"

"Prophesying. Isaiah wrote this about Jesus almost four hundred years before these things actually happened."

CJ nodded. "You kids are doing good tonight. Let's read another couple of chapters and see what else Isaiah has to say."

The wind whistled around the corner of the house with its icy blast. Snow fell in sporadic fits and dusted the prairie with more of its arctic chill. Even though the world and her inhabitants were continually fretting, spring would eventually come, and God's Word would not come back empty or void.

18

July 1, 1913

Elko, Nevada

Western Union

Viper in camp. Beware. Headed your way. IS

CJ read the cryptic telegram several times. He ran his hand over his mouth and jaw and looked with puzzlement at the telegraph operator from the Belvidere Depot.

"I know, CJ. It's a strange message. But I'm pretty darn sure that's what it said." Henry Watts scuffed the toe of his shoe on the wooden platform of the depot. "Is there a reply?"

CJ expelled a deep breath. "Well. Let me think a minute. You say it just came in?"

"Yessir. I couldn't believe the luck when I saw you and John pulling in with the team. That's why I'm thinking you could answer it, and they'd know you got it right away."

CJ nodded, and the two men walked back into the depot. "Well…I guess you can say…" CJ read the telegram again. It had to be from Isaac, and he was obviously trying to warn them about something. There could only be one viper. Apparently, Parker Vinue had been to see Isaac at the ranch at Elko. How the man traced him there was another question. It would be logical that Vinue would be going through on the train back to Mankato. And obviously, since Isaac sent a telegram, he was worried that a letter would take too long to warn them. Whatever Vinue had up his sleeve must have bothered

Isaac enough that he made the long ride into Elko to send them a telegram.

CJ made a swift decision. Reaching for paper and pencil, he hastily scratched out a message.

Henry Watts read it and glanced at CJ. "'Ready and waiting?' Nothing more? I mean, nothing more besides 'CJ'?"

"That should do it, Henry, and thanks. What do I owe you?" CJ counted out the correct change and slowly left the cool interior of the depot. Other than being forewarned trouble was coming, there was very little he could do to be ready. He would carry his pistol. He would make sure Joanna had hers. But how far was the man willing to go? What would he stop at to have his son with him? Isaac called him a viper, which meant, CJ decided, that he thought Parker Vinue was utterly contemptible.

John was already unloading cream cans and collecting the empty ones that had come back on the train. They had come in early to beat the mugginess of early July. It had been a pleasant ride, but now CJ began to see snakes behind every rock. He decided they would quickly take care of business and shopping and head back home. It made him nervous to think that Vinue might go to their ranch and find Joanna home alone. However, Joanna the woman would be a different story than Joanna the vulnerable teenager.

They were halfway home before John asked him what the telegram said. How much could he tell a thirteen-year-old boy? Yet on the other hand, how much should he conceal from him?

Oh, God, help.

"Well." He stalled for several seconds. "Well, it was from Isaac. And there is a…a man who wants to cause some trouble for him and for us, and Isaac was trying to tell us he might be headed this way."

"Did Isaac do something wrong? Is that why he left and never came back?" John's brown eyes, so much like CJ's mother's, expressed genuine concern.

"Isaac did not do anything wrong. But this man has the idea he wants Isaac to work for him, and he isn't going to let matters rest until Isaac does. It goes clear back to a time when he knew the Swanson family after Joanna's father passed away. The guy, John, is a creep. That's all I can tell you."

"So Isaac left so the guy couldn't find him, and now the guy has found him. And the creep guy is coming to Belvidere. And Sissy Tinner is already in Belvidere."

CJ felt the hair on the back of his neck stand up. "What?"

"I'm sure I saw Sissy going into the hotel before we left Belvidere."

The towns that sprang up along the railroad tracks celebrated the Fourth of July with enthusiasm. Even after the drought caused an exodus of homesteaders seeking greener and wetter pastures, there were still a great number who wanted to slip away from everyday chores and come to the closest town to enjoy friends and neighbors and a day of games and fun.

The Crezners were no exception. The kids had been looking forward to Belvidere's celebration for weeks. Most of the neighbors and their families planned to be there for ball games and horse races and fireworks.

"If we hadn't planned this for days, I'd say we should stay home," Joanna lamented privately to CJ the night before. "I hope we don't regret going."

"I think I'd rather meet the viper in public than have him come out here when you're alone with the kids. After thinking about him for a year, it'll be a relief to get it over with."

Joanna gave him a worried look. "CJ, please don't do anything rash."

"I thought you were going to say 'stupid.'"

"I was, but that didn't seem like the right word."

"I was planning on being civil."

Joanna's eyebrow raised in skepticism. "No, you weren't. You were planning on beating his sorry hide into the ground. I know you, CJ. I know you when you get very quiet and when your eyes turn the coldest color anyone can imagine. It means you are very mad. Deep-down, hating mad."

He tweaked her nose and then decided to kiss her. And Joanna kissed him back.

When they left on the morning of the Fourth, CJ had a sick feeling she was probably right. On all counts. They probably should stay home and not encourage an encounter with either Sissy or Parker. And if he was given the chance, he would dearly love to pound Parker's hide into the ground. *Help me not to do something stupid, Lord.*

Belvidere was crowded. The Bohemian band played polkas, and with only a little encouragement, the homesteaders who loved to dance swirled in the streets until they were out of breath and looking for something cool to drink.

Kids raced everywhere, throwing firecrackers. Horses reared in fright, girls screamed, and young boys were reprimanded, only to find more arsenals and repeat the whole procedure all over again.

At noon, families with their picnic hampers began to gather in the little park. It was visiting time. Crops were discussed, cattle markets were cussed, optimism for a wetter year was voiced, political opinions were aired, and if other voices expressed opposing views and the exchange became heated, a long-suffering spouse deflected the argument by offering both parties another piece of pie.

Joanna's own hamper included fried chicken, her light and delicious homemade bread, and both pie and cookies. CJ and the kids leisurely enjoyed every bite and were in different modes of despondency from being happily full and a little bit sleepy.

The midday sun was in full glory when the Indians appeared, and soon their drums were in rhythm with their chants. Circles were formed with women dressed in bright-colored dresses and shawls. They moved slowly in one direction while men in beaded buckskins, eagle feathers, elk teeth, and porcupine quills stayed in the middle. Whatever story the men were trying to express in dance seemed to move them to a frenzy of activity.

CJ noticed Joker leaning against the hotel. His eyes were closed, and CJ had the sinking feeling he was horribly drunk. After Little Sparrow's death, Joker occasionally drowned his sorrows with a bottle of whiskey. CJ discovered a drunk Joker was both quarrelsome and petulant, yet he always wanted to talk to CJ, if nothing more than to argue faith and hope. He had just gotten to his feet to speak to his friend when Sissy Tinner seemed to materialize out of nowhere.

"How sweet! A family picnic. And how are all the Crezners?" She stood as close as possible to CJ and put her hand on his arm.

"We're fine, and how are you, Sissy?" Joanna's voice was measured and cold. She kept packing items into the hamper as she spoke.

Sissy ignored her and looked at Willow and Heather. "What big girls you're getting to be. I saw you when you were bald babies." She laughed at her own remark and didn't seem to notice that no one else thought it funny.

Willow stared at her until Sissy acted uncomfortable. Heather sidled closer to her mother.

"What brings you to Belvidere?" CJ backed a step away from her and hoped she wouldn't follow.

"I thought it was time you met someone, CJ." Sissy's smile held malice. "He's a friend of your wife's family. He and Joanna were especially...close."

With a smirk at Joanna, Sissy pointed to a man coming toward them, and CJ clenched his teeth until his jaw ached. Parker Vinue moved like a man who was used to having his own way. From his haircloth telescope hat to his polished leather oxfords, he was the epitome of sophistication. His small dark eyes roamed back and forth as if searching for details that could be used for or against anyone he deemed friend or foe. His cleft chin jutted out with important arrogance. His entire attitude seemed to say he defied the world to make issue with him.

"Mr. Crezner." Vinue's voice was appeasing, and he approached CJ with a dainty white outstretched hand. "Sissy has told me so much about you."

CJ turned his back on Parker Vinue. He walked over to Joanna and gently pulled her to her feet. He smiled at her searching gaze and handed John money for an ice cream treat with Teddy and the girls. When the kids raced away, he turned and looked again at Vinue and Sissy.

Vinue had casually lowered his ignored hand and put it into his coat jacket. He was staring at Joanna with ill-concealed interest. CJ felt his blood turn to ice.

As if he could feel the arctic blast, Vinue cleared his throat. His smile was forced, but his words were oily smooth. "I've just been to see Isaac. He's going to come to Mankato and work for me. I told him I'd stop in Belvidere and tell you that." His eyes slid away from Joanna and rested on CJ's face. What he saw gave him pause, and he involuntarily stepped back.

The coldness spread throughout CJ. Everything about the man galled him. When he thought of those soft hands on Joanna, he wanted to break every bone in them. When he thought of Isaac being approached by him, he wanted to pound the guy into the ground. He looked Vinue over from hat to shoes before he answered. When he finally spoke, his words were so soft that Vinue leaned forward to hear them. "When the next train leaves, be on it. And Vinue, from what my wife told me, you should be spending time behind bars."

"CJ," Sissy began uncertainly, "don't say that. This is for the best. Surely you can't expect Isaac to be a farmer all his life when he has a chance to be so much more." She reached to pat his arm but stopped with her hand in midair. "My goodness! For a man of God, you certainly look…ungodly."

CJ heard Joanna's slight gasp. "CJ, be careful." Was she warning him of something he couldn't see, or was she trying to tell him to not do something stupid?

Vinue's laugh was as forced as his smile. "My good man, I didn't stop at this place to be threatened or insulted."

While Vinue was talking, CJ noticed Joker walking unsteadily toward them. His body tried to bob in time with the drums, but for some reason, his wobbly legs carried him in CJ's direction. He moved unnaturally fast, and when he was directly behind Sissy, he found his vocal chords and let out a Sioux chant that rent the air.

Sissy screamed in fright and plunged into CJ's arms; she needed no other encouragement or reason to wrap her own arms around him. Forgetting his Southern manners, CJ threw her aside with an ungentlemanly oath. She would have fallen if Joker hadn't grabbed her. The Indian acted as if he was sure that she wanted to join him with an impromptu ceremonial stomp.

CJ paid no attention to them. With the grace of a cat, he spun around to Vinue and gave his smirking face a backhanded slap. The force of it knocked Vinue to the ground. It may have been both stupid and careless, but at the moment he didn't care. He would like nothing more than to slap him with his other hand.

"Get up, white trash. Get up and fight, or isn't that your way?" His voice was so soft that once again, Vinue had trouble hearing him.

Vinue held up his plump white hand in a gesture of reconciliation.

"Come! Come, man, let's be reasonable!"

"I'm not reasonable when it comes to my family."

"Parker, get this Indian away from me!" Sissy's voice was loud enough to turn several heads, and the two men lost eye contact as Vinue glanced her way. Joker was bobbing and weaving around her, still in time with the drums, and he was looking at her blond hair with undisguised interest. For whatever reason, he turned to look at Vinue and, with a guttural sound, stumbled toward him. With clumsy grace, he bowed and then reached brown powerful hands around Vinue's wrists and hauled him to his feet.

"Stop, you dang drunk fool, before we're both back in the dirt!" Vinue was flustered by Joker's attention. He was ready to say more but apparently felt that the situation he wanted to control was rapidly deteriorating. He pushed Joker's hands away and, with forced casualness, reached unsteadily for Sissy's arm. He glared at them with a mixture of menace and frustration and slowly began to walk toward the hotel.

"Oh! Oh, little fat man, you forget war bonnet!" Joker realized he was standing on Vinue's hat and quickly picked up the crushed and dirty headwear. He gave it a toss when Vinue turned to look at him. Perhaps his aim wasn't as keen as usual. It fell several feet short of Parker Vinue.

Parker Vinue became disconcerted. He ran his hand through his hair, muttered some unintelligible oath of "Savages and barbarians!" and bent to retrieve the disheveled hat. Not knowing if holding it or wearing it would appear the more dignified, he nervously shrugged and handed it to Sissy before they turned once again to the hotel.

"Joanna?" CJ put his arm around her as she moved close to him and rested an unsteady hand on his arm. He pulled her close and nuzzled her cheek.

"Did you know he had a gun?" He could see the effort it took her to remain calm.

"Ah-ha.Even drunk savage knew the fool had gun." Joker grinned at both of them and stood amazingly still.

CJ released Joanna to study his friend. He finally grinned. "I think a certain drunk savage had a few tricks up his sleeve to help his old trail mate."

"Old trail mate sometimes loses his temper and gets himself into trouble. You have big burr under saddle when it comes to this guy."

"How did you know that?" Joanna leaned forward with interest.

"Must be smoke signals. Isaac sent them." Joker patted her arm and walked away. Very straight and dignified. No bobbing or weaving. The act was over, and CJ thought Joker was probably mentally patting himself on the back for rescuing his white man friend once again.

"I suppose the kids will really howl if we tell them we want to go home." Joanna straightened her own straw hat with its roll front and plaited lace. She smoothed her skirt carefully then gave a searching glance across the park to locate her children.

No wonder Parker Vinue had stared at her, CJ thought. She was a striking figure in her black-checked white lawn dress. Her looks were appealing, but her demeanor was fascinating. She had come through a storm and had found the peaceful valley. Not only had the truth set her free but it had given her strength she didn't know she possessed.

19

July 18, 1913

Elko, Nevada

Dear family,

I finally have time to sit down and write a letter explaining my telegram. Thanks for answering it right away. I was glad to know you understood me.

Parker Vinue came to our roundup in a buggy one evening. He claimed he was interested in investing, but something about him didn't seem to ring true with the trail boss. Anyway, when Vinue asked if I was on watch, someone sent him out with coffee for me, and talk about a slick salesman!

I've not been appreciative about the things Aunt Jo told us, but when he started talking, I was grateful I knew the truth. I played ignorant about knowing anything, and I think he believed me. He gave a sweet package of wanting to help the Swanson family, wanting to help me, wanting to be such a very good fellow. Had I not known what the man was about, I would have swallowed his lies hook, line, and sinker.

I never said I would come. I never said I believed him, but I acted the gullible young fellow he wanted to believe I was. He was going to leave in the morning, and after I spoke to the trail boss, we decided I would ride with him and bring back a chuck wagon we were getting repaired at Elko. Vinue felt this was a break from heaven, and he spent the ride back to Elko giving me more reasons why I needed to work for him.

Somewhere along the ride, I asked him if he knew Sissy Tinner. He sort of hemmed and hawed before he said she worked for his wife. When I asked what sort of work, he said she was his wife's private secretary and he didn't see her much. He was quite relieved when I asked about Lizzie, and even though he said he knew very little about Lizzie, he still talked about her for quite a while. She has been to nurses' training and apparently has quite a knack for it. But guess that doesn't surprise anyone.

I was glad to put him on the train and get rid of him. I would rather punch cows all my life and be a man's man than follow this guy and be a crook. I have a feeling he has several things in his past that are unsavory.

Don't know when I'll be home. Simon has asked me to come and stay with them this summer for a while. I don't know what I want to do yet. You understand, don't you?

Best wishes,

Isaac

PS: Tell John and crew I'll write to them later.

"Poor Isaac," Joanna said in the privacy of their room that evening. "I feel so bad his world is upside down over this. I suppose if he had known the truth when he was a little boy, he wouldn't feel so deceived. At least he mentions me. For a long time, I think he wished I didn't exist."

"Isaac has always loved you, Joanna. But right now he can't fit you into the mother spot because you've always been Aunt Jo. May as well leave it that way. Makes it easier for everyone." CJ yawned and stretched out tiredly on their bed.

"I know. I plan to leave it all alone. But my heart has a special spot for him." She turned to the window to make sure it was opened as far as possible. "Another hot day and hot evening. Guess it's what we should expect this time of year, but it doesn't make for good sleeping."

"Mmm." CJ was already dozing. He and the boys had been in the hayfields for the past month. John and Teddy helped all they could, but there were a lot of times when he wished for the more mature help of Simon and Isaac, especially when it was time to milk the cows.

CJ found the note stuck onto the tines of the pitchfork the next morning. He felt the hair on the back of his neck raise when he read its brusque message.

Meet me at the homestead this morning. Come alone. Belle Tinner

How had she gotten here without the dog barking? What did she want? Should he go? Should he tell Joanna? Should he milk the cows first? His mind was a jumble of questions with no answers.

"Oh, Lord. I'm a simple man who wants a simple life with his family. Why are the Tinners in my life? Take 'em away!" He brought the freshest milk cows into the barn to start the morning routine and nearly jumped out of his skin when Joanna's voice seemed to come from nowhere.

"Are you okay?" She looked at him in puzzlement and put her milking stool beside a cow named Hally.

"How come you came to help?"

"Because it's cooler out here than it is in the house and because I wanted to help you when you're so busy haying."

He told her about the note while they milked. By the time they were finished, the dawn was gilding the sky with its vibrant hues.

"I'm going to grab a bite to eat and go see her," CJ said as they carried milk buckets into the house. "If I don't, we'll never know what she wants. Uh, and if I'm not back in a couple of hours, send John over to Jake's. He can tell Jake to go check the old Tinner homestead."

Joanna pressed her lips together and set her buckets down. She reached for his pistol in its holster and handed it to him. "I'd feel better if you had this with you."

He nodded and strapped it on. It was probably a fool's folly to go. All the while he rode in the fresh air of the morning, he pondered what Belle Tinner could possibly want with him.

"Lord," he finally prayed as he topped the last hill before the Tinner's abandoned homestead, "I ask for wisdom and safety. You know this woman better than I do. Thank heavens for that."

"You took your own sweet time," Belle Tinner greeted him as he rode into the yard. The years hadn't been kind to her. She had pants on with the pant legs tucked into scuffed boots. Her hair was pulled back in one long braid, and a dusty hat sat on her head in a tilted attempt at style. But it was the wrinkled face that arrested CJ's attention. Deep furrowed lines etched their way across her cheekbones.

"Good morning to you, Mrs. Tinner." CJ sat on his horse for a while and studied her. She was sitting on a dilapidated chair beside the old barn. The corrals had long ago disappeared, and the claim shack had been stripped by homesteaders.

"I don't suppose you thought to bring anything to eat."

"No, I didn't. But Joanna did." He fished in his saddle bag and brought out a couple of sandwiches. After he dismounted, he handed them to her, and in her typical ungracious fashion, she examined them closely before she devoured them.

"Coffee?" He handed her a wrapped pint jar.

"Ain't we just having ourselves a cozy little party here." She gave him a brief smile and unscrewed the lid. "Find something to sit on. This is gonna take a while."

"Looks like you could have provided a chair since I brought the lunch." He found an old rusty bucket and set it upside down a bit upwind from her. "Let's hear it, Mrs. Tinner. I've got hay to cut."

"My daughter thinks she's in love with you. Sissy wants you real bad. She's crazy, you know."

"No, I didn't know she was crazy. And let this be on record, Mrs. Tinner: I've never done one thing to encourage her."

"Ah, no. But you were here when the old man killed her horse. She ain't never been right since then. But you've got a whole list of other problems."

"I have problems?"

"And I'm gonna help you. But you have to hear the whole story, and I'm only gonna tell it once."

CJ sighed and gazed over the prairie. "I'm listening." Although what Belle Tinner thought she could do to help him was probably as far-fetched as her thinking he had problems.

"I started out being a young and good-looking circus act, Crezner. I was a trick rider and a sharp shooter, and I turned the men's heads." Mrs. Tinner gave a short snort of laughter, but there was a faraway look in her eyes.

"I liked fast horses and fast men, and when I saw Parker Vinue, I wanted him. We were an item for a while. Then his family took matters into their own hands, and he married a young woman with money. By that time, I had his baby. And the last thing he wanted in his life was a circus act claiming he was the father of her kid. He brushed me off."

An early morning gust of wind ruffled through the grass, and CJ's horse stopped chomping for a couple of seconds.

"Anyway, one rainy spring day, I stopped him as he was riding out of town. I told him I needed money, and he laughed at me and rode on. So I followed him. He went to the Swanson farm. He skulked around until he was sure no one was there, and then he put his horse in the barn and went to the house. When Joanna let him in the front door, I let myself in the back door. A front-row seat, you might say. And she fought him like a wildcat, but he was too strong for her."

"Wait a minute!" CJ jumped up and paced in front of Mrs. Tinner. "You were there, and you didn't help her? What kind of a woman are you anyway?" CJ's anger spewed like hot lava. If it could have destroyed the woman in front of him, he would have felt justified.

"Just shut up, Crezner! Don't judge me and don't interrupt me. And sit down."

"I won't hear the details of what that low life demon did to my wife!"

"I wasn't going to give details. Sit down."

CJ expelled his breath and kicked the dirt a few times with his boot before he sat down.

"Now where was I? Anyway, I followed him back to town, and then I told him what I saw and what I wanted to keep quiet. He agreed. I got money from him before I left."

CJ shook his head. Why was he listening to this sorry dredge of humanity?

"I married Tinner. He was a loser from the start, but he gave his name to Sissy."

"What?" CJ exploded again. "Sissy is Vinue's daughter?"

"Sissy is Vinue's daughter, and she's Isaac's half sister."

CJ buried his head in his hands. "How much worse is this going to get?"

"Quit whining and listen. I ain't got all day. I'd a-thought you and Joanna would have that cleft chin of Sissy's figured out. You're slower than I thought."

CJ waved one hand as a signal for her to continue.

"When we came out here, I recognized Joanna. I could see Isaac's chin, and I put two and two together. After Tinner killed Sissy's horse, she hated him with a passion. And one day, they got into a terrible fight, and he told her all about Parker. I couldn't shut him up. And after she knew, she hated Tinner even more until finally I had to sell a horse and get her a ticket back east to a relative of mine."

CJ shivered even though the sun was beginning its climb into the eastern sky.

"Vinue is scared that Sissy is going to tell his wife who she really is. And Sissy is beginning to crack around the edges, if you know what I mean. There's a little bit of craziness in my family, and I think she's inherited it. She's transferred all her hate of Tinner to Joanna. I can't talk her out of it. I think Vinue is going to get rid of her quietly. I don't know how, but he's capable of it. And he's also capable of getting Isaac under his spell."

"What makes you think that?"

"I just know. He'll come at it a different way. He'll manipulate things so Isaac will think he's protecting Joanna to give in to Parker. I know him well."

Belle Tinner got to her feet and began to hobble over to Ben's grave. "Too many horse wrecks. It takes a while for these old gimpy legs to start working." She stood in silence in front of the pile of flat rocks that marked Ben's grave. Finally, she spoke again.

"Lizzie gathered these rocks. She wanted everyone to be sure where Ben was laid to rest. And it's Lizzie I want to talk about now."

A breeze was gaining strength as it made its way from the south. It promised another hot day. CJ sat motionless as he waited for Mrs. Tinner to continue.

"It was a mistake for Lizzie to leave you folks and go with Sissy to Mankato. I sold my favorite horse and sent her the money and told her to get out of there. Lizzie always did know when to run, and she hightailed it to a different state and got a job. She didn't keep in

191

touch with Sissy, and Sissy doesn't know where she is. I want to keep it that way. And that's where you come in."

"I thought we'd get to my part pretty soon."

"When I'm gone, Lizzie ain't got nobody. I want you to keep track of her and help her if she needs it. I'm giving you the few things I have, and I want her to have 'em. It ain't much."

CJ slowly rose to his feet. "Mrs. Tinner, are you expecting to die soon?"

"Yes."

"Have you been to a doctor?"

"Yes."

"Don't you think it would be good to go see Lizzie yourself?"

"No. You just do as I say and don't try to figure out my life."

"Well...well...I...Of course, I'll give her whatever you want me to." CJ made a helpless gesture with his hands. "I'm sorry, Mrs. Tinner."

She snorted and slowly turned in full circle to look at the prairie around them. "I did hate this place. I hated you folks. I hated everything. But I especially hated Tinner for killing that horse and my boy. I thought justice was served when the cattle trampled the cellar with him in it. Yessir. Justice was served."

She was silent for several seconds. "Hate fills a heart until there ain't much room for anything else." She limped toward her horse. "I left Lizzie high and dry. I left because I knew she'd be better off without me." She wrestled with a knapsack hung over the saddle horn before she said anymore.

"Crezner, you mind what I say about Joanna being in danger. Sissy is a keg of whiskey ready to explode. She writes crazy letters to me. She loves you and hates your wife."

CJ ran his hand over his face. "Can't Vinue control her? Or does he have his own agenda?"

Mrs. Tinner handed CJ the knapsack. "I don't know those answers. I've told you what I do know, and I've warned you. Lizzie is a better person because you folks were good to her. And anyway, I always felt I owed Joanna something."

20

September 10, 1913

Pierre, South Dakota

My very dear Joanna and CJ,

It has been far too long since we have seen you and visited with you! My goodness, Momma and I were just saying the little girls will be all grown up and we won't have gotten to enjoy any of their childhood! Anyway, Drew and I want to invite your family to come and stay with us for a couple of days. We would love to have you come when they are doing a fishing derby on the river, and also, we want you to come and tour our beautiful capitol building. Oh my goodness! So many things, and we won't take no for an answer!

Let us know what days work the best for you. We would really like to have you come on the twenty-fourth to the twenty-sixth, but as Drew says, we must wait and see what works well for you.

Besides being horribly lonesome for all of you, we are also concerned about Mrs. Ordin. She would literally throw the book at me if she knew I was writing and worrying you, but that nasty cough she caught last spring just doesn't want to go away, and I think she should go to the doctor. Of course, she won't if we tell her to, but she might if you talk to her. She always did listen to you best. We have told her you're coming. Please, please, say you will!

One more year of country school for John, and then high school for both him and Grace Lynn! How did our babies grow up so fast? I do so hope (very selfishly, so Drew tells me) that Belvidere won't get their high school finished before John starts. I so want him to stay here with us! It will make it seem like the old days when Isaac was here. We did get the nicest letter from him. I invited him for those days also, and who knows, maybe he'll get to come!

And if, I mean, *when* you come, we would love to have another trio with CJ. Everyone always asks about him and his singing.

I must close and get this posted! Hope to see you very soon!

Love in Christ,

Deborah Lynn, Drew, and Grace Lynn

"Let's go, CJ! I'm more than ready for something different." Joanna handed him another staple from her battered bucket.

"I think we're all ready for a change. Thinking about Ma Tinner and what she said can take the joy out of life." CJ put the staple over the barbed wire and with three swift blows had it secured to the cedar post.

"They're all out on this post, Daddy," Willow announced importantly. It was her and Heather's job to find posts that were missing staples to hold the wire up. Heather mostly enjoyed guessing cloud shapes and finding late-blooming wildflowers, but Willow took her job seriously.

It was a treat for both CJ and Joanna to be working outside when the weather was South Dakota at her best. For a change, the wind was just a light dancing breeze, enough to make fleecy white clouds meander across a cobalt blue sky and prairie grasses weave a graceful waltz. Joanna had packed a lunch, and it was their intention to enjoy a picnic as they checked fences and made them ready for winter grazing.

"What will we do with Prince while we're gone?" The dog's happy woofing made Joanna look in his direction as she pulled three staples from her bucket.

"I'll take him over to Frank's. I might as well have Frank do the chores while we're gone. He can keep the milk and cream and eggs for their own use. With their growing family, and as much as she bakes, Antonio won't have any trouble using the extra."

"Counting little Helena, they have five little Bohemian mouths to feed."

"Well, they have three boys and two girls, so maybe they'll call it a family."

Joanna smirked at him. "You and I called it a family with two boys. Sometimes we don't plan these little blessings."

CJ grinned at her as he finished pounding the third staple over the bottom wire. He and Joanna needed some pleasant days. They had spent the past month going over and over what Ma Tinner had told him and bounced from being horror-stricken and nervous to dubious and calm. Nonetheless, it was unsettling business, and their day in the sunshine along with Deborah Lynn and Drew's invitation gave them better thoughts to ponder.

The day before they left, CJ took Prince to Frank and Antonio's along with final chore instructions. He wondered how Frank would manage their milk cows along with his many other chores, but nothing seemed to daunt his little friend. As usual, he had three little towheads following behind him, and when Prince dashed up to the boys with his usual exuberance, all three of them tackled the good-natured dog.

"My wife just made cookies." Frank grinned. "Come, come. We put the coffee on."

CJ knew by now that declining their invitation for coffee and visiting usually hurt their feelings. He started toward the house with barking dogs and young Bohemian voices filling the air with background noise. Frank puffed placidly on his pipe and never missed a beat of the conversation.

When they filed into the house, Antonio already had cups poured with coffee and a plate of cookies on the table. She seemed to be everywhere at once: one minute greeting CJ, the next doing a headcount to make sure her little brood was accounted for, one minute scolding, the next minute grabbing the nearest child for an impromptu hug.

The youngest of the three boys stood next to CJ, studying him with blue eyes. "This must be Aldrich?" CJ thought it was quite a dignified name for such a little boy. Confusion seemed to erupt as everyone began to talk at once.

Finally, Frank tapped on the table, and the room was quiet. "We have small trouble," he said and lifted his oldest daughter, Alyse, onto his lap. "Now then, Alyse, tell CJ what your brother's name is."

She looked at him with puzzled eyes. He repeated his question in Bohemian, and she bobbed her head bashfully in CJ's direction.

"Oric." She put her chubby arm around her dad's neck and giggled.

"Oric?" CJ gave her an uncertain smile. "I thought his name was Aldrich."

The little girl nodded. "Oric."

Antonio's hands waved energetically through the air. "She can no say Aldrich. So"—she shrugged philosophically and kissed her little boy—"Oric."

Apparently, it didn't matter to the little guy what they called him. He reached for a cookie with his small hand and grinned unconcernedly at CJ as he scurried around the table to find his place on the bench.

"Deborah Lynn, that was a delightful meal." CJ pushed his chair back and smiled at their hostess.

"Momma and Mrs. Ordin deserve most of the credit. They both had some favorites of yours they wanted to make!"

"Ladies, I'm honored and happily full, and my family and I thank you from the bottom of our hearts."

"If that was a toast, I would say, 'Hear, hear.'" Joanna's laugh bubbled delightfully as Drew and Reverend Smith quickly raised their water glasses and gave a resounding "Hear, hear."

"Now Grace Lynn, you and the other youngsters are excused. You may as well finish the game of croquet you started before dinner." It didn't take long for the kids of the group to push away from the table and file outside in the crisp September afternoon.

"And the rest of us may as well have another cup of coffee." Reverend Drew Wilson fetched the glass percolator from the kitchen and soon had all cups refilled.

Reverend Smith slowly stirred cream into his coffee. "Joanna, I hear the train ride from Midland was spectacular."

"I've never seen the trees along Bad River as decked out as they were today. Golds and oranges and dark reds—just beautiful." We were lucky to come when they were in full color."

"The old Missouri is pretty fancy herself this fall." Mr. Ordin grinned at his wife. "I know 'cause I've been doing a lot of fishing."

"That's a-saying a whole mouthful of truth." Mrs. Ordin's leaf earrings bobbed wildly around her ears.

CJ favored his former landlady with a bemused grin. He had been afraid that he'd find her thin and quiet after reading Deborah's account, but quite to the contrary, she appeared to be her usual cheeky loveable self.

They discussed weather, lost souls, and new songs; and then, as if she simply couldn't contain herself one second longer, Deborah Lynn's laughter trilled up and down the scale.

"I didn't want the children to hear me, but we have a wonderful surprise for them—all of them." Deborah Lynn's eyes sparkled, and she clasped her hands together in excitement. "And it's a surprise to everyone else here also! I declare I can hardly wait another second to tell you!"

Drew looked at his pocket watch and stood up. "Excuse me a minute." He looked smug and mysterious at the same time and slowly walked to the back door.

When he opened it and peered outside, the now quiet group gathered at the table heard him say, "Ahh. You made it! Good!"

Three people filed in behind him looking immensely pleased with themselves. Joanna gave a small scream and with one leap was on her feet, running into the open arms of her mother-in-law.

There was a general scraping of wood on wood as chairs were swiftly pushed back. John Crezner's deep laugh was recognized, and soon, everyone was crowded around the new arrivals.

It was a wonderful surprise Deborah had planned, and her parents and husband had worked with her. When they invited the elder Crezners to come and join the group, they had responded eagerly, and soon an elaborate subterfuge had transpired.

After several minutes of hugs and explanations, CJ stood back and gazed at the young man who stood hat in hand with a benevolent smile aimed at the entire group. When recognition dawned on him, he gave a quick intake of air.

"Isaac! Isaac, I hardly knew you!" With one stride, he was beside the stranger and was clasping him in a bear hug.

"Hey, CJ, I wondered when you'd look my way." Isaac pounded CJ's back with hearty affection.

"Isaac!" Mrs. Ordin pushed CJ aside and grabbed Isaac's leather vest in her hands. "Honey, I ain't never been so glad to see someone!" She stood on tiptoe and planted a smooch on Isaac's whiskered cheek.

Joanna stood with hands clasped together, gazing at Isaac with rapt concentration. When everyone else had greeted him and they were walking into the parlor, she took his arm timidly.

"Aunt Jo." Isaac gave her a quick hug.

"I'm so glad you're back," she whispered, and CJ noticed that her eyes were bright with unshed tears.

"Mrs. Wilson, we're finished in the kitchen now." The bashful young woman ducked her head and left the room.

Deborah Lynn hurried after her, but it scarcely stopped the ebb and flow of conversation that had continued all afternoon. CJ slowly put his coffee cup down and walked after her.

She had just closed the door after her departing guest when CJ reached her. "You must have hired more help to clean up the kitchen. I wondered why you kept telling the ladies not to worry about the dishes."

"CJ, on this grand and glorious occasion, we ladies do not need to interrupt our visiting with dirty dishes." Deborah Lynn dimpled her lovely smile at him and twined her arm through his.

"Mrs. Wilson, it is indeed a grand and glorious occasion, and I want to thank you again, dear lady. Whatever made you decide to do all this?"

Deborah looked out the hall window before she answered. When she did, her lips were trembling. "Because, CJ, time goes so fast. My parents, your parents, the Ordins—they're getting older. We're getting older. I wanted us all to have this happy memory to share before something happens to one of them or us." She brushed at her eyes impatiently. "I'm just emotional, CJ. Please forgive me."

He gave her a scrutinizing look. "Do you know something I don't?"

"Darling, I know that sometimes a woman just has to act on her intuition. Even if it's only because she feels she's getting older and time is flying. That's all. Trust me, that's all it is."

"I just love touring our new capitol. Don't you all agree that it is a beautiful building?" Deborah Lynn walked slowly down the marble staircase that adorned the central rotunda.

"For a million dollars, sweetheart, it should be." Drew laughed at the fire his remark kindled in his wife's eyes.

"I love the goddesses best. What do you like best, Isaac?" Grace Lynn had reached the bottom of the stairway and was staring up at the mural representing the goddess of agriculture.

"I like the copper dome. But it's all pretty impressive." Isaac grinned at her. "You're going to get a kink in your neck if you keep staring at those goddesses."

CJ rubbed his own neck. They had been on an extensive tour of the capitol for a couple of hours. Deborah Lynn had been a walking encyclopedia of fascinating facts, but now he was ready to go out into the September sunshine and enjoy the fall air.

"Dad," Teddy pulled on his hand. "Could I go outside now?"

"Let's both go," CJ said softly. He didn't realize he was leading a parade until they walked down the outside steps. Willow and Heather each had a grip on Grace Lynn's hands, and John and Isaac were following the girls.

"I think my Mother has plans for us to go on a carriage ride this afternoon. She said something about seeing Scotty Philip's buffaloes." Grace Lynn looked at Isaac as she gave her information

Isaac nodded. "I'm supposed to bring the carriage here. Guess I may as well go fetch it. You boys want to go with me?" The boys were only too anxious to stretch their legs. After they left, a slightly disappointed Grace Lynn settled herself on the bench beside CJ as Willow and Heather started looking for treasures in the grass.

"What do they think they'll find?" Grace Lynn looked puzzled.

"They're always hoping someone will have lost some change. Even in the middle of the prairie, they look for treasures."

"My mother says you aren't going to sing tomorrow at church. She says you just want to be with your family."

"I hope she's not too disappointed."

"No, I think she's decided by the time tomorrow gets here, she'll be a bit tired, and it will be nice to just listen to Daddy preach."

"Isn't Reverend Smith going to preach also?"

"Not tomorrow. Just Daddy. He has a message on false prophets in the church he wants to give. He said with so many ministers listening, he wants to present this and get their opinion on it."

CJ glanced at the young girl. She made a pretty picture in her gingham skirt. Not a child anymore and not a young lady either, she was caught between wanting to play with the younger girls and yearning to be with the older boys. She and Teddy were in the same boat, but she handled her situation better than he did.

"Well. Well, he's a brave man. It's hard to get a group of ministers to agree on doctrine."

She flashed him a dimpled grin. "I bet they'll talk a lot about it, and you won't say anything. And when they get all done and are about halfway mad at each other, you'll mention a whole different viewpoint. At least my mother says that's what you always do."

Sunday afternoon found CJ and his family on the westbound train headed to Midland. Isaac was on the eastbound train to visit Simon and his family, and the elder Crezners were staying at Reverend and Mrs. Smith's for a couple of days.

It had been three memorable days of sightseeing and visiting with people whom he and Joanna held near and dear to their hearts. Joanna gave Deborah Lynn an unexpected hug when they were at the Pierre Depot. CJ didn't hear what she said, but Deborah Lynn began to tear up again and seemed very touched.

"What are you thinking about, Joanna?" They were several miles out of Pierre, and already, the twins had fallen asleep on the seats beside them.

"I'm thinking that this was the nicest thing anyone has ever done for us. Deborah gathered us all together, made the plans, got the food lined up, made places for everyone to stay, and when I asked her why, she said she wanted the people she loved to come together and have some happy memories." Joanna looked out the window at the passing scenery. "CJ, she's been reading the papers, and Europe seems in a dither. She said they talk about war. I can't think it would affect the United States, but she isn't so sure."

"Well, who needs war when we have the Tinners to think about?"

"Did you get to talk to Isaac any?"

"Some, but I never told him that Belle Tinner said Sissy was Vinue's daughter. I thought I'd tell him that when we were alone. He said he was anxious to meet little Mary Edith. She's already seven months old! He plans a short visit, and then he's coming here for a while before he goes back to Nevada."

She nodded. "My heart finally has a little peace since I've seen him. He's filled out so much, and his whiskers make him look different." She reached across the seat and squeezed CJ's hand. "Tomorrow, even though it's Monday and washday, I'll get the little house ready for your folks. I can't wait to have some long visits with them!"

21

October 10, 1913

Mankato, Minnesota

Dear family,

I thought I'd be on my way to Belvidere and the ranch this week, but I have received some news that changed my plans.

Parker Vinue just left, and he was sort of shook up. I guess Sissy Tinner hadn't been feeling well for a couple of days, and yesterday morning, Parker's wife found her in her room, and she was dead. Parker's wife found Lizzie's address and immediately wired her train fare money to come to Mankato. She told Parker she thought a relative should be there. She's been busy boxing up Sissy's things, and the way Vinue is acting, I think he's afraid she's going to uncover something he doesn't want uncovered.

Anyway, he wondered if I would stay until Lizzie got here, as he said Lizzie would appreciate seeing someone she knew. I think he has an ulterior motive like he usually does, but for some reason that I can't explain, I feel like I should stay.

It's strange business. Simon and Edith think so too. Makes me think Belle Tinner knew something more than what she was telling CJ.

Mary Edith is a growing like a weed and crawls all over. She has lots of admirers with Edith's five kids, and truthfully, I think Simon is the happiest I've ever seen him since I was little and we were living in Minnesota.

I'll be in Belvidere after Sissy's funeral. If you could take a saddle horse and leave him at Maney's livery, I'd appreciate it. When I arrive on the train, I'll get the horse and ride home so I won't have to bother anyone to come and get me.

Parker's wife bought a cemetery plot for Sissy. She seems pretty anxious to get her buried.

Talk to you later,

Isaac

Joanna frowned as she put the letter back into its envelope. Even after re-reading it for the umpteenth time, it was difficult to absorb the fact that Sissy Tinner had died. "I just wonder. It's odd for a young healthy woman to pass away so quickly. Very odd. Hmmm."

A chilly wind rattled the windows. Joanna shivered, and CJ wondered if it was because of the wind or the events in the letter. Charlotte Crezner reached over to touch Joanna's arm.

"God knows. We can only guess. It's strange business. Do either of you know Mrs. Vinue at all?"

Both Joanna and CJ shook their heads.

"Well, it's October 16 today. I would imagine Isaac will be getting here in a couple more days." John Crezner looked at his wife with a raised eyebrow. "I have a feeling Charlotte isn't going to want to head back to Missouri until she's satisfied he can't tell her one more thing about all of this."

CJ's mother gave a derisive laugh. "Charlotte? How about you, Mr. John? You've talked of little else since you brought in Isaac's letter this morning. We practically had to put a clothespin on your mouth to keep you from discussing it in front of the little girls!"

CJ leaned back in his chair with his hands behind his head. His thoughts were fragmented. One part was thinking about Sissy Tinner, and the other part was wondering if his boys had heavy enough jackets as they rode home from school. He sometimes felt he constantly worried about something. As far as the boys were concerned, it was doubtful that they'd freeze in the middle of October. The past couple of days, he had worried that Joanna had made the wrong decision in confessing her whole story to his parents. She had wanted to, she said. She felt they deserved to know the whole truth.

"What are you thinking, CJ? You've been unusually quiet all afternoon." Joanna tapped the table with her long slender fingers.

CJ set his chair back on all four of its legs and reached over to cover her hand. "Did John and Teddy take their heavy jackets this morning? That wind has quite a bite to it."

He felt three pairs of eyes looking at him incredulously.

Isaac rode in a couple of days later while CJ was finishing evening chores. He had ridden into the wind from Belvidere and was glad to head into the warmth of the barn after he dismounted.

"Everybody else at the house?"

"The two Johns carried the milk buckets up a few minutes ago. Teddy shut the hens up and gathered eggs before it got dark. We have the barn to ourselves, Isaac, so if there's something you need to tell me in private, this would be a good time."

Isaac dropped the reins of his horse and began to loosen the cinch. "Well, first of all, I need to know what your parents know about me."

"Joanna thought she should tell them everything. They're the only ones we've told the whole story to, although Joanna and Mrs. Ordin discussed several things in Pierre." CJ slipped off the horse's bridle and put a halter on. "And Isaac, we haven't even told you the whole story."

"What?" Isaac looked startled. "Dang it all, CJ! I don't know if I can handle much more."

"I know. It's a messy business." CJ paused. "Do you want to hear it all now, or wait until you've had a chance to eat and get some sleep?"

"May as well hit me with it now. I think I'm going to be glad to get back to Nevada."

"I told you Belle Tinner had a child with Vinue. What I didn't tell you was that it was a little girl, and she called her Sissy."

Isaac swung his saddle onto the rack and for several seconds said nothing. Finally he turned to CJ. "Sissy. Sissy was not a Tinner. That explains a lot of things. That was the missing puzzle piece, and I wondered about it. Vinue was having quite a hard time about Sissy's death. I thought he might have done her in, but I'm beginning to wonder about it. My gut feeling tells me Parker's wife is hiding something."

"Tell me about Lizzie." CJ opened the grain door and scooped some oats into a coffee can.

"Lizzie came in on the morning train. She buried her sister, took the box of things Mrs. Vinue gave her, and left on the afternoon train. She said she's going to be moving around quite a bit with her nursing studies, but she'll give you an address when she can. And she was pretty cool to both Vinues. She obviously doesn't want them in her life."

"Did you tell her that I saw her mother this summer?"

"Yes. She didn't act surprised. But you know Lizzie. She can be pretty tight-lipped when she wants to."

CJ poured oats into the wooden box. "Isaac, you've become quite a man since you left here last year. I'm proud of you."

Isaac led his horse to the grain, and for a while, the only sound was the horse's obvious delight in his treat. Finally, he cleared his throat and slowly walked to the door of the barn. In the gloom of the twilight, CJ could barely make out his face.

"I needed to be alone. For a long time, I just wanted to be alone and get this all sorted out in my mind. I felt deceived, betrayed, disgusted. But I also appreciated the fact, the one you pointed out, that Aunt Jo had done the best she could with a terrible situation. I decided that she still was a wonderful aunt, and Simon was a great dad. And the woman I always think of as my mother was an angel. Maybe I'm dodging the truth. Maybe I don't want to face reality, but I think I'm playing the cards the way they were dealt to me." He turned to CJ and shrugged.

CJ clasped the younger man's shoulder. "I think you've accepted the truth, and by God's grace and wisdom, you have chosen to move on in life not only with full knowledge of the facts but also with a heart to protect those you love."

Isaac met his gaze with seriousness and suddenly broke into a wide grin. "You sure have a nice way of saying things, CJ. You should have been a preacher."

"Did Mr. Vinue try to persuade you to work for him, Isaac?" CJ's father asked casually as he passed the mashed potatoes to Isaac.

Isaac took his second helping and waited for CJ to pass the gravy before he answered. "He seemed perturbed I hadn't come when he expected me or that I never answered his letters. But he had other matters on his mind when he talked to me about it." Isaac gave a short laugh. "He did say CJ Crezner disappointed him. He said after hearing Sissy speak so highly of him, he was surprised to see the man had such a temper."

"Daddy hit him," Willow proudly told her grandmother. "Like this!" She gave a demonstration of a backhanded slap.

"And he fell to the ground like this!" Heather jumped off her chair and crumpled to the floor.

"Girls, that will do!" Joanna glared at both of them and shook her head.

"Daddy, I told 'em not to look, but they just wouldn't listen." Teddy slumped in his chair, as if trying to raise two younger sisters was almost more than he could handle.

Young John shook his head in imitation of his mother. "Yeah, Teddy. You kept saying Dad was really, really mad, and then hollered 'Look at that!' Of course they were gonna look."

"How come you kids never said a word about this until now?" CJ looked at his children in disbelief. "Not one word. Good grief, what a time to bring all this up."

CJ started to take a drink of coffee, but with all eyes on him, he quickly set his cup down. "I *was* mad." He looked at his father uncomfortably. "Vinue deserved what he got. He's lucky I just slapped him."

Reverend John raised his eyebrows. "Well, Carl John, with your temper and your fighting ability, I guess he *was* lucky you just slapped him."

Teddy's eyes were wide with wonder. "Dad can fight?"

"Your father can very well defend him or us, but most of the time, he chooses to use other means of persuasion." Joanna's voice was brisk and no-nonsense. "Now what I want to hear about is Lizzie. How is she doing, Isaac?"

Truth be told, Isaac would rather have heard about the encounter between CJ and Vinue, but he recognized CJ's reluctance to say any more about it and took Joanna's hint to change the subject.

"I think the first thing I noticed about Lizzie was her voice. She used to talk so loud and nasal, and now she speaks soft. She said her head nurse took her to task for disturbing patients with her bedside manner and insisted she take a decorum class for young ladies. I gathered it was brutal for her, but she kept at it."

Charlotte clasped her hands in front of her. "That's wonderful! I always hoped Lizzie would receive the polishing she needed."

"I'd say she's still a diamond in the rough, but at least, she's got her voice problem conquered."

"I believe there was a time when you would have rejected the fact she was a diamond in any form. I think you've shown great perception!" Charlotte was so pleased that she passed the almost empty meat platter to Isaac.

CJ shook his head. "Lizzie..." He stopped and wondered how to continue with his children present. "Lizzie was...interesting. She was definitely interesting." It was the best he could do to defend Isaac in front of listening little ears.

"Did she say anything about her mother?" Joanna wondered.

Isaac speared the last two pieces of roast beef and set the plate down. "Not much. She said she'd had very little contact with her over the years. Mrs. Tinner apparently sent her money a time or two. Aunt Jo, this is a wonderful supper."

Several other voices chimed in to agree, and CJ rose to get the coffee pot. He knew Joanna treasured Isaac's praise, and when Joanna was happy, CJ was happy. When she realized that Isaac was home, she had the twins set the table with her mother's Blue Willow dishes and went to extra lengths to make his homecoming meal the best she could. He also knew she had baked a chocolate cake just for Isaac. He watched her go to the pantry to retrieve it and then to the china cupboard to get dessert plates. There was a definite lightness in her step that hadn't been there before.

Cake and coffee were served after Isaac finished his second helpings. The conversation centered around his work on the Nevada ranch. However, the special interest to the ladies was his account of Simon's new daughter.

"I think Simon must be enjoying the folk's farm and his new family," Joanna said. "I'm glad for him."

"He is, for sure. His wife has taken the house and made it quite a home. Grandma Mattie would be pleased. And CJ would love all the pretty milk cows around the place." Isaac grinned mischievously.

CJ shuddered. "I would love seeing all our milk cows at Simon's. That's what I'd really love. And I'd like to see all my old range cows back here. Maybe someday."

"Maybe you should pick up and move farther west. Buy a ranch out there in God's country."

"Sure, I think there's homesteaders there also."

"But I didn't like Sissy," Willow interrupted unexpectedly. "She said Heather and I were bald."

"Yeah. And she laughed when she said it!" Heather frowned.

"And she didn't like powwowing with Joker," Willow added indignantly .

"But she really liked Daddy holding her." Heather looked at Willow and shook her dark curls.

"Time to do dishes!" Joanna jumped to her feet, and CJ pushed back his chair with the intention of muzzling his two daughters.

They must have realized they were in trouble, and both announced they needed to visit the outhouse. They were out the door in a flash, but not before they heard Isaac roar with laughter.

22

January 16, 1914

Mankato, Minnesota

Dear Joanna, CJ, and family,

This is a very hard letter to write. I may as well start at the beginning when the sheriff came to visit me.

He said Parker Vinue had been shot and killed by a woman who seemed to materialize out of nowhere. Witnesses said she called his name and said he had killed her daughter in secret and she was going to kill him in public. He said, "Belle, as God is my witness I didn't—" But she shot him before he could finish his sentence, and then she shot herself. When they took them both to the coroner's office, all they could find to identify her was a piece of paper that she had written on. It said, *I want to be buried beside my daughter, Sissy Tinner.*

The coroner remembered that Isaac Swanson had been at Sissy's burial, so the sheriff came out to see if I could identify the corpse as Belle Tinner. I hope to never have to do such a thing again. She was scarcely recognizable.

He wanted me to make a statement about her. I said she had been a homesteader and a neighbor when I lived in South Dakota. I told him about Lizzie coming to fetch us when old Tinner was drunk and on a rampage. I recounted the details of Tinner killing Sissy's horse, of young Ben losing his arm, of his death, Sissy leaving to live with relatives, and, last of all, Tinner's death. I said Lizzie came to our place after Belle left and had stayed about nine months. I also said I thought Belle worked for some roundup crews north of the Cheyenne River.

Well, Belle was buried beside Sissy. A minister and myself were the only two there. It has bothered me a lot. A life lived by someone who made a lot of wrong choices, and in the end, two strangers are all that pay their last respects. It's very sad, yet how much can a person grieve for a woman who has committed a murder and than a suicide? I guess we grieve for an unhappy soul, and our own soul is in despair of where Belle Tinner and Parker Vinue are now.

The sheriff and Mrs. Vinue had no current address to contact Lizzie, but somehow, I just have the feeling she wouldn't have come. Isaac sort of insinuated she was through with the family and wanted to be left alone.

Parker's funeral is tomorrow. I have no intention of attending. Enough said.

I'll write family news in another letter.

Love,

Simon

The ticking clock was the only sound to be heard as CJ finished reading Simon's letter. Neither he nor Joanna could seem to think of a word to say. They shook their heads and sighed. Finally, Joanna pushed back her chair and stood.

"Maybe we need a cup of coffee," she murmured. CJ nodded.

While she was pumping fresh water into the coffeepot, CJ found the box Belle Tinner had given him. Her instructions had been to send it to Lizzie when she was gone. Belle had wrapped it in brown paper, and it was tied with dirty white string. She had practically laced it with knots. Obviously, the contents were only to be seen by Lizzie.

"I'm going to write a few lines and get this sent. Where did you put the note from Lizzie with her address?"

"Upstairs in our dresser." Joanna added another stick of wood into the kitchen range. "How are you going to tell her Belle committed murder and suicide?"

"I think…" CJ was about to put the box on the table but changed his mind and placed it on top of the ice chest. "I think I will just say she passed away and is buried beside Sissy in Mankato."

"Yes, that would be best." She gathered writing paper and an envelope and handed them to CJ. "Let's get it done with. I'll get the address."

By the time she returned, CJ's short note was composed and waiting for her approval. She raised one eyebrow and leaned over his shoulder to read it aloud.

"Dear Lizzie, we have just learned your mother has passed away and is buried beside Sissy in Mankato. She wanted you to have this package when she was gone. Our thoughts and prayers are with you, CJ and Joanna."

"Brief and to the point, CJ. It seems a little…cold."

CJ shrugged and copied the address onto the envelope. When he finished, he handed Joanna the pencil. "If you want to add something warm and fuzzy, go ahead. If I don't sound charitable, it's because the Tinner family caused my family a lot of grief right along with Parker Vinue."

Joanna stood uncertainly with pencil in one hand and CJ's note in the other hand. "I'm sure I don't know what else to add." She hesitated before she put both of them on the table. "Seal it up. Let's get letter and package ready for the mail."

She had fresh coffee poured when CJ completed his task. He thought she looked pale and drained. She fiddled with her cup before taking a drink, and then she leaned back into her chair and gave him a steady look.

"CJ, I've been on an emotional roller coaster every since the twins were born—even before they were born. My mind is worn-out trying to do what's right, not even knowing what the right thing is, and now all these deaths. I can't take it in. I'm exhausted."

He nodded and reached over to put his hand on her arm. "I know. Even when I constantly asked God to protect you from whatever evil Sissy and Vinue had in mind, I worried. Their deaths are almost a relief, as awful as it sounds."

"I'm glad you said it. I thought it and was ashamed of myself." She patted his hand absently. "I know you didn't want me to tell your mom everything about my past. Once I started, I couldn't seem to stop, and I told her things I never told another living soul. Putting it all into words, not just milling thoughts that swirled in my mind constantly was…I guess I can only say it was a release."

CJ cleared his throat and took a sip of coffee. "Mom told me there were things a woman can only tell another woman. She said she admired you tremendously." CJ heard the girls leave their room upstairs. Whatever else they wanted to tell each other would have to wait until little listening ears left them in private. He impulsively leaned over and kissed her cheek. "I love you, Joanna."

The buzz from the men lounging in the post office had nothing to with Lizzie's package and everything to do about the pending vote to divide Stanley County into three counties. Haakon, Jackson, and Stanley County borders had been drawn and waited for the vote of the people to make it official.

"We'll be Jackson County again," the postmaster announced as he weighed the box. "Been a long time since we were called that."

"It ain't happened yet. They've tried it before, and it never passed." CJ didn't recognize the speaker.

"It'll pass this time. Folks are getting tired of going clear to Fort Pierre for all their county business. Who knows? Maybe Belvidere will be the new Jackson County seat! We need to think of where we could put a courthouse!" The postmaster stamped the package with vigor and tossed it into a bin of other packages.

"CJ, you could run for commissioner. Heck, for that matter, so could I!"

CJ grinned at them and shook his head. "I'd probably yell at some nice lady and get myself into trouble."

The men laughed knowingly. It was widely acknowledged that CJ and the wife of one of his former client's had a shouting match at the Belvidere dam. The lady in question usually gave him a wide berth when she saw him.

"Did you see the automobile at Frank Obr's blacksmith shop?"

CJ hadn't, and he made it a point to stop and see it before he left town. The boys would want to know all the details. They pored over any magazine with pictures of cars.

He shivered in the January breeze as the team clipped home. One thing about horses: when they were headed home, they didn't need guidance from the driver. Bet you couldn't say the same about a car.

A month later, Lizzie acknowledged that she had received her mother's package. Her note was as brief as CJ's had been, but at least he and Joanna knew their mission was accomplished. They both breathed a sigh of relief.

"I've been wondering how Isaac feels about Vinue's death. It's one thing to dislike a person, but altogether something else to have that same person murdered. It makes it...complicated." CJ unbuttoned his shirt and yawned.

Joanna was already in her nightgown and had pulled back the covers on their bed. "I've thought about Isaac and what this must mean to him. He hasn't...well, he hasn't shared any of his thoughts with me." She sat on the edge of their bed and kicked off her slippers.

Little footsteps were heard coming from the girls' room. Usually, Willow and Heather thought they needed a drink before they gave up and finally went to sleep. CJ learned by embarrassing experience that he best wear pajamas. He grumbled incessantly to Joanna about feeling like an old man since he had to wear all those clothes to bed.

The door opened slowly. "Mama, we need a drink." Two smiling little faces peered at them through the open door.

"And I suppose you're too scared to go downstairs and get your own drink." CJ knew the ritual by heart.

"It's not that we're *scared*, Daddy. We just might bump into something in the dark." Heather advanced slowly into the room.

Joanna swiveled on the bed and put her feet under the covers. "Well, I can't get your drink because I'm already in bed." She grinned impishly at CJ. She also knew the ritual well.

"What if I stub my toe in the dark and yell and get mad?" CJ took off his shirt.

Willow giggled and jumped into bed with Joanna.

"You could carry the lamp down with you." Heather patted his leg.

"What if I can't carry both lamp and water?" CJ tried to look stern, but the sight of his little daughters with tumbled hair and flannel nightgown along with beseeching looks undid him every night.

"We'll wait right here for you." Heather crawled into bed to join her sister and mother, and the three of them snuggled together. CJ often thought Joanna's favorite time was those moments when her work was done and she could cuddle her daughters while he fetched their drink.

He shook his head and started out the door. "Daddy! You forgot to say, 'I swear, every night I have to do this!'" Willow apparently thought he was forgetting his lines.

"Fiddle on that." At least he could control some things in his house.

23

July 20, 1914

Belvidere, South Dakota

Dear Mom and Dad,

We are accepting your invitation to come and visit you this summer before school starts. I've written to Isaac to see if he would consider coming in August and take care of the chores. It would be a nice vacation for all of us, and we need a break.

If Isaac can't come, I'll ask our neighbor Frank to come over. Right now, he and Antonio are worried about their family in Prague. It's an unsettling time in Europe with Bohemian Prince Ferdinand along with Princess Sophia being assassinated in Sarajevo. Frank said his country has been under foreign control for a long time, and most of the people there would like to have their independence from the Hapsburgs. He's afraid Europe is of the mind that a war would settle some of the boundary issues. Both he and Antonio have sisters and brothers there.

You mentioned John and the excitement he must feel as he gets ready for high school. It's a big leap for him, and he doesn't seem to be quite ready for it. However, Midland has built a nice building on top of the hill, and they are offering high school classes. Some of the kids he knows might also be going there. He will have to board with someone during the week and maybe even stay there on weekends, but it's a lot closer than Pierre. Belvidere is making plans for a bigger school, but I think it's still on the drawing board.

You notice I'm typing this on your typewriter. Hence, all the mistakes.

Our plan is to leave Belvidere on the train on August 15 and be at Springfield two days later. We will try to stay about a week.

Looking forward to being with our loved ones.

Love,

CJ, Joanna, and family

"We might need a vacation, but I don't know that Missouri in the summertime is what I had in mind." CJ groused as he rolled the sheet of paper from the typewriter carriage. He wasn't sure he was on speaking terms with this new and annoying gadget, but it was easier to type than write. Easier, but not necessarily faster. He spent considerable time cussing it, much to Joanna's amusement.

"Darn Deborah Lynn anyway." CJ pushed his chair away from the library table and began to rummage in a drawer for an envelope.

Joanna looked puzzled. "What does Deborah Lynn have to do with any of this?"

"If she hadn't gotten all mushy and sad about everyone getting older, I probably wouldn't have noticed it. First I find Mrs. Ordin coughing her head off, and when I ask her if she's been to the doctor, she swatted me. Then I notice how slow Deborah's folks walk, and when my own parents get there, I see how they've aged in the past couple of years. I would have been blissfully ignorant if it wasn't for her."

Joanna broke into peals of laughter. "You goose. You're being silly." She stopped snapping beans for a few seconds and looked at him with eyes full of merriment. "If typing puts you in such a bad mood, maybe you better stick to paper and pencil."

CJ muttered unintelligible sounds while he found a stamp. "And besides all that," he said when letter and stamp were on the envelope, "how come the kids aren't helping you?"

"I sent them out when you started yelling at the typewriter."

CJ raised himself to his six-foot-one-inch height and shook his finger at her. "Do you know Miss Swanson that on some days I hate progress? I hate typewriters. I hate my open range settled by homesteaders. I hate fences. I hate trains. I hate milk cows. And I hate Missouri in the summer. So there." He stomped out of the house and glared at his four kids sitting on the porch watching him with wide-eyed wonder.

"I don't suppose it makes sense to ask if you feel any better when you're sitting in a hot barn milking cows and fighting flies." Joanna set the milking stool beside the cow next to him.

"Woman, put the stool away. You've canned beans in a hot house all afternoon, and you don't need to come out here and milk an ornery cow. Besides, I'm going to turn their calves in and let them finish up." With the last squeeze headed toward the waiting cats, CJ got up and wiped the sweat off his face with his sleeve.

"How could Missouri be hotter than this?" Joanna took the milk pail from him while he opened the gates to let hungry calves find their mothers.

"It's humid hot there, and I'm so sweet I just melt." He gave her a rueful smile. "Let's stand outside in the shade."

A slight breeze hit them when they stepped outside. "Oh, that feels good!" Joanna murmured.

CJ touched her shoulder. "Did you know when you married me that I was a spoiled brat?"

She softly laughed. "You're a delightful spoiled brat, darling. And I love you. It was the quietest bean-snapping project I've ever had with the kids. In fact, when we were done, John and Teddy went to the garden and hoed. I've been after them to do that for ages."

The little breeze came again. It lifted the bangs on Joanna's forehead and then slid over CJ's perspiring face. He walked over to the corral fence and looked over the poles to the creek. "The thing of it is, I wanted to take all of you to the Black Hills for a week. Cool, nice streams where we could do some fishing and swimming and just rest for a change. I know what will happen at my folks. There will be this little social and that little social and would I please sing for this or that, and it will be hot and humid. Truthfully, Joanna, I'm dreading it. And I'm ashamed of myself for even thinking it. My folks..." He turned and met her gaze. "My folks have aged a lot, Joanna. Have you noticed it?"

"Yes."

He turned back to his view of the creek. "Dad always says it's good that we have eternity to look forward to because this life flies by."

She moved to the fence and stood beside him. "Life does fly by. I guess that's why it's important to enjoy the good moments we have every day."

Even if it was ninety-nine degrees in the shade, he put his arm around her shoulders and gave her a gentle hug.

His folks were waiting for them at the train station. It was hot. And humid. Almost too hot to offer hugs. They felt wilted as they rode in the carriage to the Crezner's home.

"Just leave your luggage in the carriage for now." His father seemed anxious for them to come into the house.

They were given a brief tour of the little cottage, and CJ was struck by the fact that there was only one guest room. Apparently, his mother had some plan in mind to house them for a week, but he could see no evidence of it.

Instead, she poured them cool draughts of fresh lemonade and seemed as anxious as her husband.

"Uh, Dad, don't you think we should unhitch the team?" The horses stomped continually as flies buzzed around them, and CJ thought it odd his father didn't take off the heavy harnesses and turn them loose in the adjoining pasture.

"No, no. In fact, what we should do now that you've had something to drink and a chance to stretch your legs is get back into the carriage. Your mother and I have a surprise for all of you. With Doc Regis's help, we've rented a big cabin by a lake in the Ozarks. Our plan is to head out there this afternoon and get settled in for a week of swimming and fishing."

The weary travelers were incredulous. After a lot of whooping and excited laughter, they bounded over to the carriage. The cottage was shuttered and closed for the week, and within the hour, the horses clopped down cobblestone streets on their way to the Ozark Mountains.

"Grandma, this is the funnest thing I've ever done." Teddy sat on the pier next to Charlotte and watched the cork on his fishing pole bob merrily in the water. "I've already caught five fish, and I never ever catch that many. Never ever."

"You're right! I believe it's the funnest thing I've ever done myself!"

"Will we get to have them for supper again tonight?"

"Oh yes! Nothing better than fresh fish all fried up. With corn bread and butter and syrup, we'll have a dandy meal!"

"I wish we could stay longer." Willow sat on the other side of Charlotte with her own pole. She should have caught fish, but she was forever checking the hook to see if she still had bait. Young John finally gave up trying to instruct her and let her flip her pole out of water every other minute. He and his grandfather and Heather wandered to another fishing spot.

"I wish we could stay longer too," Joanna murmured to CJ.

He nodded sleepily. The hammock by the dock had called to him steadily since they had arrived. Other than fishing, it occupied most of his time.

He could scarcely believe that his folks had planned such a perfect retreat for his family. It had been paradise for five days, and he was as reluctant to leave as the rest of them.

"Grandma! Where's my cork? My cork's gone!" Willow started to whip her pole out of the water, but it seemed to have a life of its own; and to her consternation, Teddy and Grandma Charlotte started yelling at her.

"Pull it out, Willow! You have a fish! Pull it out!"

Willow screamed and started running backwards as she pulled pole and fish toward the shore. "I have a whale! I have a huge fish! I have to have help!"

Since she couldn't see behind her, she clipped Joanna as she raced by. Her fish was not far behind her, and before Joanna could move, wet fish and line and pole slapped up and over her.

"Whoa! I mean you, Willow! Stop or you'll have this thing beat to death!" Joanna had bits of moss in her hair and was wiping excess water off her face. She kicked at CJ, who jumped off the hammock to chase the fish and was having a laughing fit.

It was a pan-sized trout. By the time they convinced Willow that it wasn't a whale and that she needed to take it off the hook, the rest of the group had joined them.

"With all these good fishermen, we better get to cleaning the catch! We'll have a bountiful supper tonight!" CJ's dad was beaming from ear to ear.

CJ flipped the sizzling fish that was frying over the campfire. "Dad, I want to thank you and Mom for all you've done for us. This was by far the nicest vacation we've ever had."

The elder Crezner sat on an upturned wood stump and gave a contented sigh. "Your mother and I had it in mind since last fall. We thought you both looked weary. It had to be draining to have the Vinue and Tinner episodes always in the back of your mind."

"Especially for Joanna. She's had some rough years."

"But she's a strong lady. I always knew she was." The elder Crezner gazed at the reflected sun on the water. The frogs had begun their chorus, and the night birds added their own harmony. "I remember the time you came back from the trail drive to South Dakota." He stopped and cleared his throat. "You were so unsettled. We were particularly busy, and we never got a chance to talk. When Deborah Lynn came and you sang together, I thought she would be the perfect wife for you. However, your grandfather insisted she was not. He was right. I believe God made Joanna just for you. Charlotte and I love her very much."

The fish were fried to perfection, but CJ's mind was on other matters. "When she told you about Isaac, whatever you said to her gave her peace of mind she hadn't had for years. I've thanked God for that many times."

His father handed him a platter and watched in silence as CJ flipped fish onto it. Finally, he cleared his throat again. "We told Joanna what Parker Vinue meant for evil against her, God used for good. Isaac has been a blessing to many people since the day he was born. And Simon told Isaac the same thing. The words Joseph spoke to his brothers are as true today as they were in Bible times: 'Ye thought evil against me; but God meant it unto good.'"

24

March 16, 1915

Belvidere, South Dakota

Dear Simon,

We are always pleased to get your letters and learn your family news. You're very welcome for little Mary Edith's gift. Joanna spent delightful hours making Mary's quilt for her first birthday, and Willow's and Heather's squares were made with love, not with skill.

I can't begin to tell you how much it means to us to have Isaac home. He became a man while he was gone and does more than one man's work. He isn't sure what he wants to do. In fact, at times I think he's quite unsettled. I imagine the war in Europe contributes to his unrest. Some articles say American forces should help fight, and others say keep out of it. I think we all feel uncertain about the future.

The election for the county seat in Jackson County has been causing a stir. Most folks seem to think it will go to Kadoka because that little city is central to everyone, but quite a few around here think Belvidere would be the better choice.

Frank and Antonio also added a little Mary to their family. She was born last September and is another little towhead with a sweet disposition. Frank talks a lot about "the old country." I think all the war news bothers him a lot and brings back memories. Antonio just shakes her head. With six little ones, she has her hands full. How she finds time to bake I'll never know, but whenever I visit them, she wants me to come in and have coffee and kolaches. Who could refuse? One thing that cheers Frank up is the new Bohemian hall going up on Frank Halva's land east of Belvidere. I understand it will be a big enough building to hold some dances.

With the winter bringing storm after storm, we're glad we decided to keep John home this year. I've never seen snow so deep. Teddy and the girls looked relieved when we told them their school was cancelled for the winter months. Joanna does a good job of keeping them lined up with schoolwork.

The hay is lasting if I use it sparingly, but I'm running low on oats. When we get a break in the weather, we'll bring out some from town.

Greet your family for us.

Love,

CJ, Joanna, and kids

CJ's typing skills had improved enough to keep him reasonably calm when he composed a letter. With a little coaching from Isaac, he mastered the keys and discovered he could change the ribbon without a calamity. LC Smith and Brothers would probably get rich and famous for inventing this clattering beast.

Spring was going to be a wet and soggy affair when all the snow melted off. Maybe it was selfish of him, but he was glad both John and Isaac would be helping him when his range herd started dropping calves. Some cattlemen said they didn't check their cows when they birthed. They claimed nature would let the fittest survive and they would have a stronger herd. CJ checked his cattle often and usually had a good calf crop for his efforts. He didn't know which way was best but he enjoyed riding through the pastures and seeing live baby calves.

A brisk wind was blowing from the west when he stepped outside. He pulled his Scotch cap down a little tighter around his ears and headed toward the barn. Some homesteaders' wives became depressed from the ceaseless prairie wind. He'd heard Joanna mention several women who felt they couldn't handle another day of it whistling around the house. It made chores a challenge. He learned to fasten down any article that could blow away, or he set it inside. Yet, for some strange perverse reason, his soul felt a kinship to its facetious ways. He grinned as he blew into the barn. Milk cows hated wind.

Buggies and wagons surrounded the new hall, and by the time CJ had his team unhitched and tethered, polka music was coming through the open doors and windows. It didn't take long for his children to vanish into the crowd of kids, and he and Joanna leisurely made their way to the open double doors of the Bohemian hall.

The community gathered in the lingering June evening to enjoy feasting and dancing. ZCBJ not only was oriented to help the Bohemian population learn about their new country but it was also there to help with insurance needs and to provide a meeting place for the population. It boasted a small platform for speakers or musicians, and on this rare lovely evening, the musicians were playing with gusto.

CJ noted that Frank was there with his accordion, and another neighbor, Mr. Kejsar, was also in the band. The music had a beat that was hard to resist. He winked at Joanna when he saw her foot tapping to the irresistible strains of the lively "Baruska."

"Mrs. Crezner, may I have this dance?"

"I thought you'd never ask, Mr. Crezner!"

They whirled and twirled through the dancing couples until they both were out of breath. When the rousing dance ended, the musicians began a slow waltz, and CJ took the opportunity to hold his wife close to him.

"Remember when we danced under the stars at old Stearns?" Joanna said softly as they dipped and swayed.

"I remember. I thought you were feisty and formidable, and for some unexplained reason, I poured out my whole sad story to you. I never have understood what made me do that."

"It's my sweet nature." Joanna quirked her eyebrow at him and smiled. "That was almost seventeen years ago. Time flies. We've been through a lot of valleys since that time."

"We've been on a couple of good mountaintops too. And have some great kids."

"Is it wicked of me to feel so relieved our antagonists are gone?"

He chuckled. "If it is, we're both wicked."

Joanna granted him a quick hug, and they danced in silence for a while until they noticed several people smiling and pointing at the band. When they swung closer to the podium, they saw Mr. Kejsar's three-year-old son Frankie standing close to his father with one little arm wrapped around Mr. Kejsar's leg. He swayed to the music with his eyes closed, and his expression looked as if he were completely enchanted with the music.

"What a precious little boy," Joanna murmured. "I wonder how long he's been standing there?"

The blacksmith's wife, Mrs. Obr, overheard her. "A long time," she answered. "A long time."

The supper break gave everyone a chance to visit, and CJ soon discovered the foreign homesteaders were well aware of the war's progress in Europe. Many of them subscribed to their native country's newspaper and were following battles and the progress each side was making.

"The Italians have come in on the Allied side. That'll make a difference."

"I read where the Canadians really mopped up at Ypres."

"Yeah, but the Russians got their butts kicked. The Germans drove them clear back to Poland."

"Think of all the damage the bombs with gas will do to the land."

"Land? Think what it'll do to the soldiers breathing the blasted stuff!"

CJ wandered away from the group discussing war. It was personal to them; they knew where the battlegrounds were, they knew the country, and they had families involved.

He found Willow and Heather playing London Bridge with a group of girls their age. Looking around, he saw Teddy and John and an army of other kids playing Red Rover. It looked like intense competition.

Over by the buggies, enjoying the long twilight evening and the young ladies, were a group of young men and Isaac. CJ grinned to himself as he checked his team. Some things never change.

The hot summer sun beat down unmercifully over the mourners clustered around a tiny grave at the cemetery in the Belvidere Township. CJ thought it ironical that these sacred plots of ground were gaining more residents than some of the towns. Death took its toll in this harsh land. The Fred Barth family had donated three acres in 1910, and already there seemed to be a sizeable amount of graves.

The minister spoke reassuring words of heaven and of little children; however the mourners stood with bowed heads and with heavy hearts. Homesteaders expected hardships, but to bury a child was almost beyond what they could bear.

Little Frankie Kejsar, the boy who loved music, had been fatally bitten by a rattlesnake. Everything had been tried to prevent death, but to the community's chagrin, nothing prevailed. Those who had been around the area for a long time said August was when rattlers shed their skin and strike in irritation at whatever they feel threatened by. Every mother felt a cold fear that a blind and striking snake could be around the corner. Every father cast a wary eye and felt trepidation whenever a rattling sound was heard.

A couple of days ago, at the news of the little boy's death, Joanna and CJ had joined the neighbors at the Kejsar homestead with offerings of food and comfort. But, CJ asked himself afterwards, how can one comfort when words won't come?

"Children should be able to grow into adults," he had told Joanna the evening after their visit to the Kejsar home. "They shouldn't lie in homemade pine boxes because of a miserable rattlesnake. I just couldn't think of anything to say to comfort the family."

Joanna had nodded tiredly. Her eyes were puffy from grief, and she was as exhausted from her emotions as he was.

The girls hadn't come into their bedroom for the usual drink-of-water routine. Instead, CJ and Joanna had heard muffled sobs coming from the bedroom down the hall.

Joanna had sunk onto a chair by the dresser and had begun to brush her hair in weary strokes. "I suppose we should think about this from a different perspective. Little Frankie is with God in paradise. But boy howdy, CJ, I just can't get his little happy face out of my mind when he heard the music." She had stopped brushing her hair in mid stroke and had stared at him.

"What?" He had known she had some thought in mind.

Joanna had spoken slowly. "Maybe instead of thinking of how sad we feel, we should think how happy this child is, at this moment, listening to angel choirs."

It was those very words that were on his mind as he walked over the dry buffalo grass in the cemetery to the boy's family huddled in anguish over the small casket. The brief service was over; yet no one talked or moved but stood instead with bowed heads. The men clutched their caps and hats in their rough hands, and the women dabbed their eyes with cotton handkerchiefs.

CJ, uncharacteristically, put his arm around the mother and patted her shoulder. She looked at him in surprise as he smiled at her. "Joanna tells me that your son is in paradise, listening to angels sing. And she's right. He's hearing the most beautiful music you can imagine."

The woman looked at him, not understanding English well enough to catch the full meaning of what he said. However, the expression on her face gave evidence she knew he was trying to comfort her.

CJ motioned to Little Frank, his neighbor, and the small man was beside him instantly. "Tell her what I just said," CJ implored him.

"Say again," Frank asked. CJ repeated what he had said, and with great care, many gestures, and several pauses, Frank translated CJ's words into Bohemian loud enough for all to hear.

Heads nodded in agreement, slight smiles indicated they understood and approved. Mr. Kejsar shook CJ's offered hand and said "B'yt zavazan tebe." Even before Little Frank's interpretation, CJ knew the grieving father had expressed thanks, for what CJ thought, were words that probably only gave small consolation for such a huge loss.

Several men stood back as the mourners left. CJ was among the volunteers who had offered to fill the yawning grave with the clumped prairie sod. It was a silent task, without the usual banter the neighbors usually tossed back and forth to each other.

They were patting the last of the dirt over the grave with shovels when someone asked what an angel choir would sound like.

One of the neighbors leaned on his shovel and said, "It would have to be polka music to make little Frankie happy."

Someone else spoke up. "CJ, is there polka music in heaven?"

CJ was on his knees straightening the small wooden cross that would soon be replaced by a stone marker. He glanced up to see all eyes upon him as they waited for his answer. He slowly stood and dusted the dirt off his pant legs.

"You betcha. Beautiful music, sang by an angel choir, accompanied by accordions and happy Bohemians."

They grinned at that. Little Frank put his suit jacket back on and gathered shovels to put in the wagon that waited for them. "Maybe not a bad place to be, yeah?"

25

August 15, 1916

Belvidere, South Dakota

Dear Simon,

I understand your concerns about Isaac. I'm afraid none of us can stop him from enlisting in the army. Ever since Congress passed the National Defense Act, the newspapers have been saying we'll be going to war before another year is over. Both the *Belvidere Times* and the *Midland Reporter* have editorials and articles on the subject.

He thinks if he goes now, he will be in better shape physically and mentally to handle situations when they go overseas. He said he'd rather enlist than be drafted. He talks a lot about the airplanes. I can't believe they'd be used in the war, but he seems to think they will. I guess I'm old-fashioned. It's all I can do to type letters.

As you mentioned, I've noticed the change of attitude from wanting to be neutral to wanting to put the ones who started this mess in their place. I think when the German submarine torpedoed the *Lusitania* and when men, women, and children died (plus 124 Americans), everyone was outraged. War had come to our back door.

Joanna is, of course, upset, but she says she'll pray him to Europe and back and he will come home again. I hope she's right. And she is right about praying for him. Like every family who has loved ones preparing for war, we pray.

John and Teddy continue to lament that they are underage to fight for our country. Good grief. I hope the blasted mess is over with by the time they are of age or else they'll all be on the boat to the battlegrounds.

Take care, Simon. Enjoy little Mary and your stepchildren and our lovely Edith. As you said, worrying won't help. We both know

Isaac's faith is strong, and as in Bible times, the battle belongs to the Lord.

Love,

CJ

A year can bring so many changes, CJ mused as he addressed and stamped the envelope to Simon. From the vague uncertainty that the United States might join forces with France and England, the country now seemed certain that its young men had a duty to fight.

Not only young men but also young women. Lizzie wrote to Isaac that she had joined the Red Cross and suggested if he wanted to write to her to send it in care of that organization. When Joanna told Dr. Sullivan, she snorted and said it didn't surprise her one little bit. According to Joanna, Doc added quite a bit of colorful language to describe foreign kings and American politicians.

The house was quiet. Joanna and the girls had taken the buggy and joined some of the neighbor women and kids for a church cleaning. The boys had taken their horses and left early to herd the milk cows home. Isaac left in the early morning with a determined look on his face. CJ knew without being told the day had arrived when Isaac was through talking and was taking action to enlist in the army.

"A rare August day," CJ informed Prince as he walked outside into surprisingly pleasant temperatures. He bent down to scratch behind Prince's black ear. For some reason, the dog seemed to have more itches on his black ear than the brown one. "A person could feel right peaceful if there wasn't all this brewing in the world."

In the hills toward the east, he could see the boys and the milk cows slowly meandering home. The chickens were clucking contentedly in their pen, and the countryside had a tinge of green even in August.

"Hay looks good, crops look good, threshers lined up, boys old enough to help. Life could be perfect now. What do you say about that?" Prince evidently thought life was great. After CJ quit petting and scratching him, he raced in circles on their way to the barn.

"If this blamed war lasts and lasts, all three of these boys will leave home and fight. It's a thought that could ruin a perfect day." Prince seemed convinced no thought could ruin his day. He nipped at CJ's hand and barked happily as he made another turn in his circle.

Isaac received his enlistment orders and Mrs. Parker Vinue's letter the same day. He brought them to the house to show CJ and Joanna.

It was official now. He would report for training on September 25. CJ couldn't tell by his look or tone if he was nervous about his new adventure.

"But this," he said flatly as he gave Joanna Mrs. Vinue's letter, "is another kettle of fish."

The letter was brief. She had tried to contest an account Mr. Vinue had set aside for Isaac, but the judge declared that it was legal and valid for Isaac to have the money. She had enclosed a check for one thousand dollars.

Joanna's eyes widened when she saw the check. Without a word, she handed the letter and check to CJ.

"You met her. What was she like?" CJ scanned the note and looked closely at the check.

"She was cold and calculating. And she wanted everyone to know she always done her duty and it was her duty to make sure Sissy had a proper burial. She said several times she believed in doing what was right, even if it caused a great hardship for her." Isaac took the letter and check CJ handed him.

"She's one of these unchristian women who like to announce to the world how Christian she is and in her heart begrudges every penny and every kind deed she rations out." He shook his head as he looked again at the check.

"I don't know what to do with this. It's like receiving filthy lucre."

"You don't have to decide tonight, Isaac. You have enough other things to think about." Joanna was brisk, and she brushed her hands together before putting them in her apron pockets. "There's not a lot of time to gather all the things the enlistment note says you'll need."

"I thought maybe they'd wait to call you until the election was over. President Wilson keeps promising peace without victory if he wins the election." CJ frowned as he leaned against the kitchen sink. "I don't know if any country is going to agree with that platform though. I imagine if he wins again, we'll be at war. And if the Republican Charles Hughes wins, we'll be at war."

Isaac nodded absently. He looked at the check again and put it in his pocket. "What would you do with the money, CJ?"

CJ crossed his arms over his chest. "I'd put it in the bank. Maybe in the future you can do something with it that will be a good cause. And think of this, Isaac. War can destroy healthy bodies and minds. It wouldn't hurt to have some financial security if that happens to you."

Isaac gave him a piercing look and straightened his shoulders. "That's such a comfort to know, CJ," he said dryly.

Joanna opened her mouth to speak, but before she could, Isaac relaxed and gave them a lopsided grin. "I'll leave it in God's hands as to what my condition will be when I get back. And He'll have to tell me if it's filthy lucre or manna from heaven. But in case you're right and it becomes manna, I'll put the dang stuff in the bank."

John and Teddy and the girls weren't bashful about telling the world that Isaac had enlisted in the army. Many afternoons found friends and neighbors at the Crezner homestead to give Isaac a handshake and a mountain of advice.

On the Friday before he was to leave, Joanna baked enough food to feed an army, or so CJ thought. She smiled a secret smile and didn't act at all surprised when a nasal-sounding "Oooga" sounded in the yard.

"Look at that!" Teddy yelled as he bounded out the door with John right behind him.

A Model T Ford puttered to a stop by the yard gate, and the Wilson and Smith family gave a rousing "Hello, the house!" as the Crezners poured down the steps.

Prince didn't know if he should bark or hide. He stayed as close to Joanna as he possibly could, but when Drew sounded the horn again, he broke rank and dashed under the porch steps.

The next hour was spent admiring the car. The boys wanted to know every detail. The girls wanted to sit in the seats.

"It's a 1914 model," Drew said. "It usually costs over five hundred dollars, but I got it used from a guy who said he was going back to horses. He just wanted to get rid of it."

"I almost fainted dead away when Drew brought it home!" Deborah Lynn looked lovely in her touring clothes.

"I almost fainted dead away when Drew drove so fast!" Mrs. Smith exclaimed. "He had it going twenty-five miles an hour, and both Deborah Lynn and I said we wanted out if he was going to be reckless!"

Everyone blasted the horn several times. Prince almost fainted from the noise.

"Wow! Three pedals on the floor! And look at all the room! How many can it hold, Reverend Wilson?" John's eyes were sparkling with desire.

"It holds five. Reverend and Mrs. Smith said to bring the Ordins instead of them, but Mrs. Ordin was in no mood to ride in my Tin Lizzie." Drew shrugged. "Maybe next time I can coax her to come."

"What are all these levers on the steering wheel for?" CJ didn't know why he asked. He really didn't want to know.

Before Drew could answer, Joanna announced that dinner was ready. The travelers had left Pierre early in the morning. They had driven the Bad River road, crossed the bridge at Midland, and came on the buggy trail to the ranch. It had been quite an adventure, and they were ravenously hungry.

Even Grace Lynn had a larger appetite than usual. *She had changed in the past couple of years*, CJ mused as the ladies were cleaning up the kitchen. She was in her second year of high school at Pierre, while John, who had stayed home a year, had to be content with being a freshman at Midland. Somehow, she seemed much older than him. Maybe, CJ decided, it was because she seemed to only have eyes for Isaac.

It became apparent to the amusement of CJ that she wanted a few words alone with the soon-to-be soldier. Isaac seemed completely unaware of that fact. Heather and Willow didn't help one bit. As eight-year-old girls are prone to do, they hero-worshipped Grace Lynn and didn't want to leave her side.

Early in the afternoon, Drew cranked the motor, and after several tries, the Model T sprang to life.

"You want to take it for a spin, Isaac?"

"I think I'll wait to drive one of these when there isn't such a big audience." Isaac grinned at Drew. "But thanks for the offer."

The goodbyes were rather hastily said. The visitors were anxious to get on the road. They made Isaac promise to write, and the two reverends shook his hand and said they'd remember him in their prayers. The wives kissed his cheek and told him to be extremely careful. Grace Lynn opened the door to the back seat and said she'd see him later.

September 25 came far too quickly. Isaac was up at dawn. He saddled his horse and took a solitary ride over the hills that he had called home for many years. Whatever thoughts he had were camouflaged by a gentle smile and congenial banter.

The morning hours seemed to take wings. Much quicker than he would have wished, CJ loaded his family in the buggy and they were on their way to the depot. He thought Isaac probably would have preferred riding away by himself, but both CJ and Joanna were insistent that Isaac should have a grand send off.

When they arrived at the depot, the train hadn't made its appearance yet, but a large group of friends had come to wish their soldier good luck. There was the usual serious handshaking, the shy young ladies coming forward for a light hug, and kids wanting just one more look at a person who was going far away.

Little Frank edged his way around everyone until he was standing beside Isaac.

"Isaac," he said, struggling to say what he wanted to in a language he wasn't sure of. "Isaac," he repeated and then shrugged. The words weren't there. He shook Isaac's hand vigorously. "God go with you."

The train's whistle wailed as it pulled into the station and John took his little sisters' hands and led them away from the steam and noise. Teddy, however, seemed glued to Isaac's side, and even after the engine had gulped its new water and the conductor yelled his 'all aboard', Teddy stayed voraciously close.

Isaac put his hand on his shoulder. "Teddy, you'll have to help John take care of everybody while I'm gone. And, right now, I can see he needs your help with his sisters." He pulled Teddy's cap a little further down on his head. "See you later little buddy!" Teddy blinked several times. Clearly he didn't want to leave, yet to stay might make him look, oh heavens; it might make him look childish. He gave Isaac an awkward salute and raced toward John and the girls.

CJ and Joanna walked with Isaac as he mounted the steps to the waiting car. He turned and waved at the home folks and hollered above the train's steam as it snorted from all sides. "Goodbye, Belvidere! I'll be back soon!" CJ wished that it would be soon, but a whisper in his heart told him it might be otherwise.

One last handshake with CJ, and then Isaac bent and spoke softly to Joanna before he gave her a quick hug and disappeared into the car.

CJ led her down the metal steps and away from the tracks. When the train pulled out, they stood with their children and waved until it disappeared around the far bend of the tracks.

Joanna's eyes were brimming with tears, but she wore an ecstatic look as she waved and waved and waved.

"I don't think he can see you anymore," CJ told her softly.

She nodded and buried her face into his chest.

"What did he tell you before he left?" CJ wrapped his arms around her.

She looked up at him and her lips trembled slightly before she spoke.

"He said, 'Goodbye, Mother. I love you.'"

TO BE CONTINUED!

Join the Crezner family in the next (and last) book of the Goodbye, Belvidere series. The war years, the prohibition years, and the hardships of the thirties brings new challenges to the family and to their friends. Watch for *Goodbye, Belvidere, I much love you!*

The first book of the Goodbye, Belvidere trilogy is entitled, *Goodbye, Belvidere, A Hundred and Sixty Acres.*

This is the second book: *Goodbye, Belvidere, His Eye Is on the Sparrow.*

The third book is called *Goodbye, Belvidere, I much love you.*

If you have enjoyed Joyce's style of writing, you'll want to read her western romance novels.

My Lady is the intriguing story of young Jolene O'Neil and the men she loved. With its setting in the Nebraska and the Dakota prairie, *My Lady* is a contemporary novel that carries mystery and romance to an unusual ending.

Laughter in the Wind brings British nanny, Abbie Miller, to South Dakota's capitol city and the Jackson ranch. Redneck Wade Jackson, and red-haired Abbie cuss and discuss the strange decorating habits of Mrs. Jackson. Will the old ranch house give up its secrets?

The juvenile book, *The Countries of Whine and Roses* is an allegory that beautifully describes God the Father, God the Son, and God the Holy Spirit, in an easy-to-understand story set in the Kingdom of Roses. Ages 8-12, but enjoyable reading for anyone.

Joyce can be contacted on her facebook page
www.com/joycewheelerbooks

For twitter users, you can find her at www.twitter.com/grasslandrose

For more information about Joyce and her books, check out her website www.prairieflowerbooks.com

If you want to contact her by e-mail, send your inquiries to joycewheelerbooks@gmail.com

CPSIA information can be obtained
at www.ICGtesting.com
Printed in the USA
BVHW091337130620
581309BV00005B/123